Blurb

Nothing more.

When I met British billionaire Kabir Spencer at Splice London, he promised me an unforgettable night and *nothing more*. One night turned into a string of satisfying encounters, each one hotter than the last.

As our dynamic evolved, Spence helped me explore a side of myself I didn't know existed until the moment I uttered the words, "Yes, Sir."

But I kept our boundaries clear. While he could have my body, he couldn't have my heart.

Then my secrets and my sorrow became too much to bear, and I well and truly broke.

But Spence didn't leave.

He stayed, and he cared for me in all the ways I needed during my lowest lows.

Now, he's come to my rescue once again, while also unceremoniously dropping a secret bomb on me when he showed up unexpectedly in North Carolina.

I know I have a lot of explaining to do to my current boyfriend, Levi, and my ex/stepbrother, Greedy, but I'll have plenty of time to do it since all four of us are headed to a remote cabin for the holidays.

Levi. Greedy. Spence. And Me. All under one roof.

Nothing more didn't last, clearly. But no one I love ever stays.

It's probably for the best—I doubt the possessiveness and sizzling tension between the three men in my life will last before it explodes and starts to feel too real.

Copyright © 2024 by Abby Millsaps

All rights reserved.

paperback ISBN: 9798990077027

No portion of this book may be reproduced, distributed, or transmitted in any form without written permission from the author, except by a reviewer who may quote brief passages in a book review.

This book is a work of fiction. Any resemblance to any person, living or dead, or any events or occurrences, is purely coincidental. The characters and story lines are created by the author's imagination and are used fictitiously.

Line Editing, Copyediting, and Proofreading by VB Edits
Cover Design © Silver at Bitter Sage Designs

Contents

Dedication	IX
Content Warning	1
Author's Note	2
Sincerest Gratitude	3
1. Greedy	4
2. Kabir	10
3. Levi	13
4. Greedy	19
5. Hunter	23
6. Hunter	26
7. Hunter	33
8. Levi	38
9. Kabir	44
10. Hunter	48
11. Levi	55
12. Hunter	59

13.	Kabir	63
14.	Hunter	66
15.	Hunter	74
16.	Hunter	78
17.	Hunter	85
18.	Hunter	90
19.	Greedy	99
20.	Hunter	102
21.	Hunter	107
22.	Hunter	110
23.	Hunter	122
24.	Hunter	126
25.	Kabir	130
26.	Hunter	136
27.	Hunter	142
28.	Levi	145
29.	Hunter	151
30.	Hunter	157
31.	Greedy	162
32.	Greedy	171
33.	Hunter	178
34.	Greedy	182
35.	Hunter	185

36.	Kabir	190
37.	Levi	195
38.	Hunter	201
39.	Greedy	206
40.	Hunter	213
41.	Hunter	222
42.	Hunter	231
43.	Hunter	236
44.	Kabir	238
45.	Hunter	243
46.	Kabir	246
47.	Hunter	249
48.	Levi	252
49.	Levi	256
50.	Greedy	266
51.	Greedy	270
52.	Kabir	274
53.	Hunter	279
54.	Greedy	285
55.	Hunter	290
56.	Levi	293
To Be Continued		299
Afterword		300

Acknowledgments	301
By Abby Millsaps	303
About The Author	305

To Mr. Abby—
Who witnessed and suffered the lowest lows right alongside me, and never loved me less for any of it.

Content Warning

Potential triggers for So Real include BDSM dynamics, degradation, and impact play. Additional triggers include on page emotional abuse and manipulation of an adult child by a parent, mention of past miscarriage, on page mental health crisis, on page suicidal ideation, and an unintentionally missed safe word during intimacy.

Additional context for the trigger warnings is available on the next page in the Author's Note. Reading the Author's Note will reveal spoilers for the story.

Author's Note

Dear Reader—

So Real is the hardest book I've ever written, full stop. Hunter's journey is gut-wrenching and raw. When she arrives in London, she's at the lowest she's ever been, and yet she still has so much farther to fall.

Suicidal ideation is a significant theme within this story. It occurs in detail, on page, through Hunter's POV. Three separate incidents occur between chapters 22 and 24. Physical self-harm does not occur in any of the situations because of outside interruptions and interventions.

The BDSM dynamic within this story was written with consent as the central theme of every scene. Communication and on-page aftercare are also prioritized. The unintentionally missed safe word mentioned in the content warning occurs in chapter 32. A thorough debriefing as well as apologies are issued after the incidence.

The storyline of Hunter's miscarriage that was first introduced in So Wrong continues in this book. In chapter 25, Hunter experiences her first menstrual cycle post-miscarriage. She is not entirely lucid in this scene, and she breaks down when she sees the blood between her legs. Please note that these chapters were written with care and from a place of lived experience. My heart goes out to anyone who has also experienced the physical, emotional, and mental pain of pregnancy loss.

Please prioritize your mental health when reading this book. If you have questions about any of the triggers mentioned, feel free to reach out to me directly via email at authorabbymillsaps@gmail.com.

Sincerest Gratitude

Thank you to the following individuals who beta read and provided sensitivity reading for So Real:

Adah Kruszlinski
Alina Xiong
Amy Sykes
Brittany Bailey
Jen Adams
Linds Sunshine
Mica Garcia
Robin Leung
Tricia

Chapter 1
Greedy

NOW

Red orbs cloud my periphery as I home in on the overdressed asshat standing in the doorway. He's pretty and polished in a way that screams money, exuding arrogance and privilege.

It's not just his smug expression and ridiculous suit that have me gritting my molars.

The words are what really send me for a loop. A cutting jab at Hunter—which would bother me on principle alone—along with a confession woven in his hurtful words leave me reeling.

With my heart in my throat, I turn to Hunter, searching.

Searching. Seeking. Silently praying that it's not true.

It can't be.

She wasn't pregnant. She wouldn't keep something like that from me.

Except...

My stomach rolls.

The truth is written plainly on her face. The panic emanating off her further confirms the confession from her—what? European lover?

Fisting my hands at my sides, I narrow my eyes, willing her to look at me.

She's fuming at Sir Kabir What's-His-Ass, shaking her head slowly. Every few seconds, her attention drifts to Levi, who looks exceptionally uncomfortable, but also at the ready to come to her aid.

"Hunter."

She hears me. I know she fucking hears me. Her eyes shutter closed, her lashes trembling in a way that tells me she's fighting back tears.

Fucking hell.

I still need her to say it. I need to hear it.

More than that, I'm desperate for the truth.

"Hunter." I suppress the urge to claw at the hidden tattoo on my skull as I wait for her to finally acknowledge me. I settle for scratching the back of my neck as I step directly in front of her.

Her eyes open, then immediately widen in surprise.

When our gazes lock, a million lifetimes flash through my mind.

A million scenarios.

A million ways I wish it could be different.

She closes her eyes again, shutting me out like she always does.

I tip her chin up with two fingers. She startles, and her eyes fly open.

Choking back the venom churning in my gut, I lean close and focus on keeping my voice soft as I force the words out. "Where is our child, Hunter?"

A gasp escapes her, and tears track down her cheeks.

A set of perfectly manicured fingers encircle my wrist, and a flashy gold ring glints in the light. Then my hand is being peeled off Hunter with more force than necessary.

"She miscarried, you insensitive wanker. You don't have a child."

The world around me goes dark and hazy, and a sharp pain radiates through my knuckles.

"Greedy!" Hunter screams. She flies toward me.

I still haven't fully processed what I'm doing when I wind back and prepare to hit Sir Wanker What's-His-Ass again.

"Greedy, no!" Hunter shouts, clutching my forearm.

A second set of hands grasps my other arm, and then I'm pulled off the man I'm fully prepared to beat the shit out of.

I shift, fighting Levi's hold. But he's too strong, and I won't risk hurting him or Hunter just to get another hit on our British Invasion, so my efforts are halfhearted.

Once they've put some space between the two of us, they release me. Clawing at my head, I stare up at the cloudless blue sky and take a long breath in, then let it out slowly.

I force myself to take two more deep breaths before I right myself. Instantly, I wish I hadn't. Hunter's hands are all over Kabir.

My blood, which has just cooled to a simmer, heats again. She doesn't get to get away with this. "When?"

She's silent—they all are—as I search her expression, desperate for answers.

"Come on, man," Levi insists. "Let's go inside. Give them some space. Cool off." He smooths one hand down my forearm and grasps my wrist.

With a scoff, I recoil.

Space.

All I've done for the last three-plus years is give her fucking space. Where has it gotten me? To what fucking end?

"Answer me, Tem," I grit out, shaking.

Beside me, Levi sighs, garnering my attention. I shoot him a glare, but the look on his face is like a punch to the gut. Though his expression is filled with hurt, there's pity there, too. What's missing? Shock. There isn't a single iota of surprise...

"Hunter!" I bark.

She freezes, but she still won't look at me.

"Come on, G," Levi pleads, his voice rough. "Give her a minute."

I turn to him, fists balled and blood pounding in my ears. "Why aren't you more surprised?"

He averts his gaze, glancing at Hunter, then settling his focus on the ground where his bare feet are planted wide on the stamped concrete pathway.

"Did you—"

My heart cracks in two, and my throat closes up, leaving the sentiment hanging between us. He couldn't have known. If I had no idea, then he couldn't possibly have—

"I only knew because I was with her at the hospital when she found out."

The confession is mumbled to the ground, yet the weight of it slams into me like a 270-pound linebacker.

My knees hit the grass, pain ricocheting up my thighs as I sink back on my heels. Memories flood my brain. Regret churns my gut. A wave of devastation swamps me.

She kept it from me.

He knew.

Then she left.

She was gone.

He was gone.

Back then, he knew. He left me anyway. He never told me.

"Greedy," Hunter whispers, crouching in front of me.

Bile burns up my throat, but I ask the question anyway. "You were pregnant with our baby?"

With her lip caught between her teeth and tears still streaming down both cheeks, she nods.

The misery I've existed in for the last three years transforms into bitter betrayal. From heartache to fucking anguish.

I plop back on my ass, crossing my legs and tenting my elbows on my knees. The dew still clinging to the grass glistens along the edge of the pathway. The smell of cold and changing seasons blends with the sweetness of Hunter's strawberry-scented shampoo.

Breathe. I have to remind myself to inhale, then exhale again. The task feels so unnatural I want to scream.

In front of me, Hunter worries her lip. She keeps looking from me to Levi, then back to Kabir, as if she's waiting for one of them to swoop in and save her.

Except this is her doing. This was her lie. It was my life—my fucking future. She owes me the truth, and we both know it.

She has to say it. She owes me that much.

"Levi knew?" The words are jagged, like broken glass, as I force them out.

Her eyes shutter closed. She sinks to her knees, wincing when her bare skin scrapes against the pavement, and reaches for my arm.

I flinch, pulling quickly out of her hold.

"Levi knew," I grit, tugging on my hair. "Sir What's-His-Ass knew. You decided what, Hunter? They were worthy enough to know, but I wasn't?"

Pain lances through me, the cut of it so sharp it takes my breath away.

"It wasn't like that, Greedy. I found out the—"

"I don't want to hear it!" I hop to my feet and press my fists against my skull. "There's nothing you could say. There's no fucking excuse. You chose not to tell me, Hunter. You chose to cut me out.

"I thought your disappearance was the worst thing that ever happened to me. But this? It's so much worse."

"Greedy," she pleads, rising to her knees like she's going to get up. To follow me. To chase me for once.

An hour ago?

That's all I fucking wanted.

But now...

"You made your choice, Hunter."

"Come on, G—" Levi pipes up.

"No!" I scream, pointing at him. He betrayed me, too. He's right up there with Hunter at the top of my shit list.

He looks absolutely wrecked, his face drawn and his dark-blue eyes filled with anguish as he looks from me to Hunter and back again.

"You made a choice, too," I whisper to the ground between us.

He could have told me. Urged me not to give up on getting through to her. Given me some fucking indication of what she was going through. *Alone.*

Knowing what he did, how could he let her go?

Why did she seek his comfort and solace, but not mine?

Heart shattered, I back up a few steps and take in the scene.

Kabir is off the side of the pathway, rubbing at his jaw like a fucking pussy.

Levi's hovering near Hunter, desperately looking from her to me, his expression full of uncertainty and fear.

Hunter is on her fucking knees. Defeated. Out of defenses.

Three fucking years.

For three years, she ran. For months, she's rejected me over and over. She's ignored me. Pushed me away and held me at arm's length.

For what? So she could continue to hold on to a secret that wasn't hers to keep?

She had no right to keep it from me—to flee the fucking country and leave me behind.

That wasn't just her baby. She wasn't the only one who experienced a loss. She couldn't even give me that heartache.

"You made your choices," I say, regarding Levi, then Hunter. "Now it's my turn. And I'm choosing to walk away."

Chapter 2

Kabir

NOW

Every cisgender American male stereotype there is just played out in real time right before my eyes.

Bloody hell.

"Well, he seems reasonable and well-adjusted." I approach Hunter with caution, wishing I could better gauge her current mental state, unsure of where she's at in her cycle. Is she well? Is she thriving? I know so little about the life of the woman still kneeling on the concrete in front of me.

Yet when she tilts her head up and hits me with an unamused glare, I'm catapulted back to our first encounter at Splice. To every encounter after that in which she consumed me.

My Italian loafers squelch in the damp earth below my feet as I step closer. I shudder at the sensation. Americans and their ridiculous expanses of plain green grass. Has no one ever heard of a garden?

Squatting, I cup Hunter's cheek with one palm. "I take it he wasn't aware of the circumstances prior to my arrival?"

Tears well in her pretty green eyes, and her face crumples. She's heartbroken. Dammit. It wasn't my intention to show up and make things even harder for her.

I caress her cheek, capturing a single tear on the tip of my thumb and sweeping it away. "Chin up, love. I'm here now. We certainly have loads of catching up to do."

She sinks into the touch, turning her head and letting me palm the weight of her skull.

Bloody hell. This woman. I missed her more than I've allowed myself to admit.

We've been apart for two years, and there has been a Hunter-shaped hole in my life since she fled from London and left me behind.

Her departure hurt.

Even if it was for the best. I told myself that she wasn't leaving forever. That she'd be back.

It helped that I kept up with her whereabouts.

At the thought, I shift my hand, dragging my fingers against the soft skin at her nape, and cup the back of her neck. With my thumb, I brush over the tiny implant—a tracking device I installed during her lowest point.

It's no bigger than a grain of rice, yet the comfort it brings is enormous. It's the assurance I need. A reminder that I can always find her. That she and I are endgame, in this lifetime and through all the rest.

That's the only reason I ever fucking let her go.

"Shall we go inside?"

Her glossy green eyes search my face.

"Or we can go somewhere else? We could check into a hotel, or—"

She shakes her head, snapping out of her stupor. "I'm not going anywhere. Levi and I—" She surveys the sandy-haired man watching her warily from a few feet away. "This is our home, too."

"Then I'm not going anywhere either." Standing, I brush off the front of my trousers.

The blond man shifts forward instinctively. Protectively.

Noted.

Where was his gumption when Garrett was drilling into her, I wonder?

I offer her my hand, which she scrutinizes as she worries her lip. The sun glistens off my gold rings, casting brilliant beams of light across Hunter's face.

"Come, love," I try again, taking a small step closer.

My patience is wearing thin. I traveled for upward of fourteen hours to be here, all the while tempering the adrenaline that flooded my body and forcing myself not to stress too terribly about what I might find when I finally got to my girl.

The call came in from her old counselor's office yesterday.

Hunter requested an emergency appointment, which she hasn't done since leaving London. When the team was unsuccessful in their efforts to contact her, they alerted me.

"I can't believe you're really here," she tells me as she rises to her feet.

Pulling her into my arms, I squeeze tightly, savoring the solidness of her pressed against my chest. She smells of berries and sugar: tart and sweet, exactly as I remembered.

With a deep inhale, I cup the back of her head once more and kiss her hair.

"I'm here," I assure her. "I'm yours."

At those words, that assurance, I swear she gives me more of her weight, sinking deeper into my arms.

"Let's get you inside. I would kill for a cup of tea."

Chapter 3

Levi

NOW

I fetch three mugs and force myself to focus on the task at hand, though I can't stop myself from shuffling from foot to foot, despite how badly my thighs ache. I'm itching to check on Greedy, to plead my case, to comfort him if he'll let me.

Only, Hunter needs me too. Maybe more?

Hell if I know.

She's sitting at the kitchen island while her friend leans against the marble counter, all broad-shouldered and broody. He hasn't taken his eyes off her since he arrived. I don't know what he's looking for. What he thinks he might find.

The way he just showed up, along with all the trouble he caused? Fuck, I dislike him. Strongly. How could I not, when he so blatantly and disrespectfully shared a truth that wasn't his to reveal?

I pull open the microwave and set the first mug inside with a loud clank.

Gritting through the frustration, I set the microwave for ninety seconds and hit start. That should do it. Now to find some tea...

I pull open one drawer: spoons and utensils. Then another: a grill spatula, meat thermometer, a few lighters, a random pot holder. Hunter told her friend we live here—the both of us—yet I'm nothing more than a houseguest. That's obvious by my inability to find anything in this stupid kitchen.

I doubt I'll be a houseguest much longer. Now that Greedy knows Daisy's secret, now that he knows that I was privy to details that she should have shared with him instead, it's only a matter of time before I'm kicked out.

It's probably for the best.

Hunter won't want to stay much longer anyway. Not now that her mom is here. Not under a cloud of Greedy's anger and bitterness. If she stays, it'll be because of me. If she stays, she'll be stuck. Because of me.

I shove both drawers closed, rattling the contents.

"Duke," Hunter hedges from behind me.

Panting and fuming, I turn to face her, hands on my hips.

Straightening, her friend regards me, scanning from my bare feet to the ballcap on my head.

"You're a duke?" he asks, a brow raised, his expression somewhere between confused and impressed.

For fuck's sake.

The urge to laugh is just as potent as the urge to scream.

Hunter wraps one hand around Kabir's forearm, the touch easy, familiar. They're very clearly physically acquainted. I hate him even more now.

"Levi doesn't have a title," Hunter clarifies. "Duke is a nickname."

The microwave dings, so I snag the mug and gingerly carry it over to the island.

Kabir scowls at the hot water, the expression full of disdain. "What's this?"

"You said you wanted tea."

Hunter snorts, and Kabir scoffs, his face twisted in disgust.

"Bloody hell. One does not microwave water and call it tea. What sort of deplorable conditions have you been living in, Firecracker?"

His words are in jest—I think—but I'm done.

"Make your own bloody hell tea, then," I murmur, weighed down by defeat. "I'm out."

Intent on finding Greedy, I turn to leave the kitchen. What awaits me there likely isn't any better than this, but I might as well get it over with.

"Levi."

The sound of my name on her lips hits at the same moment she grasps my hand.

"Don't leave me," she whispers.

That's all it fucking takes to lower the defenses I've erected over the last several minutes.

Halting in my tracks, I pivot and assess the girl before me.

The girl who rode me in the front seat of the truck yesterday. The girl who came to me at her most vulnerable. The girl who made me see stars not once, but twice in the last twenty-four hours.

"I'm not leaving." I survey Kabir, who's watching us intently from his perch against the island. "I thought you could use some alone time to catch up."

She smooths her fingers over my knuckles, and then she's taking my hand. Interlacing our fingers. Shaking her head ever so slightly. "Stay with me."

I gulp past the trepidation brewing in my gut. Her request is simple, but it feels like we're on the precipice of so much more than me being present in the kitchen.

"Okay." I nod without taking my eyes off her.

Her expression softens, and her lips tip up in a hint of a smile—a hard-earned smile that hits me straight in the solar plexus.

"So you two are together?"

The question is even, cool, offered up in a smooth accent.

I swallow, prepared to come to Hunter's defense.

But she beats me to the punch.

"Levi is my boyfriend." She pulls gently on my arm, guiding me back to the barstool she was just occupying.

"Boyfriend?" Kabir smirks, giving me a once-over so intense it makes me itch to shift my weight or turn away.

"It's new," Hunter offers, hopping back up on the barstool. She drops my hand as she situates herself—but then pulls me closer and interlaces our fingers again.

Kabir catches the movement, his blue-gray eyes homing in on our touch, then searching Hunter's face.

"Right. Okay, then," he says, his tone full of wild amusement. "I'm here because I thought you needed me." He trails off, tracing the natural veins of the marble countertop with one finger. "Once I'm sure you're all right, I can be on my way."

Rolling her lips, Hunter side-eyes me, then regards Kabir.

After a few seconds, she lets out a long breath. "I'd like you to stay. If it's okay with Levi."

I'm unsure what she's actually asking. Does she want him to stay at the house? Is she asking that I be okay with whatever exists between them? Ultimately, it doesn't matter. When it comes to Hunter, it's always yes.

"That's fine."

She nods and gives me another small smile, but it slips away the moment she focuses on Kabir again. "To answer your question, no, I'm not okay. My mom showed up unannounced yesterday." With a thick swallow, she lowers her head a fraction. "She's never actually lived in this house, yet she's here. And now Greedy knows, and—" She cuts herself off, but not before her voice trembles and her lip quivers, giving away the hurt plaguing her.

"We've got you, Daisy," I promise, slinging one arm around her and pulling her into a hug.

For a long moment, Kabir is silent, but eventually, he gives me a subtle nod, then turns to Hunter and lifts her chin with two fingers. "I'm here. I'll stay. There's nowhere else I'd rather be."

Hunter licks her lips, her pupils dilating. The tension and heat between them are palpable. It's clear they were so much more than friends. Maybe even more than lovers.

He knows her. He sees her.

But to what end? Why aren't they together now? How did he even find her?

His appearance brings more questions than answers.

Answers I'll have to wait for.

She wants him here, and she wants me to stay.

That'll have to be good enough for now.

Hunter leans forward—away from me, toward this man.

I hold my breath as her tongue darts out to moisten her bottom lip.

Commotion in the hall off the kitchen startles us all, and her eyes go wide.

"We're home!" cries a voice coated with sticky sweetness and inauthenticity.

Magnolia.

"Ah, good. You're still here." She breezes into the kitchen.

Dr. F trails behind her, wearing a bright smile and carrying multiple shopping bags.

"Hunter, darling, we were hoping you and your brother would join us at the club tonight. A family dinner, if you will."

Under her breath, Hunter mutters, "He's *not* my brother."

"It would mean a lot to me," Dr. F adds, stepping up beside Magnolia.

Hunter deflates, her hackles lowering. She has such a soft spot for him. I get it. Dr. F is a genuinely good guy.

"Be ready to leave by five," Magnolia calls as she saunters toward the primary bedroom on the first floor.

It's then that Dr. F catches sight of what Magnolia failed to see. We have a guest.

Kabir introduces himself and shakes hands with Dr. F, casually mentioning he was in the area and thought he'd pop in.

Hunter snorts at his smoothness, leaning back into my arms as Kabir continues to interact with her stepfather.

"I don't want to go to dinner," she whispers, the confession only loud enough to reach my ears.

"I know, Daisy. I know."

As the two men carry on, we stay locked in this embrace. She's just as lost in thought as I am. Likely concerned about the same thing. What happens now?

Chapter 4

Greedy

NOW

I'm numb, stuck in paralysis, my ass cemented to the third stair, with no desire to go up, down, or side to side.

Hunter was pregnant.

With my baby.

A myriad of emotions swirl inside me. There's no outlet for their intensity. One second, I'm angry. In the next, I'm heartbroken. When I inhale, my blood pressure spikes. Then on the exhale, tears form in my eyes.

She went through—*fuck*, I have no idea what she even went through, because she cut me out so quickly and cleanly. I never even stood a chance of being there for her when she needed me most.

And yet I still feel responsible, ashamed even, for letting her endure that alone.

I thought she needed space. Time. A minute to adjust when our parents dropped a bomb on us at the Lake Chapel Country Club three years ago.

Memories of the night play back in my mind.

Hunter, despondent and looking absolutely wrecked when she arrived.

I thought she was flustered because she was late, or still dealing with the side effects that came along with hitting her head that morning.

Another memory materializes in my mind. Hunter, arms wrapped around her waist, wincing and moving in slow, deliberate motions.

She wasn't well. She was the furthest thing from okay.

I should have known. I should have pushed.

That day, I was so worried about her head and her heart. I never fathomed there was more to the story. I had no idea the extent of her physical pain and mental anguish. How could I? She shut me out that night, then pushed me away time after time until she was gone for good.

And then there's Levi.

Rational or not, I'm more upset with him than Hunter.

He kept this from me.

He knew. He fucking knew, and I fucking didn't.

Even if she made him promise—made him swear to not tell me the true depth and reason for her pain—he made the wrong call. He should have at least given me something to fucking go on.

He let her go.

He let me let her go.

Then he left me, too. Left me in the dark. Slow-faded from my life when he moved to California and never once thought about the fucking repercussions.

I'm still glued to the stairs. I don't want to be around her, around any of them. But I need answers.

"There you are."

The voice startles me, and I grasp the banister to steady myself.

My dad slows on approach, assessing me. "Everything all right?"

The question pierces through my gut and inspires a burning sensation behind my nose.

Nothing's all right. Everything's so wrong.

Yet, as angry as I am, I won't share details of what's playing out right now—Hunter's pregnancy and miscarriage, along with Levi's betrayal, their budding relationship, and fuck, the appearance of Sir What's-His-Ass—with my dad.

When I meet his gaze, he's beaming. Grinning from ear to ear, the skin around his eyes wrinkling from the intensity of his joy.

The Magnolia effect.

I haven't seen him this happy in years.

He looks younger. Carefree. More like the version of my dad I remember from childhood: vivacious and lively, humming off-key to my mom's music as they danced around the kitchen.

I want him to have this—to feel this way. I hate the very thought of tarnishing his spirit when he's like this.

Why does his personal bliss have to be delivered in the form of a viper?

"I'm fine," I assure him half-heartedly, rising to my feet and cracking my neck from side to side.

He takes a step closer, practically gliding across the floor. "Magnolia and I would like to invite you and Hunter to dinner tonight at the club."

Heart lurching, I bite back every cutting remark I want to throw.

I hate her. Hunter hates her.

His infatuation, though—the love he genuinely harbors—is real. Magnolia is responsible for putting that goofy grin on his face now.

"Yeah," I reluctantly agree, roughing a hand down my face. "Okay."

"Hunter introduced me to her friend from London. Seems like a nice guy."

There's no stopping the snicker that escapes me.

"But Magnolia asked him and Levi to hang back. She wants this to be a family dinner tonight. Just us four."

I heard her say as much as I was eavesdropping when they arrived.

The request is just as daunting now as it was a few minutes ago.

"Okay," I repeat, despite how badly I want to refuse.

My dad's too caught up in his own glee to notice.

I let him stay there. I give him that.

He passes me with a quick squeeze of my arm, then bounds up the stairs, taking the last few two at a time, with a literal spring to his step. "Be ready by five," he calls over his shoulder. "We can all ride together."

I don't know how the fuck I'm going to get through this day, this dinner, however long I have to co-exist with Magnolia and Hunter, Levi and Sir What's-His-Ass.

Even so, I'll do it. I'll see it through for my dad.

Chapter 5

Hunter

THEN

"I can do this."

Running my hands down my little black dress, I smooth away nonexistent wrinkles.

I spent nearly an hour getting ready, and yet I refuse to really look at myself in the mirror. It's like I'm waiting for a jump scare—afraid to make eye contact or focus on my own reflection for too long, in fear of what truths I'll see.

Despite digging a deep hole and burying all the emotions threatening to bubble up inside me, tears still leak from my eyes without my permission. I attempt to swipe them away without smearing my eyeliner. I fail.

"Let me see you!" Louie calls from the living area of our flat.

With a flustered breath, I hustle to fix my makeup again.

Louie's done so much for me over the last few weeks. First by allowing me to join her in London and share the little apartment she had originally rented for herself. Then with helping me get hired where she was planning to work.

It's a lovely flat. Two bedrooms with an adorable little balcony overlooking a bustling street in Mayfair. It came furnished, and the living room catches gorgeous light in the morning. The bathroom is straight out of the '80s, and the kitchen is practically nonexistent, but we make do with the espresso machine, icebox, and hot plate.

Best of all? It's only two blocks away from our new place of employment: Splice, one of the hottest nightclubs in London.

Which is where we're heading now, for our first training shift as hostesses.

I bite on the insides of my cheeks to keep the tears at bay and check my eyeliner and mascara one last time before leaving my room.

"Not much to see." A lackluster reply is all I can muster as I grab my shoulder bag and join my roommate in the main space. Despite my best efforts, by the time I approach her, my eyes are misting again.

"No, no, no!" she admonishes when she notices the tears. "You're going to ruin your makeup. We work at Splice now. We have to look posh and sophisticated." Louie grips me by the shoulders, holding me at arm's length and frowning, probably regretting allowing me to tag along. "Hunt... what do you need?"

It's not what I need. It's who I'm missing. Who I'm so desperate to call.

I haven't filled Louie in on the demise of my relationship—how I endured the worst day of my life, then made life-altering choices for Greedy and me. How I ran away.

Trouble is, my sorrow seems to have ventured across the pond with me. No matter how hard I try, no matter how badly I want to forget.

Blowing out a long breath, I stand straighter and sniff back my tears. "I need this job," I admit to my friend.

"We'll fit right in. My cousin Taylor swore it. They've been working at the club for almost a year and even have their own set on Thursday nights."

My shoulders lower an inch, and the tightness in my chest eases. Her enthusiasm settles my nerves.

"How about a shot for courage?" She marches into the kitchen and pulls a bottle of cheap vodka out of the icebox.

I shake my head and fight back a shudder.

Head tilted, she frowns. "Something stronger?"

What could be stronger than vodka? I sniffed the bottle when she brought it home, and it smells like disinfectant.

"I'll be okay," I promise, giving her a weak smile. "Let me fix my mascara and pee one more time, then we can go."

"Two minutes," she hollers after me.

I grab my toiletry bag off my nightstand and dip into the bathroom. Without looking, I unzip it and dig through it for the mascara.

While I'm searching, my hand grazes a solid mass. I freeze.

Grasping it shakily, I close my eyes and will my racing heart to settle. It's my old phone—the one I used throughout high school. It's the final connection I have to who I was, and to him.

Last time I powered it on, it had less than 40 percent battery life.

I didn't bring the charger. A choice I've regretted every day since arriving in London. I'll be lucky if I can power the thing on more than two or three more times. I refuse to waste one of them now.

Instead, I hold it. Feel it. Press it to my heart, wishing that the words he left in voicemails could take root inside me.

Eight messages. He left me eight messages, then they stopped. It took a day to realize that my mailbox was full, so I deleted a few voicemails I'd saved in the past, including one from my mom and two from my dad wishing me a happy birthday and a merry Christmas last year.

Deleted them to make room for him. To preserve. To hold on to the only piece of him I allowed myself to bring with me to London.

Within twenty-four hours, my mailbox was full again.

"Hunt! Let's go!"

I allow myself another breath. Then I put the phone away and apply one last coat of mascara. Shoulders pulled back, I tip my chin and head out into the living room.

Chapter 6

Hunter

THEN

After two weeks of training, I'm officially ready for my first solo shift as the hostess and greeter of Splice Nightclub. My heels are high. My eyeliner is fierce. I've got this.

The doors are set to open in a few minutes, and like every night, there's already a line winding around the block.

I wouldn't be surprised if it extends all the way up the hill to our flat.

Louie isn't working tonight. Only on Fridays and Saturdays do they require two hostesses, so it's rare that our schedules will match up now that training is over. But I've become friendly with Sean, the bartender, and I've got a security guard named Angelo just a few feet away to support me.

Running my fingers along the chain of my necklace, I confirm for the dozenth time that the tiny rose gold lock in the center of my chest is securely fastened.

Some of the employees at Splice offer extras. It's a burlesque entertainment club that attracts a posh crowd, and according to Louie, her cousin Taylor can make enough in one night offering up extras to pay their entire month's rent.

I'm decidedly not open to offering that kind of service, hence why my locket, part of the required uniform at Splice, is closed off and securely fastened around my neck.

My job is straightforward: Greet the guests. Check the lists. Then gently turn away about 90 percent of the patrons attempting to get in.

"All set?" Angelo asks, striding to the door.

I nod, nervous, but I'm as ready as I'll ever be.

Angelo will be stationed nearby to serve as backup if a guest doesn't take so kindly to being turned away. That's my primary task, telling people that they aren't getting inside in a way that's palatable.

I greet the guests and offer them champagne or the season signature drink, which is currently Pimm's punch. Then, once they've received their complimentary beverage, I check for their names on the list.

The *list* is actually a set of four lists, plus a running log of DNEs (do not enter) and AAAs (always allow access).

The general guest lists are ranked. There's an A list, B list, C list, and D list. The number of people I can let in from each of the lists depends on the crowd, the mood, the tone, and the attractions.

It's a bit confusing, but everything is color-coded, and worst-case scenario, Angelo will help me out.

"You've got this, kid," he tells me in his deep, gravelly voice. "Just smile and charm them with your American accent as you turn them away."

I stifle a laugh. If only it were that easy.

With a single nod at me, he heads to the door to let the other security guard know that we're ready.

Straightening, I steel my spine and take a deep breath.

I've got this.

I'm doing this.

I'm gonna stand on my own two feet, even if they are guaranteed to be aching by the end of the night.

It's only a Tuesday, yet within the hour, Splice is packed. Two DJs are spinning on the main floor. Dancers are putting on public and private shows around the club.

Several scantily clad entertainers dance on exposed catwalks above the crowd.

Louie even stops in to say hello.

She's off tonight and going out with a guy she met earlier this week.

There must be a holdup outside, because for the first time all night, there is a break in the line, and I have a moment alone to breathe. Quickly, I take a swig from my water bottle and then stash it below the podium.

When I straighten, there are three men standing before me.

They're all dressed smartly, the way rich boys in London always are, I'm learning. Two of the men hang back while one approaches my stand.

"Good evening," he greets.

"Hello," I reply coolly. "Welcome to Splice. May I offer you a complimentary glass of champagne or Pimm's?"

Smiling, he smooths his fingertips against the dark stubble on his chin.

He's got brilliant blue-gray eyes that juxtapose his warm brown skin. His dark hair is longer on top and wavy, but stylishly coifed. He's wearing a three-piece suit, but he's removed his necktie, and the top few buttons are undone.

He is undoubtedly attractive, and based on the confident way he carries himself, he knows it.

"You're new here," he tells me.

When I don't respond, he eyes the tray of drinks. "I'll take a Pimm's."

I hand him the punch, careful to pass it over on one of the signature Splice napkins, just like I was trained to do.

"Name, please?" I ask as he takes his first sip.

His smile transforms into a smirk. "You're new here," he repeats.

Rather than answer him—I haven't been trained on how to handle a situation like this—I repeat my question. "May I have your name, sir?"

"*Sir.* I like the sound of that in your pretty little American accent." He gives me a thorough once-over, as if he's really seeing me for the first time.

Ignoring his assessment, I grind my teeth to bite back a retort. Unless the man is on the AAA list that I have no jurisdiction over, there's no way I'm letting him in tonight.

"I'm sorry, I didn't catch your name," I repeat.

"You honestly don't know who I am?" he asks, his tone mocking. He throws back the rest of his drink, grins, then side-steps past me and the hostess stand, moving closer to the bar.

"Excuse me, sir." I scan the area, looking for Angelo. This is typically where he would intervene.

Angelo has his back turned and is over by the door. There must be something else going on outside, or maybe he didn't even see these guys sneak past him.

I'm on high alert as I try to position myself between the handsome man and the bar.

His friends, thank fuck, are still holding back, though they don't bother to hide their snickers.

I take a few more steps to the side and stand taller, accepting that I'll need to handle this one on my own.

"I thought the hostesses at Splice weren't ever to leave the stand," the man comments offhandedly.

Hackles raised, I plant both hands on my hips. "True," I snap, "but we're also not supposed to let in anyone who's not on the list, and considering you have not told me your name yet, *sir*, I cannot confirm or deny whether you're on said list."

"Oh, she's feisty." With both brows raised, he turns to the bar and accepts a drink from Sean.

What the hell? I didn't even hear him put in an order.

I crane my neck, hoping I can catch Sean's attention, but he's already moving down the bar. The other bartenders working tonight are hustling, bustling, and serving patrons, paying us no mind.

A hand captures my wrist, startling me.

"You're all right, love," the man trying to weasel his way into the club tells me, his voice thick with condescension. "I can assure you I'm on your list."

I've heard that about thirty times so far tonight, and more often than not, the people blustering were, in fact, not on the list.

With a huff, I twist my wrist out of his grasp and march back to the hostess stand.

"Very well," I tell him, raising my voice to make sure he hears me at his position over at the bar. "If you're so confident, why don't you allow me to check?"

He gives me a wry smile, almost as if he's embarrassed for me, and nods toward his two buddies.

"I'll meet you at my usual booth."

As the two other men breeze past me, my heart takes off. What the fuck am I supposed to do now?

I'm low-key—no, maybe high-key—panicking when the tall, dark, and handsome stranger approaches the podium once again.

"Breathe, love," he tells me. Again with the condescension.

"I apologize, sir," I force out, anger swirling inside me, "but if you are not willing to provide your name for me to check on the list, then I'm going to have to ask you to leave."

He stares deep into my eyes, unblinking in a way that both thrills me and pisses me the hell off as he sips the amber liquid from the crystal tumbler he magically procured at the bar.

Where the hell is Angelo? He better reappear before this pompous prick decides to waltz right past me and enter the club.

"Mr. Spencer," the security guard's booming voice echoes around us.

Fucking finally.

We have a name. Spencer.

A common name for sure, yet I swear I've heard it recently. Where, I have no idea. Maybe I went to school with somebody named Spencer?

I can't for the life of me recall, especially now, when I'm so agitated.

"Is there a problem, sir?"

The man smirks, his eyes dancing with mirth as he hits me with a decidedly *I told you so* look. He turns away from me slowly, looking to the bodyguard who has to be at least six-five.

"No problem at all, Angelo. Looks like our new hire is doing an excellent job keeping entry rates low. Although she probably could use a bit of a refresher on basic manners."

An exasperated gasp escapes me.

"See?" the man adds. "Testy, this one."

"I am not," I snap.

Instantly, I raise a hand to my mouth.

Oh, shit. Yes, I am.

The man—Mr. Spencer?—holds back a laugh and taps his knuckles on the podium twice. "What's your name, love?"

My blood pressure spikes. The nerve of this asshole to turn the question he refuses to answer back on me.

Angelo addressed him as Mr. Spencer, so at least I have something to latch on to.

"Well, *Mr. Spencer,*" I enunciate, "my name is Hunter St. Clair. You can call me Hunter, and I can call you...?"

He leans into my space, still wearing a devilish grin. I can smell the rich, warm scents of cardamom and whiskey on his breath. A hint of mint, spice, and something oh so masculine infiltrate my senses the longer he lingers.

"Can I tell you a secret?"

Without my permission, my body angles closer.

"I very much liked it when you called me sir," he says under his breath.

I inhale sharply in response to this man's brazenness. Is he for real right now? I can't tell whether he's bullying me or flirting with me. Rather than engage, I offer my most saccharine smile, stand taller, and repeat for the umpteenth time, "Your full name, please, *sir.*"

"Kabir Kareem Alexander Louis Cornelia Spencer."

Oh.

Shit.

After all this time, I didn't actually expect him to reply. Kabir Kareem Alan what? He rattled off at least three names before I started truly paying attention. To make matters worse, all my lists are alphabetical by last name, but which one of those is his actual last name?

I'm spiraling into a panic when he jabs the portfolio containing all the lists for the night with one finger.

"You won't find my name on any of your lists, love, but you will find it on the business card if you inquire about the owner of this establishment."

Stomach plummeting, I snap my mouth shut.

He breezes past me, lifts his glass, and calls back over his shoulder. "See you around, Hunter St. Clair."

It's not until I turn to Angelo that the pieces all fall into place. Shuttering my eyes closed, I pull in a sharp inhale through my teeth.

"That's Mr. Spencer, the owner of Splice?"

"One and the same," Angelo tells me with a lighthearted chuckle, as if this is all a joke.

Flovely.

Fucking lovely.

Chapter 7

Hunter

NOW

The powder room hasn't changed. The fabric chair at the vanity scratches at the back of my bare thighs as I shift uncomfortably in front of the mirror.

I spent the car ride here reminding myself of what's real and true. What's different now, how I've changed since then.

It didn't work.

As soon as Greedy stormed past me and through the front doors of the country club, I felt myself slipping.

I've sunken into disassociation. My mind is empty, my emotions turned off. Every barrier and protective layer in my arsenal has been erected. I'm a hollow shell of a human, but at least nothing can touch me in this state.

The toilet flushes.

I shudder.

Movement in the mirror catches my attention.

I track the threat as she approaches. I don't take my eyes off her—don't even allow myself to blink—as she stops directly behind me.

She looks older. It makes sense, since I haven't seen her in person in over three years. Though she's aged, her features haven't softened a bit. There's a sallowness—wrinkles that can't be smoothed out cosmetically, a sickly paleness that her makeup doesn't quite cover—I've never seen before.

When she meets my gaze in the mirror, I quickly look away.

That's my first mistake.

Averting my eyes. Submitting.

When she puts her hand on my shoulder, I can't help but flinch—my second misstep in as many seconds.

"Darling," she coos, a saccharine sweetness to her tone that makes my stomach turn. Her fingertips ever-so-lightly graze against my earlobe as she tucks a strand of hair behind my ear. "I'm so happy you're here. Gary is thrilled to have us all together again."

I nod, the movement jerky, and rise, shrugging her hand off my shoulder in one motion. "Let's not keep him waiting, then."

Sorrow swirls low in my belly as I follow my mother through the foyer where my life literally and metaphorically fell apart three years ago. I can still feel the pain as it came in waves, twisting up my insides in acute, throbbing contractions. I can see the boy standing before me, trying so hard to comfort me without knowing the extent of my anguish.

It was too much then.

It's still too much now.

With a shake of my head, I banish the memories and hurry through the lobby, hoping like hell I can leave the past behind me.

But once we enter the dining room, I'm transported there once again.

"Here are our guys," my mother singsongs. She stops next to Dr. F and plants a kiss on his cheek, then settles into the seat by his side.

Our guys.

If she only fucking knew.

The only seat left puts me between Dr. F and Greedy. I sit down, gaze set on the expensive place setting laid out before me.

"Anything to drink, miss?" our server asks.

"Water's fine. Thank you."

"I'll take two more of these," Greedy grumbles, holding a lowball glass up. "Keep them coming."

He won't even acknowledge my presence as I shrink into my seat and hope like hell this is as awkward as it's going to get tonight.

It got worse. So much worse.

Greedy is so drunk he's leaning on the table, head propped up in his hand, glaring at me wordlessly.

My mother is putting on her very best show for Dr. Ferguson.

Dr. Ferguson is buying it all, completely entranced by her every move and hanging on her every word.

"I hope this is the first of many, but this is more than just a family dinner. Hunter, Garrett. Magnolia and I wanted to formally invite you to spend the holidays at the family cabin."

"Fuck," Greedy mutters under his breath just loud enough for me to hear.

"For how long?" I ask, not taking my eyes off Greedy.

My mother tsks, probably itching to scold me for being rude. I don't care. I don't want to disappoint Dr. F, but I have to know what I'm getting myself into before I commit.

"As long as you'd like," he says. "I can only get away from the hospital for a few days, but you're welcome to spend the entirety of winter break at the cabin. Unless you have other plans?"

Greedy barks a snide laugh. "Do you have plans, Hunter? With your boyfriend, maybe?"

He's goading me, but I'm the only one at this table who seems to have any grasp on reality, and I'm sick and tired of falling in line and worrying about the feelings of everyone around me.

"In fact, I do," I tell him. Then, turning to Dr. F and my mother, I say, "Levi and I plan to spend the holidays together. I'll come to the cabin, but only if he can come along."

"Of course," Dr. Ferguson says with a warm smile.

Greedy snickers, wobbling beside me. "Great. Fucking great. Might as well invite your British bitch boy to join us, too."

"Garrett," Dr. Ferguson bites out with a disapproving frown. "Any friend of your sister's is a friend of this family."

Greedy looks me dead in the eye when he mutters, "She's *not* my sister."

"Hunter, your friends are welcome to join us. In fact, I insist. I just want my family together on Christmas Day."

I thank Dr. F just as our server returns with dessert. Stomach churning, all I can do is push pie around my plate and pray the night is almost over.

By the time we're ready to leave, Greedy is so sloshed he's swaying on his feet.

"Christmas at the cabin," he sneers, getting right in my face while we wait for the valet to bring around the car. "I used to love that place."

Heart sinking, I turn and catch his gaze.

His mossy-green eyes are red and squinty. He attempts to scowl at me, but it doesn't last long. His anger slips, and his expression softens the longer we consider one another. Eventually, he swallows, his Adam's apple bobbing in a motion I can't help but track.

"Greedy—" I start.

He looks away, shoulders slumped. "I used to love a lot of things," he whispers, so softly I almost don't hear it.

Then, with a shake of his head, he stands straighter, his expression going hard again.

"Time to go home, sis. Wouldn't want to keep all your special guests waiting."

Chapter 8

Levi

NOW

I'm restless and useless, pacing like a caged animal as I wait for updates from either Hunter or Greedy.

They've been gone for more than two hours. It's strange to be in this house all alone. Although I'm technically not alone, Considering Hunter's visitor is holed up in her bedroom, making himself at home.

To give myself something to do while I wait, I go through my usual isometric workout and strength routine using my body weight. Every muscle is coiled tight through my limbs. But even working up a sweat doesn't get rid of the anticipatory adrenaline circulating through my system.

Knowing just how precarious dinner is bound to be makes me all sorts of anxious. I don't have the first clue how to help. Her *or* him. That I'm not there to act as a buffer for either of them doesn't sit well for me.

Eventually, it feels like the walls of my room are closing in on me, so I wander the house. I consider watching TV, but finally end up back upstairs.

My leg aches from the workout and all the pacing. I need to rest and stop going up and down the stairs.

Deciding it would be best if I relax until they get home, I head out onto the balcony.

When the sweet scents of tobacco and cardamon hit my nostrils, I halt in my tracks.

Fucking hell.

I forgot I wasn't alone.

"He finally appears."

Kabir's tone is husky and melodic—two descriptors that shouldn't make sense together but do.

It's too late to pretend I don't see him. Even if it weren't, I'm trapped between wanting to ignore him out of respect for Greedy and being tempted to learn everything I can about the man who appeared out of thin air and instantly commanded Hunter's attention.

It's not just my curiosity that's piqued.

I want to figure him out. Unpack what sort of relationship he had with Hunter and suss out where he thinks—or hopes—things might still stand between them.

"Mind if I join you?"

He regards me, stormy blue eyes boring into mine as he sucks on the end of his pipe.

"If I say yes, I do mind, will you bugger off?" He exhales, filling the space between us with sweet-smelling smoke.

"Unlikely," I offer, more determined than before to stand my ground and figure this guy out.

"Good to know you're not easily scared away," Kabir remarks, one brow arched.

My phone vibrates in my pocket. I'm so anxious for an update, I fumble to fish it out and almost drop the damn thing.

> Hunter: We're on our way home

That's it. That's the message. She doesn't give me a single damn clue about how the dinner went, or how she's holding up.

"They'll be back soon." I hold up my phone and tip it from side to side. Then, to clarify, and maybe to boast a little, I add, "Hunter texted me."

He hums noncommittally, never taking his eyes off me. Then, with an outstretched hand, he offers his pipe.

I don't reach for it immediately.

With a scowl, he holds it closer to me. "Well, go on, then."

I'm about to shake my head, but I saw the way he looked at Hunter. The way she melted into his touch. I won't deny her what she needs, ever. If that means finding common ground with this character, that's what I'll do.

I can play nice. At least until I figure out what he's playing at.

"Thanks," I reply, taking the pipe. After another second of hesitation, I bring it to my mouth and take an easy pull. Caramely smoke fills my mouth and lungs, the tobacco notes sweet and flavorful.

An ease and lightness swirls through me as I hold the smoke in my lungs.

I let it out slowly, watching the cloud grow between us. "Does this have—"

"It's my own proprietary blend," he declares with a pompous air of distinction.

That doesn't tell me shit about what I just ingested, but it feels nice. Enjoyable, even. Maybe it'll be okay, waiting out here on the balcony with him.

That thought has barely formed before Kabir speaks again.

"Your first name's Levi?"

I nod, handing back his pipe.

He accepts and twirls the stem between his forefinger and thumb, then looks me squarely in the eye. "She never mentioned you before."

Ouch.

I spread my arms wide on the back of the lounger and blow out a long breath. "We were just friends back then." I'm not looking for a fight with this guy. At least not tonight.

"And now?"

Fucking hell. He's nosy, and for such a proper asshole, his manners are terrible. He may be a big deal over in England, but he wouldn't last a day on his own in the south with this attitude.

"Now we're more," I tell him, meeting and holding his gaze.

More.

I leave it at that.

Kabir examines me, his light gray-blue eyes piercing into me with an unnerving intensity.

Doubt pings around my gut. I'm not sure of anything after the events of the last twenty-four hours. I ignore the sensation. Hunter's given me no reason to doubt her.

"Fair enough," he eventually says with a shrug. "It's not like I was celibate during her sabbatical."

This time, it's anxiety hitting me hard. The emotion twists my gut. He may not have been, but someone else was.

Fuck.

Greedy waited.

When he confessed it this morning, I swear something fundamental shifted inside Hunter. For one perfect moment, I thought maybe we had a shot.

Greedy waited, and Hunter clearly did not. Yet that's not even the worst of the secrets that were revealed today.

Despite the easy feeling the British Invasion's "proprietary blend" has instilled in me, my anxiety grows.

I have no idea what to expect once Hunter and Greedy get home, nor do I have any idea what'll happen next.

Half an hour later, a car turns into the circle drive out front. From the balcony along the back of the house, the idling of an engine is audible.

The car turns off. Doors open and close, then all is quiet. Kabir and I are silent, waiting. A few moments later, we hear voices on the stairs.

Two distinct voices.

Two distinct, angry, raised voices.

Fucking hell.

"Shall we greet them?" Kabir suggests, straightening as if he's about to rise.

I shake my head. They'll both be eager to get away from their parents after an evening together, and there's a very good chance they'll need a few minutes to cool off.

"Let's give them a minute. They know where to find us."

I already texted both Hunter and Greedy individually to tell them to come to the balcony once they're home.

Sitting forward with my elbows on my knees, I wait. Kabir's expression remains even, but one of his legs bounces just a little.

I can't help but look from one door to the other. Greedy's room is off to one side, Hunter's on the other.

Their voices grow louder, but rather than split up, both have clearly gone into Hunter's room.

Kabir's eyes widen with interest. He stands but doesn't make any moves to go inside. With his hands in the pockets of his suit pants, he looks ridiculously out of place.

We're both quiet, both clearly attempting to eavesdrop as the voices become more distinct.

When Hunter snaps at Greedy, Kabir's lips tilt up into a lopsided smile.

I don't know what she actually said, but the venom behind it? Damn.

Kabir sets his sights on me, then tips his chin. "Brace yourself, champ. I know that tone."

Brace myself? That's what I've been doing for the last several hours. Nevertheless, I take the bait.

"And what tone is that, exactly?" I rise to my feet and cross my arms over my chest.

Size-wise, this guy's no match for me. I've got a few inches on him, and although he's in shape, it's clear from the fit of his suit that I'm much broader through the arms and chest.

Nevertheless, when he meets my gaze, the instinct to cower is strong.

There's no denying that this man is intimidating. It's the intensity of his gaze, the sharpness of his jaw. It's the way he smiles. Not like he's happy, necessarily, but like he knows he's right.

"It sounds like Garrett Reed unlocked Brat Mode."

I bite back a snicker. He's not wrong.

Now, all we have to do is wait for them to join us.

Chapter 9

Kabir

NOW

I'm on high alert as I step through the French doors off the balcony.

Hunter and Greedy are standing toe-to-toe, fuming with such ferocity the room is drenched in their energy.

I make it all of three strides into the space before it registers: what's happening right now. What she needs from me.

Halting, I throw out one hand to stop Levi in his tracks, too.

Hunter's arms are crossed over her chest, her hip popped out to one side. Her chest heaves as she glares up at her stepbrother.

"You're a liar," Garrett Reed accuses, his words slurred as he sloppily points a finger at Hunter.

"He's drunk," Levi murmurs beside me.

That he is.

"All you do is lie!" he shouts, his voice cracking. "To me. To yourself. You're a fucking liar, and a sneak, just like your fucking mother."

Hunter rears back as if she's been slapped.

"Oof," Levi mutters under his breath.

"Right." I remove my first cuff link and take a tentative step toward them. This won't fucking stand. Garrett Reed has another think coming if he reacts to his own hurt by lashing out and hurting others in return. "Hunter?"

She whips her head in my direction. Her eyes are filled with unshed tears, her brows knitted in a visible effort not to cry.

"I'm here, love," I remind her. "May I step in?"

The question lingers between us all for a breath. Then another.

Her shoulders lower, and she bows her head slightly when my words properly land.

"Please," she replies.

That's the consent I need.

"You." I stalk toward Garrett, venturing close enough to fully take in just how glassy his dark-green eyes are.

He sways as I approach, then finds his balance and stands taller, as if he's preparing to face off with me.

I tip my chin, remove my second cuff link effortlessly, and cock one brow. "Out."

He opens his mouth to protest, but I've already turned to Levi.

"Get him out of here."

Then I turn to Hunter, my chest going tight.

We haven't been together in ages. Time and experience have created craters between us that I ache to fill in.

Yet when her glassy green orbs meet my eyes, her yearning is palpable.

"On your knees, love. Now."

She drops before me so beautifully—my perfect, obedient girl.

I step closer, reveling in the position she's put herself in. It's a gift. She's the prize. I can't resist brushing my palm against the soft skin of her jaw.

Her lips part on contact. She tilts her head back slightly and locks eyes with me.

"This is what you need?" I murmur.

"Yes, Sir."

Bloody hell.

Those two words zing right through my nuts, inspiring a half chub in my pants before I've even taken my next breath. This woman. What she does to me. The power she has over me when she submits.

"Out," I bark over my shoulder, waving my free hand absently toward the other men in the room.

"Hunter," Levi hedges, his voice laced with trepidation.

"She's fine," I reply on her behalf.

Hunter's submission speaks for itself. She doesn't so much as twitch as the other two men scrutinize her, silently begging for her attention.

Hunter sits quietly at my feet, palms resting on her thighs, her gaze focused on the floor directly in front of her.

Such a good fucking girl.

"Tem—" Garrett Reed starts. He catches the nonsensical nickname coming out of his drunk facehole, then self-corrects. "I mean Hunter. Get up, Hunter."

My perfect girl remains motionless before us all. I can't help but grin.

"You're doing so well," I murmur, running one hand over her golden tendrils and letting the ends slip through my fingers. Gods, I missed this. I missed our dynamic, sure, but at the heart of it, I just fucking missed her.

"Hunter," Garrett Reed growls out again. Louder. Closer, in fact, as he attempts to snag her attention.

I hold up one hand to warn him off, then hit him with an unamused glare. "She will not speak unless I command it."

Garrett Reed halts in his tracks. "Comm—hand it?" he slurs. "What sort of fucked-up shit is this?"

Levi takes a step forward then, whether to hold back his friend or get to his girl, I don't know. Nor do I really care. They're delaying the inevitable at this point.

I regard them both, feigning boredom to mask the agitation their defiance inspires in me. "My little slut doesn't answer to either of you."

Garrett Reed lunges. "Don't you dare call her that!" Before he can make it a step, Levi catches him by the arm.

"You're not in control here, Garrett Reed Ferguson the Third. I am. And I said get out."

"Tem—"

"Out!" I shout. Then, softer, I drive my point home.

"Do you see how she submits? How she obeys? She's not yours to command. That is irrefutably clear. Leave this instant and do not address my pretty little cum bucket again unless you're prepared to see what sort of right hook *I'm* packing."

He doesn't bother sassing back this time, but when he lunges again, Levi has a much harder time containing him.

"Take him away," I tell Levi, waving one hand toward the door.

The blond man's jaw ticks, and the fingers of his free hand curl into a fist. He looks from me to Hunter, then, chin raised, at me once more. Perhaps our little rendezvous on the balcony instilled enough trust for him to see what's happening here.

She's safe. She wants this. She's the one in control.

With a subtle nod, he tugs his friend's arm and heads for the door.

"Stay, love. I'm not leaving. You're safe," I murmur, following the other men. I usher them into the hallway, then lock them out of the room.

I pivot, then quickly stride to the balcony doors.

Garrett Reed is fast in his inebriated state. I'll give him that.

Not fast enough, though.

He must have used Levi's room to get out onto the balcony so quickly.

As I turn the lock on the French doors, I meet his eye, keeping my expression hard.

He bangs one fist into the glass block panel between us, his face red and his eyes wild.

Smirking, I reach for the curtains, but instead of drawing them closed, I pull them open even wider.

Chapter 10

Hunter

NOW

Shame courses through me as I lay down every defense and wait.

I've spent so much time running. Worrying. Keeping secrets and keeping to myself.

I needed to be done tonight.

Spence clearly recognized it, even before I did.

He gave me an out. I took it.

Consequences be damned. Greedy will never forgive me anyway.

After enduring the dinner from hell with my narcissistic mother, my inebriated not-brother, and my clueless stepfather, all I wanted was for the night to be over.

Except the longer we were there, the more Greedy drank. The more he drank, the more agitated he got.

His muttered insults and taunting didn't stop when we left the club.

He followed me up the stairs, followed me into my room. The man wouldn't stop pushing.

He pushed until I was so rattled, so perfectly backed into a corner with nothing but my own self-loathing and shame to keep me company, that I had no choice but to snap back.

Only, that did nothing but escalate the situation. Every counter remark and reply to his prodding spurred him on.

It's terrifying to think about what would have happened had Spence not stepped in.

Honestly, I don't know how I've navigated the last few years without the outlet and release I can only find with this man.

"Look at me, love."

Kabir's tone brooks no argument—it never does. Even so, there's a gentleness to the way he speaks to me. It caresses the most broken, vulnerable pieces of my heart. He's a dichotomy of power and care, dominance and grace.

When I lock eyes with him, his are swimming with concern. His motive is clear and his intention pure. He wants to help me. He's always been willing to do whatever it takes for me.

In an instant, that concern morphs into heat, and his tongue darts out to wet his bottom lip. It's a familiar tell. One I love. One I've come to crave.

"Is this what you need?" he asks, one eyebrow raised.

"Yes, Sir." I drop my chin and bow my head to assure him there's no doubt or hesitation on my end.

"You're going to be a good little slut and do exactly as I say?" "Yes, Sir."

"Don't you dare look at that balcony door. You understand?"

My heart clenches. "Yes, Sir."

"Your safe word is the same?"

"Yes, Sir." My pulse picks up.

"You're on birth control?" "Yes, Sir."

"I had a vasectomy," he murmurs. "You know that, but I need you to remember that when I'm fucking you raw and filling your holes until the very essence of me is seeping out of your pores." I throb at the promise of what's to come.

"Undress, then get back on your knees."

I hurry to do as he commands, flustered and hot and aching. As I drop back to my knees, I can't help but survey him, transfixed by the sheer power of Spence undressing above me.

"You'll never escape me, love. I know you feel like you need to keep running, but we are inevitable. I'll follow you and I'll find you, through every trial. Through every lifetime. Tell me you understand what you mean to me."

"I do. I—" I don't say the first thought that comes to mind, despite it being true. "I understand," I breathe, my chest heaving as I will the frantic rhythm of my heart to even out.

Kabir shucks off his shirt, commanding my full attention. He whips off his belt and unbuttons his pants.

He lowers the zipper at a tantalizingly slow rate, putting on a show for me and for whoever is outside watching.

I cut off the thought and choke back the shame. I can't think about them now.

Kabir specifically said not to look at the door.

Swallowing thickly, I focus on the erect cock he's wielding in his hand. On the drop of precum collecting on the exposed head.

I want to please him. I want to show him just how good I can be.

"Needy little bitch. I bet you're soaking your thighs just from the sight of my cock."

I lick my lips.

"Do you want it?"

"Yes, Sir."

"You're a desperate little slut, aren't you?"

Air whooshes from my lungs. "Yes, Sir."

"Look at you. On your knees, panting like a bitch in heat. I bet you haven't been properly fucked since you left London."

I stay silent this time, peeking up at him through my lashes. He'll know if I lie.

He lazily pulls on his cock, then lets out a soft hiss. "Ah. I see. So you've had plenty of cock since I last saw you, love. Is that it? My little slut let other people fill her holes whilst she was aching for me?"

I remain silent, lowering my gaze again.

"Answer me," he demands, still jerking himself inches from my face.

"Yes, Sir," I admit, trembling on an exhale. "I'm a dirty fucking slut."

"How right you are," Kabir murmurs, drawing closer.

"Open."

Without hesitation, I open wide, prepared to take his length. Instead, he pins his cock to his stomach, straddles my face, and sinks his balls into my mouth.

"Dirty little cum sluts don't deserve cock. Suck my sack until I've blown my first load all over your pretty face."

Despite the harshness of his words, they soothe me. I open wider, letting the weight of his balls fill my mouth. I suck and lick, hum and lightly tug.

Kabir jacks his cock above my head, chanting awful, degrading insults through his teeth.

Dirty little slut.

Desperate, needy whore.

His words wrap around me in a comforting embrace, as if he's smoothing a balm over the most jagged, rotted pieces of my self-loathing.

Nothing he says truly hurts me.

I'm safe, and I'm whole.

Even in our most intense moments, no amount of degradation could match the awful things I've thought about myself. Especially at my lowest. I deserve it. I deserve it and so much more.

"Fuck, love," Kabir warns with a grunt. "I'm going to paint you with my cum and not even pretend to aim for your mouth."

With a step back, he lifts my chin with two fingers.

Mouth open, I stick out my tongue, desperate and aching for what comes next.

The first rope of warm, sticky release lands along my jaw.

Instantly, the switch is flipped. The insults stop. His words transform.

"Fucking perfect, Hunter. My perfect angel girl."

Kabir jacks himself harder, burst after burst of semen shooting out from his fat cock and landing on my face. Cum coats my lips, my cheeks, trickles down my neck.

"You're so fucking pretty, painted in my seed. My perfect darling girl."

I preen, basking in the glow of his release as if it were my own.

A heartbeat later, my chest tightens with emotion, my eyes burning with the need to cry, to just let go.

"So pretty. So beautiful." He pets my face, smearing his seed along my jaw. When his thumb caresses my lower lip, I open wider.

He inserts the digit, and I suckle him clean.

"You're perfect," he whispers, his crystalline blue eyes blazing. "So perfect the sight of you makes me weak in ways nothing else ever has or ever will."

A wicked smile tugs at the corner of his lips as he pulls his thumb from my mouth.

"Maybe you should go to the doors and show your boyfriend and your brother just how perfect you look covered in my cum."

I blink, and hot, indignant tears spring from my eyes. My face heats, and my hands shake.

Through gritted teeth, I snap, "He's *not* my brother."

Kabir freezes as we both register how badly I just messed up.

My heart pounds and blood whooshes in my ears as I watch and wait for what he'll do next.

What the hell, Hunter? Where did that come from? We slipped back into our dynamic so effortlessly just now. For me to sass back is completely out of character.

Kabir tips his head, no doubt taking in the guilt and shame written all over my face.

He knows me. He gets me at my core. Or, at least, he used to.

Living with Greedy over the last several months has changed me. He's rewired my brain and reinstalled defense mechanisms I never had to rely on with Spence.

"Stand up."

Heart in my throat, I do as he says.

"Turn toward the doors."

I hesitate.

Are they still out there? If so, then based on the lighting, they can very clearly see inside my room.

So far, I've been okay with them watching, observing, seeing me in my element, submitting to Spence, willingly letting him control the scene, degrade me, then shower me in praise.

This moment is different.

This feels cruel.

All I ever do is hurt Greedy. I'm so fucking tired of pushing him away and hurting him, even if it is to protect him.

He knows my secret now, so what am I even protecting him from anymore?

"Go and show them how pretty you look, love. Walk to the doors so those boys can see you painted in my cum."

My entire body seizes. I couldn't move if I tried. It's as if my feet are encased in cement blocks. Every fiber of my being is screaming to stay put, to leave them out of this. To protect Greedy and try in vain to undo even a fraction of the hurt and pain I've caused him.

Kabir hums impatiently.

I swallow past the emotion bubbling up in my esophagus, desperate to find my voice.

Quietly but confidently, I whisper, "*Loot.*"

It's not my safe word. I don't want to stop. I need more of him, of that, I'm sure. But I'm walking a fine line, and I'm dangerously close to causing irreparable damage to the first man I ever loved. If I do that, I'll never forgive myself.

Loot means hold up. Slow down. It's our signal that if he keeps pushing, there's a likely chance I will need my safe word.

Hurting Greedy more than I already have is a soft limit I didn't know existed until this moment. Once the realization clicks, I double down.

"Loot," I repeat, louder this time.

Kabir wraps his arms around my shoulders and turns me to face him. He scans my face, searching, assessing, looking for answers.

I swallow slowly, inhale deeply. Then, decidedly, I meet Kabir's gaze.

"I want to keep going. Just you and me. Can you please close the blinds?"

"Of course, love," Spence assures me. "Thank you for telling me. Go wait on the bed."

"Yes, Sir," I reply obediently.

He smiles warmly, bends to brush my cum-covered lips with a chaste kiss, then turns on his heel and marches to the door to pull the blinds closed and block out the rest of the world.

Chapter 11

Levi

NOW

"Let me in!" Greedy snarls, getting right up in my face as if he can intimidate me into bending to his will.

Teeth gritted, I keep my arms crossed over my chest, holding my ground.

There's no point in blocking the door, really. It's locked, and he knows what's going on behind me. We both heard enough—witnessed enough—to know exactly what Kabir and Hunter are getting up to.

The way he spoke to her was hard to swallow, but when she responded, almost as if she was grateful to submit and let go, my trepidation eased. There's something there—a whole helluva lot of something—and no matter how I feel about it or where things stand between us, Hunter makes her own decisions. She's so smart. Independent. Thoughtful and assertive.

I may not like what's happening in her bedroom, and I may not understand it, but I have faith that she knows what she's doing and that she trusts the man who kicked us out and locked the door.

"She's okay, G," I say, grasping his arms.

He shakes me off, then shoves into my shoulder. When I don't budge, he sucker-punches me in the gut. Thankfully, he's so slow and deliberate enough in his movements that I see it coming and brace my abs before he makes contact.

I hit him with an unamused glare. He's drunk, and he's clearly looking for a fight, but he won't get one out of me.

There's nothing either of us can do, even if I agreed with him. Even if I step away from the door, neither of us is getting into that room unless Hunter or Kabir unlocks it from the inside. Or one of us breaks the glass.

On second thought, I better stay put.

A whooshing sound at my back startles me, and I spin just in time to see Kabir closing the floor-length blinds. As they sway, I can make out his retreating form through the gap. I also catch one more glimpse of Hunter—completely naked, standing in the middle of the room—before the curtains settle and we're shut out entirely.

"He closed the blinds." Greedy blinks rapidly, as if he's trying to process the move. "He closed the fucking blinds." The second time he says it, his tone is edged in panic. "Levi," he begs, grasping the door handle near my hip and jerking it a few times in vain.

It's locked. He knows it's locked. But he's a masochist. A glutton for punishment. Especially when it comes to our girl.

Our girl.

Is that what Hunter is? Will that ever be a possibility for the three of us now?

What about the British Invasion currently dominating her behind these doors?

Frustrated, I run one hand through my hair, then look Greedy in the eye.

"Come on," I coax, clasping his shoulder. "Let's go hang out in your room. Or maybe get out of here, go for a drive."

I would be the one driving, of course.

"He fucking locked her in there!" Greedy rages, shaking the handle with even more effort. "Hunter! *Hunter*!"

Fucking hell. He's drunk and so damn heartbroken. Somehow, I'm stuck out here with the responsibility of explaining to him that Kabir isn't doing anything that Hunter doesn't legitimately want him to do.

"G. Stop," I say, my chest aching, even as frustration bubbles up inside me. "It's okay. She's—"

"It's not," he cries. "It's not fucking okay. She locked me out. She locked us out."

He's vibrating with fury now. I'd be surprised if they can't hear him inside.

"*Greedy*." I grip his shoulders and angle closer, trying to catch his gaze.

He's frantic and harried, desperation emanating off him as he trembles under my hands.

"G, please," I try, desperate for him to look at me, to focus, to be okay.

"She locked us out," he repeats. "She always fucking locks me out."

In slow motion, his face crumples and his anger dissipates. He pulls in a gasping inhale, then lets out a pained, mournful cry.

He collapses, his body racked with sobs as he gives me his full weight and pounds one fist against the glass next to my head.

On instinct, I wrap my arms around his waist. I pull him against my chest, pressing his body to mine as tightly as I can, aching to be his anchor.

I cup the back of his head and stroke along the base of his skull. "It's okay," I promise. "It'll be okay."

He slumps farther, sinking into my hold completely and burying his face in my neck. His chest shudders as another sob works its way out of him.

"She always does this. She runs. Why does she always fucking do this?"

He cries out again, a pained, anguished sound that sends fissures through my heart. Then he sinks to the ground, taking me down with him.

My knee hits the wooden planks, and pain sparks up my quad. Quickly, I shift to a seated position, sure to keep my back against the glass door of Hunter's bedroom in case Greedy lashes out again.

On his knees between my legs, he continues to cry, but he allows me to guide his body to a position where I can best comfort him. I wrap my arms around his neck. He places his head into the crook of my shoulder.

I smooth one hand up and down his back tentatively, then give him a firmer, steady rubbing when he doesn't pull away.

It takes a decent amount of resolve to fight the urge to kiss the top of his head. *Too much.* Instead, I channel all my energy and empathy into comforting my best friend.

"It'll be okay," I murmur in what I hope is a soothing tone.

Greedy shakes his head minutely, grinding his forehead into my clavicle in the process. "It won't, Leev," he whispers. "Not this time."

Sighing, I hug him tighter.

This whole situation is a big fucking mess. All I can do is hope that Hunter realizes sooner rather than later that what she seems to need in order to be well has the power to be Greedy's undoing.

Chapter 12

Hunter

NOW

The crown of my head rams into the headboard in a steady, soothing rhythm as Kabir fucks me from behind.

I've lost track of my orgasms. I've lost track of everything.

I've stopped thinking entirely.

I move where he tells me. I do as he commands.

For the first time in ages, I'm back in subspace. I'm floating on ethereal clouds of mindless bliss.

We've been at it for hours, only breaking to hydrate and so Kabir can pop a Viagra.

I'm in a constant heightened state of arousal, fueled by his words and the way he commands my body with such familiarity.

"Such a tight little hole," Kabir praises as he works a second finger into my ass. "My little slut loves being all filled up." With a grunt, he thrusts his cock deeper into my cunt.

"More, Sir. Please," I whimper, desperate to hold on to this high. I want him to use me so thoroughly I can't walk come morning.

"More?" A dark laugh escapes him. "My whore wants more? Of course you do, you needy little cum skip."

He spanks my ass hard, and in response, I clench around his cock.

"Naughty," he huffs with a slap to the other cheek.

This time, I squeeze him so tightly he can't pull out.

Growling, he freezes. "Oh. So that's how you want to play, Firecracker?" He thrusts to the hilt with so much force my head slams into the headboard.

Yes. Fuck.

"I'm going to fill this cunt, then suck all my cum out of you and shove it up your ass."

Whimpering, I buck my hips, meeting him thrust for thrust. Before long, I can't keep up. My arms and legs give out, and I sink flat onto the bed.

"That's a good girl." Kabir's voice is gravelly and sultry at the same time. "Such a meek little whore, giving up and letting me fuck you into the mattress."

I have no words. No thoughts. No desire to speak. My mind is empty, and the world is quiet as I focus on each slap of skin and the pounding in my pussy.

"Good girls love to be filled up, don't they, my little slut?"

Words are hard.

Talking is near impossible.

"Yes, Sir," I eventually mumble into the mattress. Tears fill my eyes. Fuck, letting go and giving myself completely to this man fills me with such an overwhelming sense of relief.

The flames licking up my insides demand my attention. I try to temper them, to hold them at bay. I can't come until he gives me permission. He told me that before we began this round.

"You're close," he accuses, his tone harsh, as if he can read my mind. "Don't you dare come, Firecracker."

"No, Sir. I won't. I swear. Please, Sir," I plead. "Fill me. Fuck me and fill up my holes."

I'm panting. Breathless. Boneless. Spineless.

With a groan, Kabir comes. He holds himself inside my body, all the while milking his cock with two fingers through the thin wall separating my rectum from my vagina.

He unloads deep inside me, then he pulls out and hikes my hips up until I'm on my knees once again.

The heat of his tongue against my sensitive flesh has me biting down on the edge of the duvet. He licks through my thoroughly fucked folds, flicks my clit, then dips his tongue as far into my cunt as he can get. Then he sucks. He makes a meal out of slurping and sucking every drop from my weeping pussy.

The pleasure is so intensely concentrated that fresh tears spring from my eyes.

The second his face leaves my cunt, I whimper.

Slowly, he pulls his fingers out of my asshole, and I'm so empty I break. On a sob, I beg, "Please, Sir." The cathartic need for him to fill me and use me is the only lucid thought left in my brain.

With both hands, he slaps my ass cheeks and spreads me wide open.

The sound of him spitting is accompanied by a wet warmth on my puckered hole.

In the next breath, he uses his tongue to push the fluid past the tight ring of muscle.

He makes quick work of feeding his cum into my asshole, holding me in place with a tight grip on both cheeks.

Then he pulls away, captures my legs, and rolls me to my back.

"Spread and let me see it, love."

I do as he says, focusing on the curves of his muscles and the contrast of color as he grips my pale thighs with his manicured hands.

He holds my legs apart, admiring my thoroughly fucked cunt and cream-filled asshole.

Smiling, he drags one finger through my sex. His touch is soft, reverent. He caresses and pets me in slow motion, as I lie spread out before him, aching and needy.

"I've traveled the world, studied the great artists of every century. Yet I've never witnessed anything as breathtakingly beautiful as your needy little cunt and perfect rosebud leaking with my cum."

Preening, I spread my legs wider. My inner thighs burn from the stretch in my effort to show him everything.

"Look at you, all spread out for me. Such a pretty pussy," he purrs directly into my cunt. He lowers his head and sniffs, wafting up the scents of sex and cum, submission and desire.

When he straightens, he zeroes in on my face, his expression going serious. "Are you well, love?"

"Yes, Sir," I assure him.

I'm more than well. I'm soaring. I'm floating. I'm whole.

I'm breathing fully for the first time in months. Finally free.

"You have one more in you, then."

It's not a question, but rather a command.

"Hold yourself open for me, love. I'm going to give this needy cunt everything she wants now, yes?"

"Yes, please," I beg, digging my nails into my thighs and holding my breath for what comes next.

"No counting," he reminds me. "This isn't a punishment. It's what you need, so say thank you."

"Thank you, Sir," I rush to offer, bracing for impact.

He raises one hand, then with perfect aim, he slaps my pussy so hard I scream.

Tears paint my cheeks as I gasp for air. I blink rapidly, trying to clear out the moisture, desperate to see him do it again.

He slaps my pussy again and again. Higher each time. Until my clit is burning. Until my insides gush out and sobs rack through my chest. Until I crash off the side of the cliff and all I can manage to do is feel and fall and cry, "Thank you, Sir. Thank you."

Chapter 13

Kabir

NOW

I scrubbed every inch of her skin, then gave her hair a thorough washing.

Thankfully, the bathroom is well appointed, and I found nearly everything needed with minimal effort. I've wrapped her in a robe, and we're sitting on the plush shag rug in front of the vanity.

"Eat, love," I encourage, nodding to the package of Tunnock's tea cakes I procured from my travel case. I didn't have time to pack properly, but even in my haste, I made sure to snag a few packs of her favorite snack on the way to the airport.

"I've already had four, Spence." Her tone is lighter than it's been since I arrived, and I can practically see her holding back an eye roll. "But thank you for bringing these," she adds, softer. "I love them."

Sitting behind her, brushing through her hair, I hum in acknowledgment.

More than anything, I want to ask her a thousand questions and unload all the thoughts I've been stewing over for the last twenty-four hours.

More like the last two and a half years.

I breathe in a cleansing breath and let it out slowly. My questions will keep. I'm not going anywhere anytime soon, at least not without her.

Once her hair is free of tangles and she's finished all six teacakes in the package, I rise to my feet and offer her my hand.

"Do you have any suppositories?"

She slips her palm against mine and lets me pull her up. Standing face to face with me, she regards me with a dreamy, far-away, fully sated smile that lights up my insides and makes me feel like the king of her world.

"Second drawer on the right."

I make quick work of locating what I need and hold up two to confirm we're on the same page.

She nods, then backs up against the vanity and pulls open the knot of her robe.

I drop to my knees before her and smooth my palms down her sides, over her ribs, and along the soft, delicate skin of her stomach.

I kiss her from navel to pubic bone, taking my time and savoring the feel of her skin beneath my lips. Gods, I've missed this woman.

It takes all my strength to fight the urge to bury my face in her throbbing cunt.

Instead, I tear open the foil packages, then carefully place one hand on her inner thigh to steady her.

When I brush two fingers through her folds, she hisses quietly.

I kiss the strip of hair on her pubic bone once more to soothe her, then I insert the first suppository—a blend of CBD and cocoa butter specifically designed for aftercare—then gingerly graze the tip of the other against her puckered hole.

"Breathe, love," I remind her.

On her exhale, I push in, placing the bullet-shaped suppository knuckle-deep in her ass.

"All done." I kiss her stomach again, then each of her hips for good measure. When I rise to my feet, I brush my lips against her forehead and wash my hands, then lead her back to the bedroom.

"I plan to sleep in here with you," I inform her as I pull back the sheets on the side closest to the phone charger and sparkly pink e-reader on the nightstand.

"I figured," she says. "I may not be able to sleep, though."

"Where are you in your cycle?"

"Day twenty-two," she tells me softly.

"So I shan't worry if you're up and out of bed in the middle of the night?"

Eyes closed and with a small smile on her face, she nods.

"Water?" I ask.

She points to a half-full bottle on the vanity across the way. I fetch it, then fill it with fresh, cold water from the bathroom sink.

Upon delivery, I ask, "Where are your meds?"

"They're inside my nightstand drawer, but I take them in the morning these days."

I finger the handle, but she catches my wrist before I can pull it open.

"I've got it, Spence. I have to take the mini pill at the same time every morning. Then I turn the bottle upside down on my SSRI to confirm that I've taken them. I haven't missed a dose in months," she assures me.

Concern nags at the back of my mind, but I trust her, and I know better than to challenge her when she tells me she's okay.

With a steadying breath, I release my grip on the drawer handle. I bend low and kiss her forehead once more before pulling the covers to her chin.

"Try to rest, love. You're safe, and I'm here. Whatever ails you will keep until tomorrow."

The first soft snore rises from her chest before I've even turned off the lights and climbed into the bed.

Chapter 14

Hunter

NOW

I wake up deliciously sore and deeply satisfied. I slept harder last night than I have in months, if not years. It was the most restful sleep I've experienced since I've been back in North Carolina, of that I'm certain.

Silently, I stretch, then stifle a yawn as I sit up and take in the man beside me.

He's turned away, sprawled out on his stomach, his bare upper back on full display. He's exquisite: lean muscle and definition wrapped in flawless dark skin. I resist the urge to touch him, to confirm that he's really here, in North Carolina. Back in my life, lying beside me in bed.

Then a memory of yesterday morning bubbles up, reminding me of why he's here.

Reminding me of how his arrival immediately and irrevocably shattered the foundation of trust Greedy and I were starting to rebuild.

Reminding me of how I screwed up. How I keep failing where Greedy is concerned.

I don't know how any of us will come back from this.

Greedy was so hateful and cruel last night, and rightfully so. Spence dropped the biggest of all bombs. Dammit. A sharp pain in my chest has me rubbing at the spot. I never wanted Greedy to find out like that.

It's my fault that he did. I should have told him, and I accept responsibility for this whole mess. For years, I've been keeping this secret because I can't fathom how I could ever explain to the first boy I loved that when he lost me, I lost myself, too.

The pregnancy and the miscarriage aren't even the hardest parts. I was a coward, and I ran. As shameful as my behavior was, I own up to it. I made my choice. I'm woman enough to live with the consequences.

The problem lies in talking to Greedy about what happened next and the aftermath. Once I start talking, there's no way I won't tell him everything. That's what terrifies me. Admitting how close I came to giving up completely in London.

A shadow eclipses the crack of sunlight streaming in between the blinds, pulling me out of my own head.

Someone is awake and out on the balcony.

I take my SSRI and turn over the bottle, then slip out from under the sheets. I take a minute to pee and brush my teeth, then quietly slip outside while trying not to disturb the blinds.

The smooth wooden planks are freezing under my feet as I shut the door behind me. As soon as the handle clicks in place, I beeline for the sectional couch, which is situated on an outdoor rug.

Immediately, my steps falter.

Levi is seated on the couch, his arms spread wide across the back cushions, his gaze set intently on me.

I offer him the slightest smile, testing the waters.

With a dip of his chin, he readjusts his backward hat.

He's worried, but there's not even a hint of anger in his expression.

Then I notice the two steaming mugs on the coffee table. We're okay. Or at least, we will be.

"Extra thirsty this morning?"

Brows furrowed, he assesses me, clearly not catching on. I roll my lips and nod toward the mugs.

His eyes light just a little, and he chuckles. "The one on the right is yours."

With that simple phrase, my heart stitches back together ever so slightly.

"I've gotta warn you, though," he says, holding one mug out to me. "It's tap water that's been warmed up in the microwave. It may not live up to certain standards."

I snort and take a sip of the weak but warm and soothing tea, then set my mug back down beside his. Steam billows off the pair of them, swirling and dissipating quickly in the cold morning air.

Shifting from hip to hip, I eye the empty cushion at his side. "Can I sit with you?"

"Of course," he replies, sitting just a little straighter.

I gravitate toward him, then sink into his side. He drops his arm over my shoulders, cradling me close and playing with the wispy hair that's fallen out of my messy bun.

For a few minutes, we stay like that. Silent and still. When the chill gets to be too much, I wrap my arm around his torso and snuggle closer.

It's cold this morning, so we're both dressed in sweatpants and hoodies, though the thick fabric can't hide the hardness of his chest. I take a deep, shameless inhale, savoring the scents of musk, teakwood, and peach.

I bury my face in Levi's side because I'm a coward, and mumble, "I wasn't sure what to expect this morning."

After last night and the way Kabir made them leave and shut them out, I can't even begin to sort out how to move forward. It must have been difficult to be on the outside looking in without any context or heads-up. I was just so desperate for an out—aching to escape Greedy's anger, Magnolia's meddling, and most of all, the self-loathing churning in my gut.

Levi pulls me closer and kisses the top of my head. "It's going to take a hell of a lot more than some Dom with an accent to scare me away, Daisy."

I snort at his all too accurate assessment, even as my heart leaps. "So we're okay?"

Levi is silent for a breath, then another. As quickly as it lifted, the damn organ in my chest sinks as I wait for his response.

"We need to talk. About what happened with Spence, and what it means for—" He pauses, his Adam's apple bobbing. "What it means for you and me."

Relief washes over me, and I snuggle closer into his side. There's still a possibility of *you and me* in his mind. "We'll talk," I promise. "But I don't want anything to change between us."

Easier said than done, I'm sure.

After another breath, Levi reaches for his coffee, takes a big gulp, and regards me with one brow cocked. "I don't either," he says, his tone firm. "I'm not giving you up for anything, Daisy. As long as we communicate—and by we, I mean all of us, including Kabir—I think we can make this work."

My stomach riots with butterflies. I haven't lost Levi.

He's staying.

He knows just how bad my mom can be. He bore witness to how I act—what I need—when I'm feeling low. He's not scared, and he's not giving up on us.

Levi wants to stay.

"I assume Greedy isn't going to share the same opinion."

His body goes rigid, and his grip tightens on my shoulder.

The reaction causes me to look up and really take him in for the first time since I ventured out here.

Levi's piercing blue eyes meet mine, then he shakes his head. "He's not okay. He was wrecked last night. Thoroughly and truly wrecked."

"He was drunk," I scoff.

"He was." Levi nods, his lips tipped down in a pensive frown. "But he was also desperate to save you from what he thought was a threat. Even after everything he found out yesterday, Daisy, he just wants to love you."

A whimper catches in my throat. It's the truth. There is no doubt about it. Only, I don't know what to do or where to go from here. Tears well in my eyes, and my stomach burns with anxiety.

What we had, it's gone. It slipped away, and my life changed forever that fateful day in August three years ago.

The Hunter who existed back then is no more. I've hardened around the edges. I've had to fight down personal demons I didn't even know existed until it was almost too late.

I did everything I could think of to remove myself from the equation. During my darkest moments, I truly believed his life would be better without me in it. I don't know if I have the strength to explain all that to him. It's not fair to ask him to love this husk of a person—a shell of the Hunter he fell in love with—when I couldn't even love him properly when I was whole.

Where do I go from here? It's safe to say that yesterday, Greedy and I hit rock bottom. Add my connection with Levi, then Kabir's unexpected appearance, and the complicated place we've found ourselves in is only magnified.

"I don't know what to do," I admit, swiping a tear from my cheek. My chest aches with the pain I caused and continue to cause Greedy.

"Give him some time to cool down," Levi suggests. "He's hurting, and his feelings are valid. I think a little space would do us all good." He cups my head with one hand, smoothing over my hair and kissing me again.

"Easier said than done, considering our parents asked us to spend the holidays with them in the mountains."

A surprised huff escapes him. "Are you serious?"

"I told them I wouldn't go unless you came with us."

There is no way I'd leave Levi out, especially knowing that if he was stuck in South Chapel over the holidays, his mother would do her best to guilt him into visiting.

"I may have also insisted Spence come along, too."

Levi blows out a long breath, his chest deflating. "You sure that's a good idea, Daisy?"

"No." In fact, I'm sure it's a certifiably bad idea to invite my European lover and my boyfriend to spend the holidays at my ex-boyfriend/not-brother's cabin. Yet here we are.

For a long moment, I focus on the steam billowing out of the mugs. A yawn catches me by surprise—I'm always groggy for an hour or so after taking my meds.

"Just so we're on the same page, I don't have a problem with Spence being... in your life... on principle. But what he said to you—"

And there it is.

Sitting up, I place my palm on the center of Levi's chest, relishing the warmth that radiates from him and the feel of the rock-solid muscle beneath the thick fabric of his hoodie.

Keeping my gaze set on my hand, I focus on the steady rhythm of his heart and tell him, "I like that."

He stiffens. "You *like* that? Hunter, he called you—" "A slut. A useless hole. Yeah." The words are strange outside the confines of the bedroom where Spence and I have an established dynamic, but I need Levi to understand. "I like when he degrades me."

Heart pounding against my sternum, I sit taller and check the solidness of my defenses, mentally preparing for battle.

Levi gapes, and his jaw ticks with visible irritation, but he doesn't lecture me.

Always the southern gentleman.

I wrap my arms around his neck, willing him to understand.

"I've asked him to say those things," I explain, burying my face in his shoulder. "I crave it. When Spence is in control, when he's degrading me or talking to me like I'm worthless while worshipping my body, I can let go. The berating voices in my head go silent. When someone else takes over, I can rest."

Cool hands find the hem of my sweatshirt and work their way up my back. Then Levi is holding me just as tightly as I'm clinging to him.

"You like it," he murmurs, the words slow, like he's testing out how they sound.

I nod, my nose brushing the warm skin at his neck. "If I wanted him to stop, he would. Immediately. Without question. We have safe words. He knows me better than…"

I cut myself off, because I can't honestly say that Spence knows me better than anyone. There are parts of me that Levi sees that no one else understands. There are pieces of who I used to be that only Greedy knows. Then there's the version of me who healed herself—a woman who was raw and vulnerable with a man who's still on the other side of the world.

There are parts of me that are only his to know. He knows me so well, but so do three other men, along with my bestie Joey.

"He knows me really well," I finally say. "He and I, we understand each other. He was exactly what I needed, when I needed it."

For several heartbeats, Levi says nothing, jaw ticking. Finally, he clears his throat. "I need to tell you something."

"Okay." If this is going to work between us, we need to be honest with each other. I want him to feel like he can tell me anything.

"He… Spence," Levi clarifies, "He mentioned last night that he wasn't surprised you had a boyfriend, because he hadn't been celibate either over the last few years."

Worry pulls between Levi's brows, though I don't know if the concern is over how I'll take this news or over sharing something he isn't supposed to share.

"Thank you for telling me," I say with a soft peck to his lips. "I'm not surprised to hear that. I assumed we weren't together the day I left London."

"Yet he's here," Levi reminds me.

"He is," I whisper. Spence traveled all the way from London to check on me. I get the sense he's not in any rush to return home.

He's here.

He's not the only one. For the first time since waking, I think about my mother. About her identical green eyes meeting mine in the mirror at the club last night. About her saccharine smile and the singsong voice she employs around Dr. F.

Why is she here, and more importantly, when will she leave?

"So if he's here," Levi pushes, "what are you now?"

Good question. "I honestly don't know," I admit. "But I promise we'll figure it out."

Chapter 15

Hunter

THEN

"I can barely keep up," I bemoan as Sean loads another tray of cider cocktails for me to take to the hostess stand.

"Get used to it," he tells me with a rueful smile. "This is pretty typical for the happy hour crowd."

Being one of the newest hostesses at Splice means I've worked nothing but night shifts until today. Typically, those shifts begin at eight, even though the doors don't open until ten.

Today I'm scheduled for an afternoon shift, which covers the after-work and happy-hour crowds.

There are no lists for happy hour. I stupidly thought that meant my job would be easier.

If anything, we're seeing double or triple the number of guests I'm accustomed to because there are no bouncers on duty.

I'm the first point of contact for each and every person who steps through the door, eager to accept their complimentary beverage. The cocktail offerings change with the seasons, I've learned. Now that we're deep into fall, it's an apple-based cider that's as tart as it is refreshing. We sampled it during our staff meeting earlier this week. It's delicious. By the time the meeting ended, Louie and I had made plans to come back to the club in a few nights when neither of us is working so we can properly imbibe.

I take the tray from Sean and precariously lift it with both arms over to the hostess stand.

"I'll bring you another round right away, kid," Sean tells me.

I'm grateful for that. I'm not supposed to leave the hostess stand, and yet we're also not properly staffed for a crowd this size.

Frazzled, I approach the small group of young, smartly dressed professionals waiting at the stand. "Here you are. Sorry about the wait."

After they've taken their drinks and headed deeper into the space, I have a moment to breathe. There's no entertainment during the afternoon happy hours, but one wouldn't know it based on the size and eagerness of the crowd. I've only just caught my breath when the stream of people starts up again. The line is so long that many bypass the hostess stand altogether. I can't say I mind at all.

"You again."

Startled, I snap my head up, and I zero in on the man I now know to be the owner of this establishment.

"Me. Yes. Um, hello..." I stumble over exactly how I'm supposed to address him.

"Sir Spencer?"

He makes a gravelly sound of approval under his breath, then comes to rest both forearms on the hostess stand. "For as much as I like the sound of that, my friends call me Spence."

Stomach twisting, I assess him. "Are you saying I should call you Spence?"

"Fair question. After our last encounter, I'm not quite sure whether to consider you friend or foe."

He's teasing me, I realize. In the daylight, he's easier to read. The glimmer in his eye and the upturn of one side of his mouth show his age—mid- to late-twenties, if I had to guess.

His jawline is perfectly stubbled once again, almost as if he shaves daily and yet can't keep up with the growth. The five-o'clock shadow suits him, simply adding to the unabashed sex appeal he oozes.

Not that I would ever tell him that.

"I consider *you* to be the owner of my place of employment," I reply, posture rigid and tone as professional as I can make it. "So you should consider me to be your employee and nothing more." I pick up a glass from the tray at my side. "May I offer you a drink, sir?"

He drags his teeth over his bottom lip, as if trying to hold back a laugh. "Well done, love. But Sean already has my drink waiting."

A glance over my shoulder confirms his statement. Three fingers of amber liquid in a crystal tumbler, no ice, sits waiting on the polished bar top.

"I take it you're well?" he asks, shifting past the hostess stand to reach for the drink at the bar, taking care to not touch me but coming intimately close, nevertheless.

"I am," I say, telling myself not to overthink that move he just made. The space is cramped, but it's the most direct route to the bar, so I suppose it was logical. "Thank you."

"You're finding your way here?" he asks, bringing his glass to his lips. Without taking his eyes off me, he takes a long sip, then lets out a satisfied sigh.

"Um, yes, sir. I'm... Splice is great. I received proper training."

He scowls as he assesses me. "I meant here in London."

Instantly on edge, I snipe, "How do you know I'm not from London?"

His eyebrows shoot up at my tone.

Flovely. What is it about this man that makes me react so instinctively? It's like all my manners evaporate around him. And he very clearly knows it, considering he's smirking down at me once again.

"Just as fiery as the first time we met, aren't you, love?"

He tosses back the rest of his drink, then angles in and places the empty glass on the bar behind me. As he rights himself, his fingertips caress against the ruched fabric at the hip of my dress.

"I'll be up in my office," he says, his rich voice low. "Second floor, past the entrance to the catwalk, at the end of the hall. I'm available if you need anything. Or if you need *me*, specifically."

I'm tempted to sass back again, but I'm too stunned at the implications of his word choice to actually form a response.

What in the world would I need him for?

I watch, bewildered, as he walks away from the hostess stand without looking back.

It's not until a throat clears nearby that I blink back to the moment and dig deep for the wherewithal to do my job. With an apologetic smile, I offer the next group their complimentary drinks.

Throughout the entire shift, every time there's a lull, every moment in which I'm not welcoming guests, refilling punch, or prepping the guest list for that night, his words play back in my mind.

He's available if I need *him*, specifically.

Was that an invitation?

Chapter 16

Hunter

THEN

Sweat drips down my jawline and into my exposed cleavage.

My heart beats in time to the rhythm, as if the bass reverberates straight from my soul.

I lose myself in the crowd of gyrating bodies and chaos and energy.

Splice is wild tonight. The dance floor is packed, and for the first time since I arrived in London, I'm filled with something other than sadness.

Louie and I have a rare night off together, and yet here we are, in the middle of the dance floor at our place of employment.

Before we left the flat, we agreed to stay close and to go home together at the end of the night. Now that we're a few drinks in, I'm not so sure Louie can keep her word. Not with the way she's gleefully grinding with a hulk of a man who claims to be an Australian body builder.

Despite being the third wheel, I keep up and shift with them every time they move.

Trouble is, they're getting more handsy as the night goes on and the drinks keep coming, and it's becoming awkward.

A twinge of anxiety creeps up my spine. Louie could decide to continue what they've started elsewhere. I don't know which scenario I fear more: that she'll go to his place and I'll be forced to go home alone, or that she'll bring him back to our flat and I'll have to share a bathroom with this stranger tomorrow morning.

With a huff, I push the worries from my mind and throw both hands up in the air. Head tipped back, I relish the way the lights dance around me and let the music fuel my soul.

As the music builds, I laugh. The energy on the dance floor is palpable. Being in the middle of the chaos instead of working front of house is a whole new experience. When the beat drops, the crowd goes wild.

I'm lost in the music when a large hand brushes over my left hip. When instead of disappearing, the touch turns into a caress and then a firm hold, I spin around to swat it away.

Before I can free myself, a set of blue-gray eyes sears into me and stuns me stupid.

Spence, with his plush, dark-pink lips surrounded by thick black stubble, and a gorgeous full head of hair, hits me with a smirk so intense I swear I'd stumble forward if his hand weren't still holding my hip so tightly.

"Hello, love."

Notes of cardamom and another profoundly masculine scent overwhelm my senses as I shift forward and put space between us.

"I'm allowed to be here," I huff, my voice barely audible over the crowd.

Spence cocks one brow and pulls me closer.

Craning my neck, I cup my hands and speak directly into his ear. "I'm not working tonight."

The last thing I need is for the owner of the club to think I take my breaks on the dance floor.

"By all means, then," he says with a low chuckle, "carry on."

I scoff at his dismissiveness while also noting the way he's still gripping my hip.

"I can't just carry on," I grit out. "You shouldn't be here."

His eyes go wide in shock.

My stomach plummets. Did I really just snap at my boss's boss's boss in his own club?

"Might I remind you—"

"Sorry. Shit," I say as a wave of panic hits me. "I just meant you shouldn't be here on the dance floor. With me."

Oh, brother. I'm talking myself into a hole. Finding me on the dance floor doesn't mean he pursued me.

"I just mean," I fumble to explain, "I'm your employee—" My words are cut off when I'm hit from behind. Not hard enough to make me lose my footing, but I have to lean forward to dodge an elbow to the head. Which, unfortunately, places me far too close to the man I'm trying to get some space from.

Spence wraps his arms around my low back and holds me securely in place. We're so close our thighs are touching. Then he's pulling me impossibly closer, holding me tighter, his hips swaying to the beat. My body willingly follows.

"I'm your employee." The words are barely more than a breath. I tilt my head back, exposing my neck. Wetting my lips, I part them ever so slightly, then follow his lead and swivel my body in time to the music.

His touch sets my skin ablaze. Butterflies riot in my belly as my hips follow his in time to the music.

What the hell am I doing?

The noise of the crowd is deafening. Maddening.

Yet it's as if we're the only people on the dance floor.

Our eyes lock. I lick my lips. Again.

"I need this job," I whisper.

"Okay." He nods once, his face hovering over mine, inching closer and making it abundantly clear he doesn't plan to let me go.

"You own this club." I find my voice and speak louder this time. "I need this job."

My meaning is clear, yet rather than backing off, I splay my hands on his chest. Then, of their own accord, they creep up to his shoulders, then lock around his neck.

I press my body to his while the music sets my soul burning.

Our faces are close, our breaths mingling. It only takes the slightest shift for his lips to brush mine. Then he's kissing me.

At first, it's so soft I barely feel it. It doesn't take long, though, to build into so much more.

As the beat quickens, my heart rate increases.

Spence grips my face and feeds me his tongue, taking what he wants and giving me everything I didn't know I needed.

With one hand, he cradles my head. He keeps the other firmly planted on my low back. Our tongues dance as our bodies come together, a cacophony of sensation overwhelming me far beyond that of the volume of the club.

When he finally pulls back, we're both breathless.

Breathless and still.

Panting and staring at one another in awe.

"I'm selling the club," he announces, his voice gravelly. One hand remains splayed against the small of my back, keeping me pressed up against his body.

I'm sticky and sweaty, tipsy and so fucking turned on.

We're not even moving. We're just standing here, pressed into one another, as the world moves and gyrates and thrums around us.

"Wait, what? You're selling this club?"

Confusion and panic flood me. New ownership could mean cleaning house and hiring new staff. I really need this job.

He hums. The sound is drowned out, but the rumble of his chest vibrates through me. "I wasn't planning on it until this moment, but now that I know what's at stake, I have every intention of letting it go."

My stomach drops. "*What?*"

Eyes softening, he brushes the hair off my damp forehead.

I should be embarrassed. I'm dripping with sweat and on fire in more ways than one. But the gesture is more intimate and lovely and real than anything I've experienced in weeks.

"If my position as the owner of the club is off-putting or a barrier to this," he says with a squeeze to my hip, "then I'll sell."

I stumble back, reeling and so out of my depth.

This man... this night... it's all too much.

Popping up on my toes, I crane my neck and search for Louie. Eventually, I spot her in the corner sucking face with her new friend from down under.

"I've got to go." I pull away from Spence and stride over to my friend.

"Hey, I'm ready to head out," I tell her, not caring that I'm interrupting.

She pulls away. She's dazed and tipsy, but her eyes quickly clear, making it obvious she's with it enough to consent to whatever's about to happen between her and Boomerang Bob.

"You're good?"

"So good," she breathes with hearts in her eyes. "We're going back to Ernie's place. Do you... do you want to join us?"

Oh.

Oh my.

"No thanks," I quickly tell her, staving off a laugh. "You two have fun and be safe."

Satisfied that she's all set, I turn on my heel and head to the door.

I wave goodbye to Angelo and the bouncer standing near the hostess stand with the girl working tonight—Rose, I think.

Rose is gorgeous, with natural red hair and freckles along the bridge of her nose. She's wearing the signature locket, of course, but hers is open and turned out, making it clear that she's not as innocent as she looks.

"Wait." A hand circles my wrist, stopping me in my tracks. "Where are you going?" Spence demands. He steps up so close I can feel the heat of him at my back.

"I'm going home," I tell him, keeping my expression cool. "Alone."

Yes, the kiss we just shared was one of the hottest of my life. But that's all it was. That's all we'll be. I need to keep my head on straight and keep my wits about me around this man.

"Let me at least call you a cab."

"I'm good," I insist with a wave. "I live two blocks from here."

Spence scoffs, his eyes flashing. "You can't walk."

I yank my wrist out of his hold. "I absolutely can." The way this man barks out commands makes me all sorts of haughty and defiant. "Despite your ruse of a monarchy, I believe this is a free country, so I'll walk where I please, when I please."

His lips part, and a breath escapes him. "There's no way I'll let you take even a single step alone in London after midnight. I'll call a cab."

I shake my head. "I'm not paying cab fare for two blocks!" Plus, my feet are killing me. I'll have to stand out there and wait for longer than it would take me to walk.

"Fine, then," he relents. "I'll have my car brought around."

Hackles raised, I stab his chest with a finger. "I'm not getting in the car with you."

Spence's responding expression is deadpan. "I don't drive my own car, Firecracker."

I fight the urge to roll my eyes. Of course he doesn't.

He lifts the phone to his ear, says something quickly, then hangs up. "Gerald will take you home."

The frustration this arrogant man brings out in me bubbles up. "And how do I know Gerald isn't a murderer who's about to kidnap me and turn me into a meat-suit sex doll?"

Spence's eyes widen in horror. "A—a what? Good grief. All that American media really does take its toll."

It's my turn to cross my arms over my chest and glare.

With a sigh, Spence runs a hand along his jaw. "Gerald is seventy-eight years old and has been employed by my family for six decades. I assure you he is kind, deeply devoted to his wife, and has no interest in turning you into a meat suit. He will get you home safely."

My feet ache, and it's hard to deny that a ride is appealing. One side of Spence's mouth twitches. He thinks he's won.

That does it. My defiance comes rearing back full force. "And how long am I going to have to wait around for Geriatric Gerald?"

"I'll do you the courtesy of not telling him you said that. You're going to love this man."

"Doubtful," I sass back.

Spence glances down at his phone, nods once, then looks up at me.

"Go on, then, love. Gerald's waiting for you outside."

My face flames. *Oh*.

Arguing seems futile if the car is already here. Plus, I want to get these heels off and sink into my bed. I might even sleep in tomorrow, considering Louie won't be home and I'll have the entire flat to myself.

I haven't moved an inch when Spence bends low, bringing his lips to my ear. "Don't make me tell you again, Firecracker. Go."

A thrill zings through me at his command. Dammit.

Affecting a cool expression, I turn over my shoulder and say, "I'll be sure to give Gerald a five-star rating on the app." Then, because I want to see him react, I call out, "Good night, sir."

His response? The man closes his eyes as if he's in physical pain. When he opens them again, he shoves his hands into his pockets and shakes his head.

With a smirk, I head toward the door, hips swaying, feeling his attention the whole way.

Chapter 17

Hunter

THEN

I pace out of my bedroom and into the small living area. With a weary sigh, I flop down on the couch and stare listlessly at my Kindle.

I'm restless and exhausted, but also brimming with energy.

Alone once again, I'm at a loss for how to entertain myself, an issue that's been happening more and more often.

When Louie and I started working at Splice, we got to train together and work together every day.

Since we settled into our places there, though, we've been working opposite shifts more often than not. Our days off don't align, and even when they do, Louie is a much bigger partier than I am.

The girl doesn't stop. Even after she gets off her shift at Splice, she'll venture out to after-hours clubs. Half the time she doesn't come home at all.

In the last few weeks, she's been bringing guests home with her more frequently. I'm grateful we at least have separate bedrooms.

Still restless, I heave myself up and meander back to my own room. It's still pretty bare, which is intentional. What's the point of adding personal touches? I have no idea how long I'll be here. I can't even bring myself to read a new book. I just keep going back to my comfort reads, but even those aren't holding my attention lately.

I stopped by Waterstones in Piccadilly Circus last week. It was trippy to see the alternate UK covers. I found a few of my favorites on the shelves, and I went as far as to stack them up and carry them around for a bit before abandoning the haul on an end cap and leaving the store empty-handed.

It's not about the money. I have Dr. Ferguson's AmEx, and I'm making great use of it out of spite toward my mother.

I just have no idea how long I'll be here or where I'll go next. The lease on our flat will be up in December.

After that, Louie has every intention of heading back to North Carolina and starting the winter semester at LCU.

Me, on the other hand?

I can't imagine going back.

Though I can't imagine staying here by myself either.

I plop down on the edge of the bed and pull open the nightstand drawer.

Heart aching, I lift my pink phone out of its hiding place and cradle it in my palm.

I haven't powered it on in over a week.

It's only got a small amount of battery left, and I swear, the battery drains faster here in Europe.

With a fingernail, I trace the outline of the power button.

As my breathing speeds up, I stop and clutch it as hard as I can.

I can't bring myself to turn it on. It hurts too much. It all feels too deep. What's waiting for me in the form of desperate messages won't make me feel better. If anything, hearing his voice, witnessing his longing, listening to his pleas for me to come home, will just make the wounds I'm trying to ignore fester further.

Choking back a sob, I put the device in the back of my drawer. Then I pull out my new phone.

I need a distraction to pull myself out of this funk. Maybe Louie will want to go out after work.

With her contact pulled up, I hover my thumb over the keypad, then stop myself from typing out a message. Honestly, I don't think I can wait that long.

I scroll through my very few contacts and home in on one name in particular.

Spence gave me his number last week.

Or rather, he told Angelo to save his number in my phone.

It didn't seem peculiar at the time, but when I asked Louie about it, her eyes grew wide with shock—and maybe a smidge of jealousy.

"Wait, wait, wait. Kabir Spencer, the owner of Splice, the richest man under thirty in the United Kingdom, gave you his number?"

"I guess?" I said, my face heating. "He had Angelo put it in my phone."

"Hunt, be real." She rolled her eyes like she thought I was clueless. Maybe I was. "You work for him. If he wanted access to your number, he already has it. He gave you his number because he wants you, full stop."

She's right. He has my number. I spent a week wondering if he would call before it hit me: he's waiting for me to make the first move.

Tonight, my listlessness makes me bold.

I open up a new text thread and find his contact information.

Angelo added him under *Spence*, a casual moniker that I've discovered only a select few members of the staff are allowed to use.

I type out a text and hit Send before I lose my courage.

> Hunter: Let's say you were to sell the club. How much do you think you can get for it?

His reply is immediate.

> Spence: Doesn't matter. I'll fucking give it away if this message means what I think it means.

My insides light up at the response.

Spence is powerful. Filthy rich. From the few Google searches I've conducted, it's clear he's also a brilliant and prolific businessman.

He's made it very clear that he wants me.

I don't have it in me to want anyone, and I'm not sure I ever will again.

Tonight, though, I could use a break. An escape. A release by way of an orgasm.

Would he be interested in a casual arrangement, maybe?

Even casual is probably more than I can give. I have too much baggage. Too many layered emotions I'm fighting like hell to keep buried inside.

There's no part of my heart or soul that's seeking any true connection. After the love I walked away from, I can't imagine truly connecting with another person ever again.

The promise of release, though, and the arousal that washes over me when he's near are feelings I wouldn't mind chasing.

I realize I'm lost in my own head when the phone vibrates in my hand again.

> Spence: What are you after, Firecracker?

Double texting.

From another guy, it might seem desperate.

From Spence?

I love it.

His directness makes it easy for me to be direct, too.

> Hunter: Sex.

> Hunter: Nothing more.

> Spence: Deal.

I smile to myself, giddy at the prospect of all my pent-up energy finally having an outlet. It's been so long, and I've never done just sex before.

Hell, I've never been with anyone except…

I shake my head. No. I can't go there.

I want to be *nothing more* to someone tonight. And that's exactly what Spence can give me.

> Hunter: Do you want to come over?

His reply is instant once again.

> Spence: No, you're coming here.

Okay, then.

My stomach flips over itself.

I trust him, and I'm not opposed to going to him in theory. Nevertheless, I feel compelled to argue. He brings out the sass in me, I swear.

> Hunter: Bossy

His quick reply has me grinning.

> Spence: I take it that's how Americans say "Yes, sir."

My cheeks heat, and my jaw aches from grinning. I'm genuinely smiling for the first time in weeks. Maybe even a month.

> Spence: Text me your address, love. I'll send Gerald with the car.

Chapter 18

Hunter

THEN

My hands were sweaty and nerves skittered through me when Gerald pulled up to the Pyrentha hotel.

Yes, the plan is to meet up for casual sex. But when Spence said I was coming to his, I assumed he meant his home, not some random hotel room.

Gerald escorted me inside and brought me up the lift all the way to the top floor. Only when the doors opened directly into a residence did it hit me: this *is* his home.

Spence greeted me warmly, kissing me on the cheek and giving me a quick tour. He offered me a drink, which I refused. Then he took my hand and led me into the most gorgeous, well-appointed bedroom I've ever seen.

The entire space screams billionaire bachelor sex god, from the deep wood of the poster bed frame to the sleek, modern lines of the windows treatments. The décor is a blend of classic elegance and modern edge.

With a few taps to the buttons on a long panel of controls, he lowers the lighting, closes the curtains, and cues up a slow, sultry song that filters in from speakers hidden around the room.

We agreed to sex and nothing more, but now that I'm here, with the mood lighting and the sexy music playing, the stakes feel impossibly high.

I swallow down the lump in my throat, hoping like hell he can't tell how nervous I am.

Spence makes his way over to me, his movements languid and intentional, and when he's close, I'm enveloped in the spicy scent of his aftershave.

He tucks a tendril of hair behind my ear, then cups my jaw with one large hand and lowers his head until his lips brush against mine.

"You're nervous," he gleans.

Instead of feigning calm, I go with the truth. I bite my lower lip, look up into his sharp gray-blue eyes, and nod.

"I am. But I promise I want this."

Lips curling up into a half smile, he hovers lower still, but he doesn't truly kiss me.

A hint of emotion—or concern, maybe?—sparks behind his eyes.

Pulling back quickly, he assesses me up and down. "Please tell me you've been with a man before."

To answer the ridiculous question, I shoot him an unamused look.

He visibly relaxes, but he uses his thumb and forefinger to tip my head from side to side as he continues to assess me.

"Right. It's clearly not a lack of experience. Or attitude." He smirks. "But there's something else bothering you, yes?"

He's perceptive as hell.

I shrink under his gaze as he continues to analyze me.

Though I find that the longer I look into his eyes, the more relaxed I become.

I want to be here. I want to do this with him.

"You came here tonight asking me for sex and nothing more. That tells me that not only have you been with a man before, but that whomever it was is a person you want to forget."

My sharp intake of breath catches me by surprise. The ache that throbs behind my breastbone is nothing new, though.

Do I want to forget?

Never.

Do I need to forget so that I can move on and move past the daily temptation to book a one-way ticket back to North Carolina and beg for Greedy's forgiveness?

I do. I may not have realized it until this moment, but this is what I need to move on.

"Are you still okay with this arrangement, knowing you're a rebound?" I hedge.

Spence traces his thumb along my lower lip, then presses down until I open.

"So sassy, yet so damn responsive," he remarks. "I appreciate candidness and clear communication, Firecracker. There's no reason we can't be open and honest about what we're both after. Nor is there any denying the magnetic pull between us or the desire I have to fuck you into my mattress all night long."

Breath hitching, I scrutinize him, but only for a heartbeat. Bolstering my nerve, I suck his thumb into my mouth and swirl my tongue around the tip.

"We are aligned," Spence declares, popping his thumb out of my mouth. He backs up and, sitting on the end of the bed, plants his hands on the mattress and lounges back. "Strip for me, love."

Okay, then. We're doing this.

Though my heart is pounding, I smile coyly, then reach off to the side for the hidden zipper of my dress.

"No," Spence scolds, halting my movements completely. "I didn't ask you to undress. I said *strip*."

I meet his gaze, searching. His tone is firm, and the way he watches me, with so much scrutiny but also desire, lulls me into a type of trance that has me hanging on his every word, waiting for him to continue.

"Put on a show," he commands, his tone rich and dark. "Reveal your body slowly. Tease me until I'm physically aching for you, Firecracker. I want there to be so much pre-ejaculate leaking from my cock you could lap it up off the floor like a dog."

My lungs seize in shock, and my pussy throbs with want. Did he really just call me—

"There she is," Spence murmurs with a tip of his chin. "Did you feel how your eyes widened just now? You're into degradation, I take it?"

My brain screams *no! of course not!* But my traitorous cunt throbs again.

"I—I don't know, exactly," I admit.

"Are you interested in finding out?"

"Yes," I reply without hesitation. With a gasp, I slap a hand to my mouth, but it's too late to take it back.

Spence's smirk turns wicked. "We're going to have even more fun than I thought," he tells me. "We'll use condoms for protection. Have you ever used a safe word during sex?"

My pulse throbs from my neck down to my toes. I'm dry-mouthed and yet salivating all at the same time.

"No."

"Pick one. It needs to be a word you wouldn't typically say during sex. My safe word is umbrella, and you're welcome to use that if you wish."

"Greedy," I whisper, saying the name aloud for the first time in weeks.

I cup my mouth again. What am I saying? What am I doing? Pain lances my chest, but Spence doesn't seem to notice.

"Very well," he declares. "Your safe word is greedy. Mine is umbrella. If either of us says either word at any time, everything stops. Communication is key, Firecracker. Do you have any hard limits I should be aware of?"

"I—"

Put on the spot like this, I can't think of any. In fact, my mind is a million miles away at the moment. I'm still stuck on the part where I said my ex's name out loud for the first time in months.

It's time to let go. I have to let him go.

I came here with a purpose, and I owe it to myself to see it through. I let Spence's aura soothe me as I shake my head in response to his question. What he's promising isn't something I knew I wanted or needed. And yet...

"Come here," he commands.

I step forward.

"No, not like that. Get on your hands and knees," he says.

Stomach fluttering, I do as I'm told.

"Now crawl to me, love. Crawl like the needy little slut you are so I can properly fuck your useless holes."

Wide awake, I lie flat on my back in what might possibly be the world's most comfortable bed.

My mind is reeling, because what just happened between Spence and me was the hottest, most satisfying sexual experience of my life.

He commanded my body in ways I didn't know it could be commanded. The pleasure was more intense than I knew was possible, sending me hurtling into a state of absolute bliss where, for the first time in forever, I felt nothing.

It. Was. Heaven.

It's also a problem.

Because no matter how I look at it, that was so much more than just sex.

He said the most vile things to me as he worshipped my body. He called me names, then praised me in a way that lit my insides on fire. I've never been turned on the way I was while being degraded by Spence.

Despite the hours-long session, I'm already craving another round.

Fuck. I need to get out of here before he wakes up.

Tonight was extraordinary. It was passionate and poignant. But it can never happen again. I don't trust myself to not latch on to this moment and chase this feeling. It's in both our best interests if I sneak out now.

When Spence's breathing is completely evened out, I slide to the edge of the bed, attempting to quietly slip out of the sheets.

Except there's nothing quiet about my escape. The damn sheets are made of slippery silk—charcoal gray silk, to be exact—and my subtle movements send me flopping onto the floor.

I land on my ass, thankfully, so the impact isn't too great. I try to stifle a laugh, but it's no use. Snorting, I cover my mouth and work to control my breathing.

Spence's head appears above me, his brows furrowed in concern.

"Are you attempting to sneak out on me?"

I shift subtly, searching for a position that is not so unflattering. But I'm splayed on the floor, naked and very thoroughly fucked. It's hopeless.

"I think it's called an Irish exit?" I offer with a sheepish grin.

He hits me with an amused smirk. "Not in Londontown, it's not. Come back to bed, love. We've barely slept. You don't need to run out in the middle of the night."

His tone is warm, his expression worried. Gone is the powerful, commanding Dom who was rocking my world a few hours ago. In his place, the serious, stoic man I'm learning can be just as gentle as he is domineering.

His offer is tempting. So very tempting.

Regardless, I know myself too well. My emotions aren't in a good place after the intensity of tonight. I promised him just sex. If I stay, my heart will be in shambles, at war with the truth of what transpired between us.

"It's okay," I insist. "I should go. I'll catch a cab."

Before I've completely righted myself, Spence is out of bed.

"You will do no such thing." He strides forward, hovering over me as he assesses my naked form.

The room is dark, but not so dark I can't make out the harsh way he's glaring at me.

"We had sex," I tell him. "That's why I came. For sex and nothing more."

He scoffs at that. "We had absolutely mind-blowing sex. Don't pretend like that wasn't the most erotic, passionate experience of your life, Hunter. You're a terrible liar."

Oh. So he felt it, too? Shit. That only ratchets up the panic already working its way through me. I really do have to go.

I scan the floor in search of my panties.

"You need to be fucked again," Spence declares.

I whip my head around so quickly I see stars. The audacity of this man.

"It was cute earlier, but don't talk to me like that," I snipe back.

Spence raises one eyebrow, regarding me. "You've still got that attitude you walked in with. Clearly, what we just did wasn't enough. I wasn't enough. I underestimated how wound up you were, Firecracker. Give me another go."

I cross my arms over my chest. "Does that work on other women?"

He tilts his head to one side, his lips tugged down. "Does what work?"

"Just... that!" I wave my hand in his general direction. "You just say words and make demands with that sexy accent and get away with being a bossy asshole inside and outside the bedroom?"

A smile teases at one side of his mouth. "You think my accent's sexy?"

With a huff, I turn away. When I spot my dress hanging precariously off the end of the bed, I shift past him. Slipping it on without underwear, I announce, "I'm going. Thank you for a lovely evening."

"You're not going anywhere," Spence tells me.

Shimmying my dress up over my hips, I peek up to challenge him once more. "Who's going to stop me?"

His eyes narrow a fraction. But he makes no moves to come toward me.

I have to admit, though his bossy side gets under my skin, this dynamic between us is intriguing. He's calling the shots, and yet it feels very much like I'm the one in control.

"You are," he tells me with a shrug, confirming the power I hold in this room.

"It's always your choice, love, but you're a smart girl. Think about it. You can leave my residence and go back home to the empty flat with a hopefully charged vibrator, since you're still in desperate need of release."

He stalks toward me, his movements fluid. He's still completely naked, his semi-erect cock bobbing between his legs.

"Or..."

He traces one finger along my collarbone and down between my breasts, then tugs lightly on the neckline of the dress I'm trying to keep up.

"You can drop the dress, spread yourself out on my sheets once more, and let me devour your cunt before I properly fuck all the fight out of you."

I let go of my dress. Accidentally. I think.

It flutters to my feet at the same moment Spence lowers his head and brings his lips to my ear.

"I swear to you, Firecracker. I'll fuck you so well your bones will feel like jelly and you'll fall into the most blissful sleep."

Desire courses through me at the idea.

Fuck.

Fine.

Now that he's called me out on it, it's clear that I need another orgasm or two if I want to settle all this pent-up energy. I didn't even realize I was still worked up.

And yet... I worry my bottom lip between my teeth as unease bubbles up inside me.

We had terms. We made a deal. I don't want to go back on my word or get too deep into something that's one-sided.

"If I stay—"

"You're staying," he interjects.

"If I stay," I repeat resolutely, "it's still just sex."

Spence cups my jaw, his palm soft and warm. "That's what you're worried about?"

My heart pangs at the gentleness in his tone.

"Sex isn't one dimensional, love. Sex can be passionate. Full of emotion. Satisfying and uniquely fulfilling. People need different things from sex."

He brushes his thumb back and forth over my jaw.

"You were very obedient earlier," he murmurs, lowering his mouth to mine. He places a chaste kiss on my mouth and hovers there. "I want to explore that side of you—to push you, test you. If you are open to it, of course. Will you let me do that for you, Hunter?" Straightening, he looms over me. "Will you do exactly as I tell you if I promise it will result in a deeper satisfaction than you've ever fucking felt in your life?"

"Yes. As long as it's just sex," I remind him once more.

"Just sex," he repeats with a smirk. "Now get back in bed. Hold your hands above your head and spread your thighs as far as they'll go. I'm going to eat your cunt until you come so hard you cry. Then and only then will the real fucking begin."

Chapter 19

Greedy

NOW

Steering wheel gripped so tight my knuckles ache, I track Levi's movement as he angles forward and messes with the radio. Again.

He's riding shotgun, insisting on controlling the music like usual.

Except the passenger in the back seat also has an opinion about every song that starts up, and for some goddamn reason, Levi cares what His Royal Highness thinks about what we listen to.

Swallowing thickly, I force myself to focus on the road again.

It's a cool day, and although there are icy patches here and there, it's nothing I can't handle.

Trouble is, every time I check my mirrors, I catch sight of the two passengers in the back.

They're on opposite sides of the bench seat.

Yet Hunter is turned toward Kabir, and he's scrolling on his phone with one hand while the other, affixed with multiple gold rings, brushes up and down her leggings-clad thigh.

It's the simplicity of the moment that slays me.

I don't think he's doing it to get to me. I don't think Hunter's even aware of how affected I am by every move and every look between her and Kabir, as well as her and Levi. The ease of the contact and lack of hostile intention almost hurt worse. Seeing them together, so intimately comfortable, is gut-wrenching.

"Holy shit," Hunter says, bolting straighter in her seat.

Instantly, I seek her out in the rearview mirror.

"Holy shit!" she repeats, smiling from ear to ear as she blinks down at her phone.

She reaches forward, the movement making me flinch. Only she's not even reaching for me.

In my periphery, she grasps Levi's arm, her perfectly manicured fingernails on full display.

"Final grades are posted."

Her voice is filled with more joy than I've observed since her return.

Levi turns around in his seat, grinning. "You fucking aced it, didn't you?"

Without permission, my eyes dart to the rearview mirror. Fuck. Her smile is brilliant.

Kabir's also watching her.

She's smiling so hard her eyes are squinty. She passes the phone up to Levi. "Twenty-one credit hours and a 4.0 GPA for my first semester of undergrad."

"I'm so fucking proud of you," Levi tells her.

He shifts further in his seat, as if he's reaching for her, only to stop abruptly, like maybe he's thinking better of it. With one last half smile at Hunter, he rights himself.

"Let me see," Kabir murmurs.

Even the sound of his voice grates against my insides.

There's a big incline coming up, and I have to breathe through the urge to floor it and whip the truck around the next bend.

I don't want to cause physical harm, obviously. But I wouldn't mind tossing His Royal Highness around in the back of the cab.

"Well done, love," he says to Hunter as he passes her phone back. "What do you say we celebrate tonight?"

His hand glides up her thigh, and it isn't until Levi clears his throat that I refocus on the road.

After a few more seconds—because I'm a glutton for punishment—I check the rearview mirror again.

This time I lock eyes with Hunter.

I clear my throat, realizing I haven't said a word, and as evenly as possible, I tell her, "Congrats. You earned it."

She offers a tight-lipped smile. The expression turns to a shudder, then she's slapping Spencer's hand away.

Fuck, I should be focused on the road.

I drag my attention to the scenery outside the windshield, but a moment later, my eyes drift back to them.

Look at the road, look back at them.

He's abandoned his phone now and is giving his full attention to Hunter, leaning over and whispering into her ear.

I clear my throat once, then twice.

Either he doesn't hear me or doesn't give a shit.

Hunter murmurs something under her breath that makes him pause.

Kabir scoffs and slips his hand up her thigh until it's almost hidden by the hem of her sweater.

"Greedy."

I zero in on the road again, then glance back up at Hunter. But she's not looking at me. She's looking at him.

Am I hearing things? Did she—"Greedy." This time, it's clear she's speaking directly to Spence.

"Yeah?" I ask.

Hunter says nothing for a beat. Then another.

"You okay back there?" I push.

She lifts her head in a jerk, her face flushing. She blinks at me as if she's just realized that I'm here, despite saying my name. "Yeah. All good," she assures me, settling back into her seat.

Chapter 20

Hunter

NOW

"Hunter. Hold up."

I freeze, which in turn causes both Levi and Spence to stop in their tracks.

We've just unloaded the car, and we're about to head into the cabin.

It's strange being here. In this place that's so deeply tied to that summer with Greedy. I'm mentally and emotionally locked in, putting on my very best face to come off as cool, collected, and unbothered.

The truth is, I'm burned out, medicated, and hanging by an emotional thread since my period is set to start soon, but I'm coping the best I can.

I look over my shoulder to find Greedy leaning against his Denali.

His gaze is laser focused on me, his arms crossed against his broad chest.

A totally different lifetime flashes through my mind as I stand before him like this, in a place that used to mean so much. A stinging wind whips between us. That's why my eyes are watering and why my throat is suddenly burning with suppressed emotion.

That has to be it.

I push down all other thoughts about what could have been.

Being here makes it all ache once again, like a wound that never properly heals. One that continues to fester and reopen over and over, no matter how many times I've patched it, ignored it, or covered it up completely.

"I need to talk to you," Greedy tells me. Tipping his chin, he squints, looking past me to Levi and Spence. "Alone."

I sigh but nod in assent.

If he wants to lay ground rules or come to terms with what's eating at him, I'd rather do it before we have the audience of our parents.

They're driving up separately, because Greedy's dad still has to work a few more days this week.

They'll arrive on Christmas Eve. It'll be easy enough to distract myself until they get here, and it'll be easy enough to ignore Greedy while I'm diligently trying to avoid Magnolia.

I turn to Levi first and hold my bag out. "Will you take this inside for me?"

With a nod, he side-eyes Greedy. Then he heads for the cabin.

Turning to my other side, I focus on Kabir. "I'd like you to go inside with Levi now."

He cocks one brow at me, clearly unamused by my directness.

"Fine. I'd like you to at least go up toward the house and give us a modicum of privacy," I say calmly, countering his unspoken argument.

He doesn't want to leave me alone with Greedy, I get that, but he's not in control right now, and he'll have to learn to deal with that if he plans to stick around.

"I'll wait on the porch," he tells me, nodding to the wooden wrap-around deck.

"We'll be quick," I assure him with a small smile.

By the time I turn back to Greedy, his gaze has darkened. I don't bother worrying about which interaction pissed him off more. Levi is my boyfriend. Spence is... well, he's Spence. And he's here.

I take a step closer, though I leave a few feet between us.

"We're alone." Hands planted on my hips, I purse my lips, silently signaling him to get on with what he felt so compelled to share with me in private.

"Are we?" Greedy counters, tightening his arms across his chest.

Rather than play into his game, I stare at him, deadpan.

He has a right to hate me. It's exactly what I've wanted for years, because I thought it would make it easier on both of us.

Standing before him now, though, and being in this place, where the foundation of our relationship truly formed, makes me feel all sorts of defensive and shaky on the inside.

His mossy-green eyes bore into me. With every second he scrutinizes me, I shrink.

The gravitational pull that's always between us pulses so intensely I can almost hear the hum of it. Greedy tears down every single one of my mental and emotional defenses with just a single smoldering look.

As we stare one another down, I'm suddenly hyperaware of my own breathing, of the slow exhales and the forced inhales.

I spent so many days and sleepless nights dreaming of our what-if.

During my lucid moments, I know what happened was best-case scenario for both of us.

That never stopped me from wondering what our baby might look like.

If it'd be a boy or a girl.

What we'd name them.

Would we be here?

Is there an alternate universe in which we're here, at the cabin, wrapping presents and gearing up for Christmas with our two-year-old?

Tears sting my eyes at the very thought of what could have been and what never will be.

"Greedy." I take one small step toward him.

He stumbles away, his back connecting with the passenger door of the car. He clears his throat and straightens, as if he's just been pulled out of a reverie, too.

"I won't let her spoil this place," he announces, tipping his chin up.

He doesn't have to clarify that by "her," he means my mother.

There'll be no argument from me on that front. I'm on the exact same wavelength.

"I told my father that I'll be taking the primary bedroom upstairs." Greedy's voice is thick, hoarse. "I plan to sleep on the second floor, across from Levi, though."

The cabin is well appointed with multiple bedrooms, so I hadn't even considered sleeping arrangements, though with as complicated as my life has suddenly become, I probably should have.

"Your guest can sleep in one of the other bedrooms on the second floor. I'm not telling you where to sleep, but the primary is available." He swallows audibly, his throat working. "If you want it."

Memories come flooding back to my mind.

Beautiful lighting, deep, dark wood. The quiet little library off to the side. The spacious, gorgeous bathroom. A place I love; a place filled with the purest, most lovely memories.

"Are you sure?" I ask, my knees wobbling.

I love that room.

Greedy loves it just as much. It was special to his mom.

"Honestly, Hunter?" He lets out a harsh sigh. "As long as your mother doesn't go anywhere near that room or near me, I don't give a shit about any of it."

His words say one thing. His tone tells me something else completely.

Clearing his throat, he grabs his duffel off the ground. He moves fast, storming past me, his shoulder brushing mine.

"Let's just stay out of each other's way for the next few days," he throws back over his shoulder.

Then he stops, turns, and delivers a final blow.

"When we get back to South Chapel, I'll move out. Get my own place closer to campus. It makes sense, with my football schedule. I'll leave, and we can forget any of this ever even happened."

His words crescendo through me like an earthquake.

Rattle.

Shake.

Rumble.

Quake.

He's leaving.

I've done it. I've pushed and prodded and cut deeply enough that Greedy's finally leaving for good.

Standing stock-still, I force myself to not breathe, to not move. I don't even blink as he marches toward the house without a backward glance.

A muted sob racks through me, splintering me at the core, but only once I'm sure he's far enough away that he won't hear me.

He's leaving.

Good things always do.

Everything I love always will.

Chapter 21

Hunter

THEN

I wake up disoriented, cracking my eyes open and taking in my dark surroundings.

Reaching out, I hit one of the paneled buttons on the nightstand, and the curtains open just a crack. Soft, hazy light streams in through the gap, although it's not particularly bright. It must still be early morning.

I stretch slowly, waking little by little. There's a little café in the hotel lobby that serves the most perfect dirty chai lattes. My stomach felt off last night, though, so the idea of espresso doesn't do it for me this morning like usual. I'm well rested enough anyway that I should be okay without the caffeine.

Spence starts his day early and doesn't ever seem to stop, so I typically wake up alone. His work ethic is unparalleled. That makes sense, since he's running multiple nightclubs, a huge music festival, an elite awards show, and, in an interesting plot twist, a highly secretive security company I know little about.

He contains multitudes.

He also excels at giving me multiple orgasms each time we're together, which has been a lot as of late.

It's my fourth sleepover at his place this week. Grinning at the thoughts, I lift the sheets all the way up to my chin.

It's just sex, I remind myself.

When I turn to my side, I'm surprised to find him lying in bed, watching me. His smoldering gaze makes my stomach flip, and when he licks his lips, my thighs clench involuntarily.

It's just sex, I silently chant.

"Good morning, love." He leans over, kisses my forehead, and pulls me under the covers until our naked bodies are tangled up in a familiar, intimate way.

"Your hair's all wet," I protest as water droplets rain down on my bare shoulders. I twist in his arms so I can face him, then run my hand up his smooth jaw.

He shaves every morning, but it doesn't last. I savor the soft skin now, knowing that it will be coarse enough to leave a rash on my inner thighs if I wind up here again tonight.

I scratch my nails against his scalp and pull on the wet ends.

"I had an early call with Tokyo," he tells me. "Then I worked out and showered."

"Why did you come back to bed, then?"

His face softens into a smile as he traces the bow of my upper lip with his thumb. "I love seeing you first thing in the morning."

Oh.

Just sex, I remind myself again. *Just sex. Just sex. Just sex.*

"Do you have plans for the weekend?" he asks before I can come up with an adequate response to his confession.

"I work tonight and Sunday, but I'm off tomorrow night."

"Can I take you to dinner tomorrow, then?"

"Spence," I softly chide, even as I secretly want to throw my arms around his neck and immediately tell him yes.

Just sex. Just sex. Just sex.

"Hunter."

The way he says my name, with that accent, is melodic. He rarely says my first name, preferring to call me *love* or *Firecracker* instead.

We're both fond of the other nicknames he comes up with in the heat of the moment, too. *His favorite whore. His dirty little American slut.*

Last night he called me a useless hole while he fucked me.

I came so hard I swear I momentarily blacked out.

Spence has the power to silence the internal dialogue I can't escape in any other way these days; when he's in control, his words are a balm.

"We're just sex." I walk my fingers up his bare chest, though I avoid his gaze.

The reminder has played on a loop in my head for the last week. This connection between us is starting to feel like... more. We're trudging into dangerous territory.

Spence captures my hand and kisses the tips of my fingers. "You need fuel for sex, love. We could be dinner companions who also have sex."

"Can we?" I have to force the question out past a lump in my throat.

Maybe he's capable of extending those boundaries, but I'm not sure I'm cut out for anything more than what we've got. I can feel myself falling for him, despite all the barriers around my heart, all the broken pieces. Because with him, I feel safe and cherished and loved.

If I can't put a stop to it, then I worry I'll get in too deep, and then there will be no way to course-correct.

"We can. I'll make a reservation for eight p.m.," he tells me as he rises from the bed and heads toward his closet.

Chapter 22

Hunter

THEN

Spence asked Gerald to take me home, which isn't unusual. I've grown fond of our conversations during car rides around the city.

Gerald has lived in London his whole life, and he's worked for Spence's family since he was a teenager. He speaks of Spence so fondly, as if he's speaking of a beloved relative.

"Ya sure this is all right, Miss St. Clair?" he asks in his thick cockney accent.

"Yes, this is perfect."

He's pulled over a few blocks away from my flat. Last weekend I discovered an adorable little grocer that sells local produce, like a farmers' market. The setup is simple and a bit rustic, but I bought the most delicious carton of strawberries, and the farmer assured me he'd be back again this week.

I can practically taste the sweet, bright berries on my tongue already. They were much smaller than what I'm used to, but the flavor was unmatched.

Gerald opens the door for me. "Mr. Spencer indicated I'll be picking you up tomorrow night," he says as I straighten on the sidewalk beside him. "What time would you like me to arrive, ma'am?"

I'm sure I'm not the only woman Spence entertains. Gerald has probably escorted plenty. Yet I've truly grown fond of the older man.

"Seven thirty will be perfect. Thank you," I tell him with a sincere smile.

Slowly, he rounds the hood back to the driver's side. "You're sure I can't wait for you?"

"No, no," I insist. "I'm going to pick up a few things, and I could use a bit of a walk before I head home."

He tips his hat. "You have my number if you change your mind."

I don't know whether that's common for Spence's acquaintances, but I appreciate the gesture. If I really did need a ride, I wouldn't hesitate to call on him.

"See you tomorrow night, ma'am."

As Gerald drives away, I scan the outdoor booths. I practically squeal with delight when I see the same vendor from last week.

Our flat doesn't have a real kitchen, so I can't bake or do much with the fruit I purchase. Even so, I still plan to pick up triple the number of strawberries I did last week. They were that good.

I take my time walking home, enjoying the brisk fall breeze and the way the leaves on many of the trees have started to change.

Fall used to be my favorite season. Now, the idea of the changing seasons makes me sad.

Every step I take serves as a reminder of what I left behind.

I think of the way the colors change in North Carolina in the fall.

About football season.

About midterms and hoodie weather. About what LCU's campus looks like this time of year.

My thoughts scatter, hopping from one topic to another, but nothing I land on feels safe.

I swipe at a stray tear, admonishing myself for the massive mood swing. I was giddy about strawberries less than an hour ago. Now all my energy has been sapped, and all I want to do is sit in the middle of the sidewalk and sob.

Thankfully, I reach our flat before I lose it.

Once inside, I shuffle through the quiet apartment and into the kitchen so I can put away a few of the items I purchased.

When I'm done, I go in search of my friend. "Louie?" I knock and check her room, but she's not there.

"Hey, are you home?" I call out.

Louie worked last night, so she may be sleeping. Or it's possible that she hasn't returned yet.

The bathroom door's open, but she's not in there either.

I check my phone. No texts. There's no note in the kitchen either.

It's a bummer, really, the way our schedules have worked out. I work tonight, and she works tomorrow. This is how our weekends tend to go. I've never had a roommate until now, but it's so much lonelier than I ever imagined.

I toe off my shoes, then, knowing I'll be too lazy to do it after work tonight, I wash all the strawberries.

Once that's done and I've sampled half a dozen to confirm they're just as delicious as last week, I head to my bedroom. I'm mentally hyping myself up to take an everything shower, then I plan to read for a bit before work.

When I open my bedroom door, I'm hit with a musty, putrid smell. It's as if an animal has curled up and died and has already started to decompose.

I flip the switch to turn on the single lamp. When I catch sight of a man lying in the center of the bed, I scream and practically jump out of my skin.

He's face down, turned away from me, and from what I can see, naked.

What the actual fuck?

I'm frozen in place, my heart pounding out of my chest for several seconds before I get my wits about me and run out of the room.

I shut the door quietly, then grab the knife I just washed in the kitchen and hurry back. With my weapon in one hand and my heart practically hammering out of my chest, I pull out my phone and dial Louie's number.

It rings and rings, but she doesn't answer.

I try her again with no success.

After a few minutes, I crack open the door and squint across the room. The guy is still asleep, or maybe dead, based on the smell that's taken over.

My stomach twists with anxiety and indecision.

Should I run? Where the hell would I even go? Would it be possible to sneak back in and grab a few things?

As I crack the door open wider, the hinges creak.

The man stirs. "Hey, babe," he calls out, his voice groggy, gravelly. "Come back to bed so I can do a line off your tits."

What. The. Actual. Fuck?

"Um, no thanks. I'll just grab my stuff and go." I blindly snatch my cell charger while weighing the pros and cons of getting closer so I can retrieve my second phone.

"Louie, what's wrong?"

My heart stutters. *Louie...* seriously?

If he thinks I'm her, that means the stranger in my bed requesting to do hard drugs off my breasts isn't some rando or an intruder. He's a damn guest of my roommate.

Flovely.

More pissed off than scared now, I plant my hands on my hips, turn to look at the man, and take a deep breath for courage. Just as I open my mouth, ready to tell him off, I realize he's fallen back asleep.

In my bed.

Ugh. So gross.

At least now I don't have to deal with him.

I snag my makeup bag from the bookshelf, then retrieve my extra phone and Kindle from the nightstand.

Quickly, I grab a little black dress and a pair of heels—I have a clean set of street clothes in my bag since I've stayed at Spence's so much this week—then I stumble out the door without a backward glance.

Eyes closed, I shudder. Ew. Ew, ew, ew.

What was Louie thinking, leaving a man in our flat? Letting him sleep in my bed?

I consider calling her again, but in the end choose to put some space between myself and the gross man in my room. So I double-check that I have the essentials, grab one of the cartons of strawberries, and quickly exit the flat.

I lock the door behind me, which feels ridiculous. Then I sit on my stoop and eat the entire carton of berries while I ponder what to do next.

It's been a strange night.

Actually, this whole day has been bizarre.

I feel like I'm watching a movie of myself. Hovering above. Judging every microexpression. Fighting back tears each time I remember what happened at the flat earlier.

I feel fuzzy, almost as if I've been drugged.

Words are too quiet; lights are too bright.

The club is as busy as always, and yet there's a softness around the edges of all my interactions.

Like I've had too much to drink or accidentally doubled up on cold medicine.

Only, I'm completely sober.

In fact, all I've had today is a carton of strawberries and a glass of water. Maybe that's the problem. Maybe I haven't eaten enough.

Or maybe I just need to let loose. To let go.

I'm even more disoriented when the front of house manager, Crystal, comes by to give me a break around midnight. I look at the clock, then I look at it again. The numbers are clearly displayed on the digital screen, and yet they don't fully register. How is it already midnight?

As I step away from the hostess stand, it feels like I'm floating. Walking on clouds.

Usually, I play on my phone in the back while I take my break.

Tonight, I want to dance.

I have thirty minutes.

Does the employee handbook explicitly forbid dancing during breaks? I don't think so. Straightening my shoulders, I weave my way through the crowd to the middle of the dance floor. As I approach, the bass sets the rhythm of my heart.

My pulse thrums in time to the music.

I thrash about, letting the music and the movements of the crowd take me this way and that. Like a rag doll being tossed around. In no time, I've worked up a sweat.

I'm drenched. But I don't want to stop dancing. I can't. I have to move.

After four or five songs, I figure I better cool down and freshen up. It won't be long before I have to make my way back to the podium for the rest of my shift.

After I've used the restroom, I wash my hands, ignoring my reflection in the mirror.

I know I'm a hot mess. I don't need visual confirmation. Sweat's trickling down my back, and my breath is still coming quickly, but I'm still restless. Wild. Desperate for more.

I pull my phone out and check the time. Eight more minutes until my break is over.

Instead of making my way back early, I stumble out of the bathroom and walk down the long hallway toward the break room.

Rather than lead me inside, my feet continue on until I bypass the door and end up inside the walk-in cooler.

Splice doesn't have a full kitchen, but we go through enough fruit and cocktails to require a walk-in fridge. Some of the alcohol is stored back here, too.

The space is no bigger than a generous walk-in closet, but I close myself in anyway.

Leaning against the doorframe to catch my breath, I shutter my eyes closed and savor the cool blasts of air as they chill each droplet of sweat against my heated flesh.

After a few slow breaths, I open my eyes, look around, and note the variety of tropical fruits perfectly sorted against one wall.

On the other side of the space, there's an icebox.

A chest freezer.

I spread my hands as wide as they'll go, steadying myself against the closed door at my back. Rubbing my palms along the bumpy texture of the wall, I absentmindedly study the chest.

Taking in the shape. The depth and the size of it.

My feet carry me a few steps forward. I approach the way one would approach a scared child: Cautiously. Curiously.

With a thumb, I swipe away the condensation gathered on the temperature gauge.

Negative twenty degrees Celsius.

I don't bother whipping out my phone to do the conversion. I know that's really cold.

How cold does it feel on the inside?

The box is long enough that if I bent my knees, I could easily fit inside.

The last time I saw the chest open, it housed only a few bottles of vodka. There was plenty of room. I could close myself in. It would be quick.

There may not even be enough time to feel the cold before I succumb.

It would feel incredible. Blissful. Soothing.

The idea of embracing the cold, and just letting go...

I want it.

I want to be inside the chest.

I try to lift the lid, but it catches.

It's locked. I'd forgotten.

Scanning the cooler, I spot the keys hanging up by the door.

But just as I make my way over to snag them off the little hook on the wall, the door swings open.

"There you are." Crystal appears, wearing a confused frown. "Did Sean send you back here? I was getting worried."

I blink. Then blink again.

Suddenly, my brain is flooded by all the stimulus of my reality.

Where I am. How I feel. What I was about to do.

Blinking rapidly, I take Crystal in, registering the clear concern etched on her face as she scans up and down my body.

What the hell was I thinking?

Shivering, I wipe at my cheeks and only then realize that I'm crying.

"I'll be right out," I tell her, willing my voice not to tremble the way every other cell in my body is vibrating.

After she's gone, I take a moment to compose myself. Then I head back to the hostess stand to continue my shift. The rest of the night slips by in a blur.

I keep meaning to tell guests who appear in front of me that we're full, and yet there's a disconnect between my brain and my mouth. People stream inside. The lists on the podium jumble together until they're nothing more than dancing text decorating each page.

Eventually, Crystal joins me at the stand, essentially taking over my duties as she side-eyes me warily.

During a slow moment, she asks, "Are you okay?"

"Just tired," I tell her with a yawn. "I'm sorry. Maybe I'm coming down with something." I can't remember the last time I felt this wiped. Everything just feels so... heavy.

She nods, her mouth turned down in a sympathetic frown. "Why don't you take off early? I can finish up here."

I consider arguing, but the prospect of getting out of here and finding some semblance of peace is way too tempting.

So with a quick thanks, I head to the break room and clock out. When I check my phone, I see a few missed calls from Louie.

I ignore them. I'm still livid about earlier, but I'm out of fight tonight. Even if I spoke to her, I don't have the first clue what I'd say. It's best to save that conversation for another day.

Spence also sent two texts, but I haven't had it in me to reply to either one of them.

I haven't even opened his messages.

It's like I'm hiding. Fading. Sheltering in place and making myself scarce.

I'm fighting against my own exhaustion as I stumble out the back.

The night air is cool, but it's no match for the chill from the cooler. Maybe if I head back inside and go—

"Hunter. Is everything okay?"

Heart lurching, I spin and slap a hand to my chest.

Angelo is leaning against the alley wall, smoking a cigarette.

"Yeah, I'm fine," I assure him, swallowing back all emotion. "Crystal just sent me home early."

He pulls out his phone and types out a quick message, then stashes it back in his pocket.

With a twist of his foot, he puts out his cigarette and tips his chin in my direction. "You live nearby, right?"

I nod. Barely. I'm so exhausted, it's a struggle to keep my eyes open, let alone form words.

"Let me walk you."

Yeah. Okay.

Angelo's a good guy. Spence trusts him. There's nothing threatening about his aura—no creeper vibes or even an iota of implication to the offer. Even if there was, I'm so out of it I don't think I could form the words to tell him no.

Mindlessly, I nod again, then take off in the direction of my flat.

Angelo walks beside me, close enough to make his presence known, but not so close that I feel compelled to carry on a conversation.

Typically, I'd be the one making small talk, asking about his weekend plans or what he likes to do for fun. Tonight, I barely have it in me to put one foot in front of the other, so we continue in silence.

I'm so tired.

So drained.

So done.

The street's mostly quiet at this time of night, save for the occasional cab and a group of people here and there making their way to the clubs and pubs that stay open extra late on the weekend.

We trudge on.

I hold on. Barely.

My steps slow as we approach the block where I live, and I have half a mind to tell Angelo he doesn't have to walk me all the way up.

I'm good. I've got it from here.

Though as I try to articulate the idea, my mind whirls, and the words don't come. So I place one foot in front of the other, keep my eyes forward but downcast, and focus on the sidewalk.

A horn sounds, alerting us to a truck rounding the corner on the road up ahead.

Head snapping up, I zero in on the big, boxy truck. As it gains speed coming down the hill, I watch.

It's going fast.

So fast.

It would be so quick.

Impulse lights up my veins, sending an alertness through me I haven't felt all night, as the truck careens down the hill.

Could I get in front of it before the driver tries to swerve?

Would it hurt?

Would it be instant?

Would it all finally feel okay?

It's approaching quickly. I have to decide now, or I'll miss my chance.

I'm fast, but not in these shoes. Decidedly, I kick off my first heel.

"Hunter."

Breath catching, I look around, confused.

Angelo is a few strides ahead of me, looking on with concern.

"Do your feet hurt?"

I assess him, his frown, the concern in his eyes, the way he's clutching his phone. "No, why?"

He gives me a once-over, brow furrowed. Then, tentatively, he says, "You stopped walking, then took off one shoe."

In my periphery, the box truck whizzes by. The moment has passed. I let out a choked sob as I spin and track its path.

As tears stream down my face, I fight back the urge to run after it. It's gone. It's over. I'm still here.

I continue to stare at the taillights as they disappear into the night, only blinking when Angelo places a hand on my shoulder.

"Hey, why don't I call Louie for you and see—"

"Don't!" I bark out, batting at him. "Don't you dare call her right now."

Angelo raises both hands in surrender. "I won't. Let's just get you home, okay?"

Home.

I close my eyes, and sunsets over the lake cloud my mind. Flashbacks of fresh-cut grass and strawberry slushies overtake my senses. I'm swimming in the quarry. I'm riding shotgun, driving through the mountains, singing my favorite country songs off-key as the boys and I head up to the cabin.

His tanned skin so close I can almost touch it. His gorgeous, taut abs hovering above me. The hardness of his chest and the softness with which he holds me.

Home.

I miss home.

I wish I could go home.

It's the only place I want to be, even if I can never go back.

Home isn't a place to me anymore. It's him.

Home.

I'm so tired of missing home.

Chapter 23

Hunter

THEN

Warm, mossy-green eyes meet mine. The sun shines behind him, illuminating his dark hair in a halo of light.

We're in a meadow, surrounded by wildflowers. Dogwood trees line the clearing, fragrant and in full bloom.

Greedy bends low to kiss me, his lips warm, sweet. He tastes like strawberries and smells like a mixture of rich cedar and sweet honey, a scent that I always associate with home.

My head lolls to the side, and my eyes connect with piercing blue orbs.

Levi.

He's spread out beside us, lying flat on his back, hands cushioning the back of his head. He smiles at me. The dimple on his left cheek appears.

He speaks, though I can't make out the words. Above me, Greedy laughs. At the sound, I grin and turn back to him. Only when I do, I no longer find warm, loving eyes peering down at me.

Instead, I'm hit with a hard stare.

Intense green orbs, the color of sea glass, glare down at me. The eyes match mine exactly. I inhale, ready to scream, but before I can make a sound, the vision of my mother blurs.

A pair of hands grasp my shoulders, pulling me out of the start of a nightmare.

Eyes still pinched shut, I bat at my attacker.

"Easy, love. Easy. You're okay."

The soothing voice instantly banishes my panic, and when I open my eyes, I find another man staring down at me.

"Spence?"

His irises are icy blue as he scrutinizes me in concern, as if trying to gauge whether I'm truly awake.

"What are you doing here?"

His face falls, then he blows out a long breath and runs one hand through his hair.

"We're at my place. You're safe."

"What?" I ask, my brain sputtering. I sit up quickly and scan my surroundings. Sure enough, I'm lying in a familiar bed. I'm not in a meadow of flowers, and no one else is here.

I'm lying in the middle of Kabir's bed, charcoal-gray silk sheets caressing my skin. The coolness of the fabric gives me pause. Peeking under the covers, I realize I'm stripped down to my bra and underwear. My skin is damp and clammy where I've sweated against the silk.

"What am I doing here?" I ask as I shakily grasp at the damp, slippery sheets.

"You're okay," Spence assures me. He reaches out as if to touch me, but stops, leaving his hand suspended in the air, and assesses me. "Angelo called me last night."

I rack my brain for a memory, but my thoughts are too foggy. I can't make sense of what he's saying.

"It's already Saturday morning?" is the best I can come up with.

Kabir grimaces and swallows thickly. "It's already Saturday evening, love. You've been asleep all day."

I slow blink, willing his words to register.

It can't be night. It was just night. I was working. Crystal told me I could take off early.

I'm lost in a blend of hazy memories that lack discernable edges when Kabir touches my shoulder, pulling me from my reverie.

"Hunter, is there any chance you took something last night? Or perhaps drank something offered to you?"

"No," I tell him, heart thudding. So much of yesterday is a blur, but I'm positive I didn't take anything or even drink anything other than the closed water bottle I keep at the hostess station.

"You're sure?" he presses. "I could call a doctor if there's even a chance—"

"I didn't take anything," I whisper.

Leaning across the mattress, he brushes my hair off my forehead, then gently places his lips on the skin between my brows.

He holds it there for a breath, the warmth of him settling into me and allowing me to relax. A few more seconds pass, his stubble tickling my forehead.

"What are you doing?"

He pulls back and offers me a small smile. "Checking to see if you have a fever."

A memory hits me then.

"My dad used to check for fever that way, too."

Kabir smiles, but a pit of pain collects in my gut at the recollection.

I miss my dad.

He opted out on so much of the last year of my life.

At first, I was sad. Now, I'm angry.

He knows I'm here in London. He assured me that we would get together soon. Yet I haven't heard from him in weeks.

"Your father checked you for fevers? What about your mother?"

I shake my head, my thoughts shifting to the even more disappointing parent.

"My mother never wanted to get too close when I was sick."

Spence studies me for a breath, his gray-blue eyes warming. "Come here." He pulls me into his arms and smooths one hand up and down my bare arm, cradling me against the side of his body. "You don't have a fever, and you're sure you didn't take or drink anything last night…"

"I'm sure," I tell him through a yawn.

"How do you feel now?"

"Tired," I admit.

What I don't say aloud is that I'm tired and so damn defeated. I've lost a full day, and last night is a blur. The last thing I clearly remember is buying strawberries at the market, then going back to my flat and finding a stranger passed out in my bed.

I shudder involuntarily at the thought.

"You're all right, love," Spence soothes. "Maybe you could use the bathroom, then go back to sleep."

Go back to sleep? He can't be serious.

"Spence, it's Saturday. We have plans."

Dinner. He wanted to take me to dinner.

He shakes his head, his chin rubbing my crown with each pass.

"Just sleep, love. If you're tired, you need rest. There will be many more Saturdays in our future."

Chapter 24

Hunter

THEN

There was no use arguing with the man. In the end, I slept for over twenty-four hours.

Now, I can't sleep any longer. It's not even dawn, but I'm up and wandering the penthouse aimlessly as Spence snoozes in the bedroom.

He occupies the whole top floor of the hotel. There's a full kitchen, multiple bathrooms, a spacious living area, and an amazing balcony with views of Hyde Park.

After drinking a glass of water and putzing around the kitchen, I find myself stepping into a room I haven't spent any time in at all: the office.

A stately, commanding desk with multiple monitors takes up the center of the space.

There's a sitting area off to one side, and one entire wall consists of freestanding bookshelves all lined up and filled, stretching from the floor to the ceiling.

I flick on a few lights, then walk over. It's impossible not to smile as I take in the titles. There are books about business and leadership. There's also a substantial historical section, as well as two entire shelves devoted to the classics.

I trace the spines of the classics. Many feature covers I've never seen, and I'm tempted to pull them out and give them closer inspection. When I remove a copy of *Sense and Sensibility*, my memory falters and snags on a deeply buried memory of another library I've tried so damn hard to forget.

The library at the cabin.

Greedy's mom's collection.

I hold the old book to my chest, then sink to my knees, overwhelmed with emotion and sick to my stomach all at the same time.

My mouth drops open in a soundless cry, my shoulders shuddering and my chest aching as I gasp for air. My every cell hurts. I don't remember how to breathe.

Flopping to a sitting position, I bring my knees to my chest, circle my arms around them, and bury my head.

I force air into my lungs, then out again, but there's no stopping the flood of memories.

Books and pages.

Smiles and kisses.

Minutes pass, or maybe hours, as I sit on the floor in front of the mammoth shelves, rocking back and forth with my arms wrapped around my knees.

When I finally exhaust myself, I tip my head back, taking in the shelves. From here, they're even more massive than I originally thought. They've got to be at least eight or ten feet tall.

They're lined up together, but they're not attached to each other. I doubt they're anchored to the wall.

How much force would it take to make them topple?

I don't need all of them to fall. One would be enough, or maybe two.

What angle would be best if I wanted them to properly crush me?

It would be awful to be conscious and trapped.

I don't want to feel it. I don't want to feel anything.

Yet, if I could get two of them to fall simultaneously, and I stretched out flat on the floor before they hit, they'd surely gain enough momentum to properly end me.

I unfurl my body, renewed energy zipping through my veins.

Crawling on hands and knees, I slip one arm between the two biggest shelves, then run my palm along the back.

I go slow. Searching. I have to be sure. I don't want to damage the walls.

Then I walk to the end of all the shelves and peer through the gap behind them. There are no anchors fixing them in place.

This could work.

I'll need a lot of strength to pull both shelves forward, then I'll have to act quickly to get on the floor for maximum impact. Getting the angle right is a must. There's no room for error or miscalculation.

Circling back to the front of the shelves, I lie on the floor. I spread my body out like a starfish, making sure my head and chest are both aligned for maximum impact.

I grip my fingertips into the plush carpet under my palms, then brush my arms back and forth as if I'm making a snow angel. By marking my position, I'll know exactly where I need to—

"Hunter."

Heart jolting, I bolt up to sitting. Spence is in the doorway, eyes wide as he takes in the sight before him.

I'm dizzy. Empty. Confused. So damn sad.

He takes one step into the room, then another. "What are you doing?" he asks in a soft, hesitant tone.

What *am* I doing?

"I don't know," I breathe. I don't even have the strength to be embarrassed. It's all too much. It's never enough.

He approaches slowly and eventually kneels beside me, cupping my face in both hands. His eyes search mine.

"What do you need, love?"

I look up at the bookshelves above us and shudder. What the hell was I thinking? If Spence hadn't walked in the moment he did...

"I don't know," I repeat.

As a sob racks through me. I pull away from him and bury my face in my hands.

"I'm so tired."

Tired of being sad.

Tired of feeling like this.

"I didn't realize what I was doing," I admit. "But I think... it could have been bad if you hadn't found me."

Spence circles his arms around me, pulling me in to a gentle, tender hug. "You're safe."

"I'm not," I whimper.

I'm the threat. I'm the problem. If I'm the danger here, then how the hell am I supposed to protect myself?

"What do you need?" he asks again, pulling back and searching my face. He crosses his legs and settles in beside me. The move alone soothes me. He's here. I'm not alone.

Even so, I truly have no fucking clue how to answer him.

I don't know what I need. Shaking my head, I choke out a sob.

"I'm not okay. I think I should go back to bed."

Nodding, Spence stands. Instead of offering me a hand, he scoops me up into his arms. "It's okay if you're not okay," he tells me softly. "But you will be. Tell me you understand, Firecracker. You *will* be okay."

I don't have it in me to argue.

Though I'm not sure I believe him either.

I let my eyes flutter closed and slip into unconsciousness almost instantly.

Chapter 25

Kabir

THEN

"I've canceled all my travel plans for the next few weeks," I explain to Gerald, catching his eye in the mirror as he stands by attentively.

He was my father's valet for years. Although I don't require his help dressing, we typically take this time to catch up on Monday mornings.

My parents passed away within a year of each other. Romantic in a way, but also a logistical nightmare in terms of settling their estates and mitigating the various business endeavors. My father retired from the British Royal Navy, where he served in a special forces unit. It was my mother who had founded and grown many of the central business entities I inherited. I miss them dearly, but as an only child, I always knew this would be my fate. Gerald is the closest thing I have to family these days.

"I've also moved all my meetings to virtual and don't anticipate leaving the flat for any reason until she's well."

"Understood, Mr. Spencer."

His tone is subdued, and when I search his face in the mirror, it's etched in the same concern rattling deep in my bones.

"Is there anything else I might assist with?"

I know what he's asking. Hunter has been holed up in my room since the weekend. She barely wakes, yet she's restless in sleep. I've tried to help as best as I can, but I'm starting to worry I won't be enough to pull her from the darkness.

"I don't know what I'm doing," I admit, my voice nothing but a whisper.

His expression falters. "You don't know what you're doing in what regard, sir?"

I huff a sigh. He's being purposely obtuse.

"About her," I tell him, nodding toward the bedroom, where Hunter's soundly asleep.

It's been more than forty-eight hours since I found her in a compromising position in my library. In that time, she's only risen to use the loo or sip a little water.

The few times she has been lucid enough to have conversations, she's not been herself. I've never felt this way about anyone, or in any situation. I'm compelled to take care of her.

All I want to do is ensure she's well.

"You're doing the best you can with the information and resources you have," Gerald offers diplomatically, his hands clasped in front of him.

Frustration bubbles up inside me for what has to be the hundredth time in two days. There has to be something else I can do for her. "Well, that's a crackpot shit way to say I'm bloody useless."

With a little too much force, I brush invisible lint from my suit jacket, then adjust my perfectly straight tie.

A hand lands on my shoulder, stilling me.

"If I may be so bold, sir?"

On an exhale, I nod. I'm desperate for any suggestion.

"Sometimes, the best way to be there for another person is to just be there. Even if it makes you feel bloody useless," he says with a roguish smile.

Fair enough.

"Do you think I'm making a mistake?" Even as I ask, I avert my gaze, not willing to show any additional vulnerability along with such a loaded question.

Now Gerald's resting both hands on my shoulders, and he gives me a firm but affectionate squeeze.

"Ms. St. Clair has been your one and only guest over the past month, to my knowledge, and that tells me that we are in uncharted territory."

I smirk at his observation. He's right. No one else has caught or kept my attention since the moment I laid eyes on Hunter St. Clair.

I've never considered myself a monogamous creature, per se, but for the first time in my life, she's the singular focus of all my thoughts and all my carnal desires. Though at this moment, those urges come nowhere close to my concern for her mental health. Helping her through whatever is going on in her head is my utmost priority.

I want her well. I want her back.

"As for whether you're making a mistake," Gerald says, pulling me back to the moment, "there are no guarantees in life, Mr. Spencer. Only opportunities. Opportunities taken and opportunities missed. You'd be foolish to let go of any of them when it comes to her."

My thoughts exactly.

Decidedly, I nod. "Thank you, Gerald."

He dips his chin, then takes his leave.

I check my attire one last time in the full-length mirror, then I quietly make my way back to the bedroom, intent on cleaning my teeth and getting on with my day.

Soundlessly, I move through the dark bedroom, but as I approach the bathroom door, a cry from the other side startles me.

"Hunter," I call out, panicked.

She doesn't respond. Dread percolates in my gut.

Grasping the doorknob, I step up close. "Are you in here, Firecracker?"

My question is met with a sob.

Fuck it.

Something's wrong.

With my heart in my throat and my pulse pounding, I push into the bathroom. When I don't find her, I stalk past the vanity and the oversized tub and open the door to the water closet.

Shock and horror ricochet through me as I take in the sight on the floor: Hunter, sprawled out, clinging to the toilet, sobbing.

But that's not the worst of it.

There's blood.

There's blood everywhere.

"Hunter."

I crouch down to comfort her, finding she's covered in even more blood than I initially thought.

My heart sinks into my stomach as nausea churns up my esophagus.

"Hunter, where are you bleeding from?"

Pulling in a deep breath, I pry her hands off the toilet and help her sit up so I can look at her properly. Did she hurt herself? Is the blood coming from a self-inflicted wound?

This is what I feared all weekend. She's not well. She's not with it.

"Hunter," I start again.

She shrugs off my touch, lifting her head so I can look into her red-rimmed eyes. "I was pregnant," she whispers.

My stomach falls out of my ass as I run the numbers, visualizing the calendar in my head.

We've been seeing each other for nearly a month. We've used protection religiously.

I look down again at the blood, trying to make sense of it all. "Are you telling me you're pregnant now?"

She shakes her head on a sob. "I *was* pregnant."

"You *were* pregnant?" I repeat, emphasizing the past tense as she did.

But she's not with me. Not really.

Without responding, she slumps back against the wall and closes her eyes.

I make quick work of wiping up the blood around the toilet. With her head back and her neck extended, I can see there are no marks on her throat or chest. I carefully turn over each hand and inspect her wrists.

There's blood on a few fingers, but it wipes clean.

"Hunter, where are you bleeding from?" I beg, the panic coursing through me growing.

"I was pregnant," she says again, the words soft and slow.

I take a big breath and stand. This isn't getting us anywhere.

The best I can do is put her in the shower, or maybe the bath.

I bend to lift her. When I hook my arm under her legs, warm moisture soaks through my sleeve.

As I assess her once more, I note the blood in the toilet that I didn't notice from where I was crouched on the floor.

Carefully, I lift her high enough to see the blood sticking between her upper thighs. Her panties fall off one foot. They're soaked with blood, too.

I'm almost certain this is menses.

Yet she keeps saying she was pregnant. Could she be miscarrying right now?

"I was pregnant," she sobs as she throws her arms around me, clinging to my neck. "I was pregnant with my stepbrother's baby."

My whole body locks, and shock whips through me.

It takes a moment to shake it off. Then I carry her to the sink and place her on the counter. "Stay," I murmur, hurrying back into the bedroom to grab the overnight bag I had her roommate pack the other day.

I fish out fresh underwear, then find what I assume is a sanitary napkin. I prepare the pad on the underwear as best I can, then help her put each leg through the knickers and pull her to standing.

She sways before me with her eyes closed, the tears continuing to fall.

I pull a pair of shorts up her legs, much more confident in what I'm dealing with now, at least physically.

She has her period. She's recalling a clearly traumatic event.

"Do you want to go back to bed, love?"

With a nod, she loops her arms around my neck and hoists herself into my arms.

I grip her under her thighs and carry her back to the bedroom. Then I tuck her in, make quick work of cleaning the bathroom, and head straight to my office, prepared to make the call I've been considering all weekend.

Chapter 26

Hunter

THEN

I wake up, but then I drift off.

I drift off, hoping to never wake up again.

The hazy pull of sleep is the only thing anchoring me to reality. Sleep and Spence.

"Rest, love," he tells me during my lucid moments and then again in my dreams. So I do.

I don't know how long it goes on, but almost every time I wake, he's there, caressing my hair, offering me sips of water.

I sleep.

Deeply. Fitfully. Restlessly. Desperately.

Eventually, I wake up again, though this time is unlike any other.

My eyes flutter open, my attention immediately pulled to the soft sunlight streaming in from the crack between the curtains.

I feel... okay. Rested. Ready to get up and greet the day. It's a sensation I haven't experienced in a very long time.

I hit the control panel next to the nightstand, and the curtains open fully.

The sunlight is overwhelming, so I shield my eyes while they adjust. But for the first time in a long time, I welcome the light.

I turn my face toward the windows, seeking the sun, craving the luminosity, and welcoming the technicolor brightness.

I feel different. I feel *better*.

After a few minutes, I sit up fully. I'm thirsty. Starving.

I really need to pee, but what I want more than anything is to be clean.

Shuffling slowly, I make my way to the bathroom. I take my time showering, scrubbing and shaving and washing my hair twice.

It's incredible. This sensation. As if I've finally returned to myself.

I'm folded over, towel drying my hair, when Spence calls my name from the bedroom, his voice panicked.

"In here," I call to him, securing the towel under my arms.

An instant later, he barrels into the bathroom, scanning me with a worried frown. My cheeks warm under his gaze.

I'm practically naked, yet that isn't what makes me sheepish. It's the knowledge of what he witnessed—what he helped me through—that makes my cheeks pink as I search his face.

What happened over the last few days... it's not normal. I wasn't myself. It would be completely understandable for him to view me differently after enduring that *episode*.

When his gaze meets mine, his expression softens. With a sympathetic smile, he asks, "Are you well, love?"

"Um, I think." I clear my throat. "I feel better, I mean. I just took a shower, and I don't feel..."

How do I categorize what I feel or don't feel? The last few days have been an absolute blur, and Spence has had to shoulder the burden of what I went through. He cared for me. Tenderly. Devotedly.

"I'm sorry you had to, um..." I grimace, staring down at my bare feet. "I'm sorry you had to see me like that."

"I'm not." He strides over and tilts my chin back so I'm forced to look him in the eye. "It was a privilege to take care of you, love. I had no idea what I was doing, but I tried my best."

"Thank you," I whisper. Pushing up on tiptoes, I kiss him softly.

He returns the kiss but doesn't take it any further, instead pulling me into a tight embrace. "I'm so glad you're well."

As we hold one another, his body physically relaxes.

"Last weekend—" he starts.

"Wait." I pull back, my heart thumping against my sternum. "What day is it?"

He lowers his head, frowning. "It's Friday, love. You've been in bed for six days."

Reality slams into me as I digest his words. Six days. Six entire days? Did he contact Louie? What did he tell management at Splice?

"Hunter."

My gaze shoots up to meet his as trepidation washes over me.

"Don't stress. Please, I beg you, let's ease back into this and take it one thing at a time."

I pull my bottom lip between my teeth. "I can't believe I was in bed that long."

What the hell was I thinking? It's rare for me to even nap during the day. Who in their right mind stays in bed for nearly a week?

"What can I do for you, love?"

Inhaling a steadying breath, I consider his words. *One thing at a time...*

"I'm hungry," I admit. Did I eat anything at all over the last week? It sure doesn't feel like it. "I'll have them bring up the entire room service menu." Spence pulls his cell out, types a message, then stashes it just as quickly. "It'll be here in twenty-five minutes. What's next?"

I lean against the bathroom vanity, unsure of where to even start. My mind is filled with so many blanks I wish I could fill in.

The biggest, most urgent question: Why did this all happen?

"Can you..." I clasp my hands and dip my chin. "I don't remember much of anything."

Spence maintains his distance this time, giving me space as he assesses me from head to toe. Eventually, he inhales steadily, lets it out again, and says, "You slept practically the entire time. When you got up, I made sure you used the facilities, drank water, ate a little toast when you were able. I got you to eat a few strawberries two days ago. Highlight of my week, really."

He offers me a mischievous smile, but I don't feel like laughing.

He clears his throat, looking unsure for the first time. "I also helped you change your sanitary pads."

My sanitary wha—

Mortification boils over, my whole body instantly going hot, as memories flood my mind.

I got my period.

I got my period, I saw the blood, and I spiraled.

It was the first period I've had since miscarrying. The ob-gyn had warned me it could take a few cycles for my body to get back on track after the loss. I hadn't fully considered what it would be like to see blood between my legs again.

Horrified, trembling, I peek up at Spence.

"I told you," I say, hanging my head and turning around so I'm facing the mirror.

"Yes." He doesn't elaborate, but he doesn't have to.

I remember now how he found me. The way I clung to him, sobbing, wishing it was Greedy who had his arms wrapped around me as I relived the physical and emotional hurricane of my loss. The sight of blood sent me right back to the moment. The aching cramps mimicked the contractions.

I held it all in, held it together the best I could the day I simultaneously found out I was pregnant, I was losing the baby, and that my boyfriend was about to be my stepbrother.

It was the worst day of my life.

This week, though, was just as awful. It hurt. Physically. Mentally. Emotionally. No wonder my mind checked out.

"Hunter," he says softly.

I look up and meet his gaze through the mirror, bracing myself for what feels like a weight that's about to drop.

"Based on what happened, I called NHS, and they referred me to a private practice."

My heart stumbles at the seriousness of his tone, but I don't understand. "What?"

"The National Health Service. They have a mental health crisis line."

I stare at him, wide-eyed, as my stomach drops. "Why would you do that?"

Spence loses a modicum of his temper for the first time. "Because you were clearly in *crisis*."

He takes a step forward, but then halts in his tracks. Whatever he sees in the mirror is clearly enough to make him proceed with caution.

"You needed help, love. More than I knew how to give."

Arms crossed over my chest, I narrow my eyes at his reflection. "You should have just left me alone."

"Absolutely not." He shakes his head in a jerky motion. "You were not well, Hunter. And there's no shame in needing help."

"I feel fine now," I tell him, lifting my arms and dropping them again.

"A psychiatrist came out the first day, then a psychologist was also assigned to your case. They've been coming by each day, taking notes. One of them will be here shortly, I'm sure."

"I feel better," I repeat, frustration turning into alarm. A stranger coming? To what? Observe me? Take notes?

What the fuck? Spence is being overdramatic.

"Call them and tell them not to bother." I meet his gaze in the mirror again. "I'm fine now."

"Hunter. I found you in my office, trying to pull a bookshelf over on yourself."

"That's absurd," I instinctively say, even as a glimmer of a memory floats through my mind.

"You could barely get out of bed, love. You couldn't speak. You couldn't function. You might feel fine now, but you were not okay."

I survey my hands, my towel-clad chest. I tilt my head back, inspecting my reflection in the mirror. I don't look different. Yet I don't feel like I truly know who I am anymore either.

"Hunter."

His proximity startles me at first. But then his lips find the delicate skin of my neck, and he wraps his arms around me from behind.

I lean back slightly at first, then eventually give him more of my weight. Resting my head on his shoulder, I peer up at him through my lashes.

"Please, love," he says, his voice hoarse. "I was so scared. I need you to accept the help that's being offered."

I study his face, his icy-blue eyes, and the stern pull of his brow line.

He softly kisses me on the lips, then pulls back. "I'm not willing to lose you."

When his mouth finds mine again, something clicks.

What happened was scary, but part of my fear is rooted in the idea that perhaps Spence wouldn't want me after what he witnessed.

But he's here.

Still.

He says he doesn't want to lose me.

I deepen the kiss, and he kisses me back just as passionately.

"Okay," I tell him gently.

Because I don't want to lose myself either.

Chapter 27

Hunter

NOW

"Lean back, love," Spence encourages. "You're far too tense."

He's not wrong. Between his unexpected arrival, my mother's reappearance in my life, and Greedy discovering the secret I withheld for so long, the last few days have been intense.

Big hands smooth over my shoulders as warm water caresses my skin. He pulls me closer and situates me between his legs in the hot tub.

As he kneads the tender flesh of my neck and upper back, his now-warm signet ring adds depth to the sensation.

Focusing on the steam billowing around us, I release a long, clarifying sigh, then tip my head back to meet his gaze. "That feels good."

Spence smirks, the subtle quirk of his lips igniting my insides. Homing in on my mouth, he says, "I live to make you feel good."

I lick my lips, eager for him to press his mouth to mine.

The sound of a door closing softly nearby pulls us out of the moment.

"Can I join you?"

With a deep breath in, I straighten, finding Levi standing before us in nothing but a pair of athletic shorts.

His nipples are pebbled and hard against the cool mountain air. The way he assesses me, his expression so earnest, makes me want to pull him into my arms and sink into his embrace.

"Of course you can." I shift slightly to put a bit more space between myself and Spence.

Spence clearly has other ideas. Before I can move more than a couple of inches, he captures me around the waist under the water and pulls me into his lap.

Possessive bastard.

"Get in before you freeze," I tell Levi.

Conceding, he takes his phone out of his pocket and sets it on the table nearby. Then he pulls the backward cap off his head, drops it on top, and steps up into the hot tub.

Kabir keeps his hand pressed against my stomach, holding me close in a way that tells me he's not letting go anytime soon. The mountain air feels amazing against my flushed cheeks. The contrast between the cool night and the heat of the water has my nerve endings sparking to life.

With his other hand, he caresses my throat, then traces the string of my bikini top. It's a clear show of possession, but after my talk with Levi, I feel okay letting him see me like this.

"It's much cooler here than it was at the Ferguson residence," Kabir remarks casually.

We're seriously going to talk about the weather? Okay, then.

"It's the altitude," I tell him. "The air is colder because we're higher up, farther from the sea level."

"By next month, there'll be snow covering the ground," Levi remarks just as casually.

He's seated across from us, his attention locked on Kabir's wandering hand. He doesn't seem bothered by it. If anything, his expression is full of curiosity.

"I love the cooler temps," Levi adds. "It was one of the things I missed most while I was in California." He settles back, arms spread wide on the outsides of the hot tub.

It was a bold choice, honestly, choosing to sit directly across from us.

Behind me, Kabir brushes my hair away from my ear, his fingertips dripping water onto my overheated skin, and angles in close, whispering, "I was planning to make you come in this hot tub, Firecracker. Is that still a possibility?"

My core clenches at the thought. God, I want it to be. But not without Levi's consent. He may be okay with sharing, but expecting him to be interested in watching another man get his girlfriend off may be a step too far. My relationship with Levi is still so new, and so far, he's had little choice in what's transpired between us.

"Promise not to purposely scare him away?" I murmur against Spence's lips. I give him a soft kiss, followed by a playful nip.

"I'll follow your lead," he promises.

I kiss him again, teasing his lips and peppering kisses along his stubbled jawline. Then, with my arms still looped around Spence's neck, I turn to Levi. "Are you okay with this? With watching, I mean?"

His blue eyes are twin flames, blazing and focused on all the places Kabir and I are connected. Clearing his throat, he shifts forward on the bench and not-so-subtly adjusts himself below the water. "Is that all I'm allowed to do? Watch?"

Spence lets out a surprised chuckle. "Captain America wants to play?"

Levi's lips tip up in a sexy smirk. "I do. But it's Hunter's call."

Grinning, I drop my arms from around Spence's neck and push forward, gliding directly into Levi's arms.

Chapter 28

Levi

NOW

Kabir sits on the edge of the bubbling hot tub, steam rising around him, making him look like actual royalty on top of a throne. Hunter is kneeling on a bench before him, moaning and choking on his cock as she struggles to take it all.

It's a fucking sight to see—so hot, the two of them together. Especially when Hunter pulls all the way back, her saliva glistening on the tip of Spence's uncut dick.

I've never seen one in person, and I can't stop fucking staring. It's not just the way she works him over that's got my blood roaring. It's him. It's them together. I don't know if I want to be him or be the one doing that to him.

Not that I have any complaints about my current position.

I'm standing behind her in the hot tub, railing her from behind. Her ass is high in the air as she bobs on Spence's cock. Spreading her cheeks, I sink deeper, groaning at the feel of her, my knees almost giving out at the sight of her taking two of us like this.

Our bodies are slick with sweat and desire. The once-cold mountain air is now thick, the sounds of our pleasure and skin slapping against skin loud and lewd in the otherwise silent night.

"How does she feel?" Spence asks, calling my attention back to him.

"Like perfect fucking heaven." It takes effort to grit the words out.

Fuck. My mouth feels like it's full of rocks.

"Don't come inside her," Spence demands.

Hissing, I slow my thrusts, tamping down the tingling sensation already building toward a mind-melting release.

Hunter's eyes sparkle as she grins at me over her shoulder. Her fingers are still wrapped around Spence's shaft. "Okay?" she mouths.

I'm fucking fantastic. But before I can reassure her, Spence inserts himself again.

"I have a plan. You'll both do as I say now," he commands.

Fuck. It takes all the willpower I have to keep my cool. I bring my knuckles to my mouth, biting down hard to stave off the desire threatening to take over. Why is his accent so hot?

I look to Kabir, waiting for further instructions. When our eyes meet, his are filled with a mixture of mirth and dominance.

I don't know what he sees in mine, but I gulp past the trepidation swirling in my gut. We're all consenting adults. He's my girlfriend's... what? European lover? Or are they something more? My chest constricts at the thought. Where does that leave me?

Before I can get too lost in the unknown, he pulls me back to the moment with a command.

"Pull out," he says, his tone sharp. "Come over here. Let me see how gorgeous your cock looks glistening with our girl's juices."

My heart stumbles, and the heat flooding me ignites.

Our girl.

Yeah. That sounds right. Whatever this is, whatever this is going to be, I'm in.

I slowly drag my cock out of Hunter's pussy. My stomach muscles tense, and an ache builds in my groin from the loss of her heat.

Hunter whimpers, completely focused on my dick, her eyes molten and her expression ravenous, as I walk through the water to stand by her side.

"Closer," Spence instructs.

Pulling in a fortifying breath, I obey, inching so close my knees graze the bench where Hunter is kneeling.

"Be a good girl, Firecracker," Spence says to her, his chin lifted regally, "and suckle your boyfriend's cock until he's coming in your mouth."

Hunter blinks up at him, wearing a look somewhere between trepidation and excitement. With a wink and a nod, she turns to me, head tipped back. Then she reaches out for my cock, admiring the coating of shared arousal all over my length.

She brings me to her lips, and the moan she emits when her tongue swirls around the tip is almost enough to send me over the edge.

"That's it, love," Spence encourages from his perch on the edge of the hot tub. "Suck his big, fat American cock. Take him as deep as you can go."

Without hesitation, Hunter takes me deeper, gagging a little when my tip touches the wall of her throat.

I'm so focused on the way she's sucking me that I don't notice Spence guiding her to a new position until her bare ass peaks out of the water.

She's perpendicular to the bench now, on her hands and knees, with half her body rising above the steamy water.

Spence straddles her from behind, lining himself up while remaining seated. "I'm going to fill you up while you choke on his cock and make him come."

Fuck. My ears ring, and my dick twitches, my impending orgasm already gripping my insides.

In this new position, I have an elite view of his thick cock disappearing each time he thrusts into our girl.

She moans around my dick, and... *Fuck. Me.*

This is the hottest moment of my life. I never want it to end. But I'm so fucking close. Soon, there'll be no stopping it.

With my chin tucked to my chest, I caress Hunter's cheek, wiping at the tears leaking from her eyes. "You're so fucking pretty like this, Daisy. So full of cock. Such a perfect little slut for us."

Her pupils blow wide. Then she takes me even deeper, lashes fluttering, humming with pleasure as she sucks and licks my length.

That word—*slut*—felt wrong as it came out of my mouth. I've never degraded a woman like that. But her wanton response was worth it.

Groaning, I give her a warning tap. "I can't hold back, Daisy. You're too good. Too fucking perfect." I grunt, gritting my teeth, seconds away from nutting.

"Come in her mouth," Spence demands. "Firecracker," he continues without missing a beat, "don't you dare swallow."

The rough command is all it takes to send me over the edge. My cock throbs and pulses as I fill Hunter's mouth with my seed.

She gasps around me, like she's struggling to breathe. Shit. Is this too much? Before I can pull out and check on her, Spence yanks on her hair, forcing her back until she's flat against his chest, head tipped back.

"Give it here, love," he commands, bringing his lips to hers.

In a display unlike anything I've ever witnessed, Spence sucks my cum out of Hunter's mouth. He's sloppy and ravenous, like he's desperate to capture every drop. When he pulls away, he sets his stormy eyes on me.

"*Fuck.*" I just finished, and already, desire swamps me.

His expression is haughty as always, but also filled with mirth.

I swear to god I'm holding my breath, desperate for him to tell me what to do.

Spence doesn't speak. He can't. Because his mouth is full of my cum. Instead, he cocks an eyebrow and crooks two fingers my way.

There's not an inch of me that doesn't want to be closer. Quickly, unsteadily, I crowd his space and kneel before him. Hunter's still sitting in his lap, still impaled on his cock. I inch closer, hit with a sudden burst of unease, hoping like hell I'm not reading him wrong.

Once I'm positioned below him, he tips my chin back, then taps my lips twice.

Chest tightening, I open my mouth.

He spits.

A full wad of my own cum paints my tongue, the salty tartness dancing on my taste buds. As the flavor registers, I search his face, seeking approval.

It isn't Spence who gives it to me, though. It's Hunter.

"Good boy," she says, her tone as coy as the small smile on her face. She loops her arms around Spence's neck behind her. "Is he allowed to swallow, Sir?"

With a smirk, he kisses Hunter again.

The way she moans when his tongue teases between her lips sends a full-body shudder through me. That's my seed she's tasting on his mouth. My cum they're sharing.

Spence pulls back, one arm banded around Hunter, and zeroes in on me. "He is."

Floating on a thick cloud of need, I keep my attention focused on him and swallow my own release. As I lick my lips, relishing the salty taste left over, fresh arousal courses up my thighs.

"Well done," Spence tells me, caressing Hunter's inner thighs. "He really is a good boy, isn't he?"

I can't fight the grin that spreads across my face.

"Maybe we should let our boy decide how we finish." Spence suggests, burrowing his face into Hunter's neck.

Their boy. Fuck. That's all it takes to have me hard again.

Biting down on her bottom lip, Hunter nods.

"Do you want to watch her suck me off?" Spence asks, tracing along Hunter's inner thighs with his ring-clad fingers, teasing through her folds and carelessly playing with her clit.

She's spread wide, so I have a clear shot of where they're joined. I ache to be closer. To see more. To... fuck, to do more. To both of them.

"What if I sucked you off while you fucked her like that?" I suggest, my voice so low and shaking it sounds foreign to my own ears.

Hunter whimpers, but Spence plays it cool.

"Let's give it a go."

Chapter 29

Hunter

NOW

Spence's words are cool and collected, but his cock is as hard as a steel pipe as he accepts Levi's proposal.

Within seconds, my boyfriend is positioned between my thighs, his mouth inches from my stuffed pussy, his eyes searching mine for permission.

Chest heaving, I give him a little nod. I want this. I want this so badly I could come just from watching them together. And yet here I am, smack in the middle of them, about to reap all the benefits of this spark igniting between us.

When Spence shifts back and pulls out a few inches, I whimper, and my center clenches around him involuntarily.

Shushing me, he glides one hand down my stomach until his fingers find my clit.

He pinches my tight bundle of nerves: a warning.

"Go on, then," he tells Levi.

Levi lowers himself below us, then takes a tentative lick of Spence's exposed length. The heat of his mouth near my pussy makes me squirm. Fuck, I'm aching to feel his tongue on me, too.

"Patience, Firecracker," Spence grits into my ear.

I fight back a laugh. His tone is low and harsh, meaning he's already fighting back his own orgasm.

Levi's licks become more confident, steady and rhythmic in their strokes.

Spence rubs my clit in tight circles, matching the pace and sending me spiraling higher.

"Can I come with you, Sir?" I breathe, arching back against Spence's sweat-slicked chest, my focus fixed on Levi as he makes a feast out of the place where we're joined.

"Not yet," Spence murmurs. He releases my clit, then brushes both palms over my inner thighs.

"I have a challenge for you, champ."

Levi perks up, his cheeks rosy and his eyes shining.

"Anything," he replies, his chest expanding.

Spence pulses inside me. He's loving this.

"I'm going to thrust all the way inside our girl." Spence teases my lips and pulls on either side of my pussy. "Once I'm in, I want you to work your tongue inside her, too."

At the prospect, liquid heat pools in my belly, and my hips buck of their own volition.

"With fucking pleasure." Levi lowers himself again and inches closer until he's perfectly lined up with us.

Licking his lips, he looks to Spence, then me, his pupils so dilated his irises are thin blue rings.

"I can't wait to feel you inside me with him," I murmur.

That's all the encouragement he needs. Levi swirls his tongue around my clit once, then licks and probes below my clitoral hood. As he continues his work, I tighten, then stretch. He backs off, licking up Spence's length, then moves back to my opening. He repeats the process a few times.

As he probes again, my breathing turns erratic. I'm so full. Too full—

"Shh," Spence soothes, his fingers finding my clit once more. "He's got this," he murmurs into my ear. Then, louder, he says, "Our boy's a champ. He'll get it in, Firecracker. Have faith."

With a moan, I will my muscles to relax, and I melt into Spence's embrace, giving myself fully to both men.

Levi probes my hole again, but this time, he doesn't stop.

He slips the tip of his tongue inside me, and as he licks against my insides, Spence moans loudly in my ear.

"Just like that, champ," he groans, one hand rubbing my clit while he grasps the back of Levi's head with the other and guides him into my tight, fully stuffed hole.

"Fuck her with your tongue. Lick me to completion."

Spence's commands are breathy. Ragged. His heart pounding a fierce rhythm against my back.

My body is just as primed. Blood whooshing in my ears and sparks traveling down my extremities. "I'm close," I warn them. "Please, Sir," I beg.

"Make us come," Spence commands.

Levi eagerly grinds his mouth into the place where we're joined, thrusting and licking us until we explode as one.

My pussy barely spasms. I'm too full. But the undulating pleasure that rolls through my body is unlike anything I've ever experienced. I'm coming and coming and coming. I'm flying and floating and soaring higher than I've ever soared.

Spence fucks into me from behind, his thrusts loose and shallow, as Levi ravishes us both through our orgasms.

My moans turn to whimpers as I come down, the intensity of Levi's mouth on my body almost too much to bear.

"Too sensitive," I pant, craning back to meet Spence's gaze.

Instantly, he stops his movements and tugs on Levi's hair, pulling him from my core.

"Can I help clean up?" I ask.

His eyes shift from questioning to confident and challenging once more. With a nod, he kisses me on the mouth. He slips out of me, then grasps my hips and guides me off his lap.

When I'm on my knees, my position matching my boyfriend's, a soft touch smooths over my back. I turn to find Levi watching me, wearing a concerned frown.

"You okay?" His mouth glistens with our joint release as he speaks.

Angling forward, I press my lips to his and kiss him deeply, savoring the way the three of us taste together. "I'm more than okay," I promise him as I pull back. "Just sensitive."

Spence clears his throat, and instantly, I'm on full alert, snapping my head back to give him my attention. He cocks one brow, his expression imperious.

I peer down at his glistening shaft, then lower my head and lick the cum off his length.

To my surprise, Levi joins me, licking in tandem, kissing me each time we reach the tip.

As Spence softens slightly, I suck on his foreskin, pulling him into my mouth and inserting the tip of my tongue the way he likes.

"Can I try?" Levi asks, his eyes glassy and wanton as he watches me suckle Spence's uncut cock.

"Teach him, Firecracker," Spence urges. "Show him how to clean up every last drop."

Grinning, I pop off Kabir's cock, then grip his length and offer him to Levi.

"Use your tongue to move the foreskin around," I instruct.

Levi obeys, bringing Spence into his mouth.

Fuck. This sight instantly makes me salivate. "Good boy," I praise, heat licking up my spine as I watch my boyfriend suck on my lover.

The groan that escapes Levi makes my head spin.

"Now, relax your jaw and let him rest in your mouth." I hold Spence's cock about halfway up his shaft. "Swirl your tongue around the tip, then probe it gently until you sink into the soft part and connect with the glans." I squeeze tightly, rapt at the sight of Levi hollowing his cheeks and working over the tip of Spence's uncut penis.

Spence is fully hard now—by my hand and Levi's mouth. I look from Levi to Spence, then back again, eager for direction, but both men are lost to the moment, their eyes closed as they chase another release.

"That's it, champ. You're doing so well," he praises.

Spence's abs are tensing and releasing in a slow, steady rhythm, a sure sign that his orgasm is imminent.

"He's getting close," I warn Levi. "Do you want me to take over?"

Levi opens his eyes, his mouth still full of cock. He pops off and sucks in a harsh breath. "Let's finish him off together."

Grinning, I grip Spence tighter. "He likes it rough. Lots of pressure on the tip. Use your teeth a little and hollow your cheeks when you pull back."

"Yes, ma'am," Levi confirms, his eyes glinting. Then he's taking Spence deep before pulling back to focus on the tip.

"Bloody hell, Firecracker. I don't know what's hotter—the sensation of your boyfriend sucking my cock for the first time or the way you're teaching him."

Spence groans, then he moans again, a deep, strangled cry filled with passion.

"He's coming," I warn.

"I know," Levi gargles out.

I jack Spence's length and watch, mystified, as he unloads into Levi's mouth. When he's finished, Levi pulls off, pushes away from the bench, and pulls me into his arms.

He pulls me to the center of the hot tub, hooks my legs around his chest, and kisses me deeply with the taste of Spence still present on his tongue.

"So good," he murmurs against my lips. Pulling back, he surveys my face, then peers over my shoulder at Spence. "Both of you. So fucking good."

He kisses me again, feeding me his salty tongue.

Behind us, Spence rasps, "Fucking incredible. Absolutely fucking incredible."

I smile against Levi's mouth as he kisses me harder. I couldn't agree more.

Chapter 30

Hunter

NOW

The next morning is mostly uneventful. Dr. F and my mother arrived at some point, but I left them to get settled in. Besides suffering through an awkward brunch, I've mostly stayed out of the way. Caterers have been brought in for the holidays, so there's not much to help with in the kitchen. I may be hiding, too.

The three of us stayed out in the hot tub for far too long, then quickly showered, chugged water, and passed out. I woke up in Kabir's bed, warm and sated. After brunch, he got to work, finally letting me out of his sight, and I headed up the second flight of stairs to the primary bedroom to hide away.

Memories of last night will be fuel for my self-care fantasies for a long time coming. Spence and Levi. Levi and me. The three of us together. The way our dynamic shifted and molded to the moment was seamless, fluid.

I'm not embarrassed by last night's escapades, but we're absolutely wading into uncharted waters. Suddenly, every emotion is more intense and every interaction is weighted.

With a long, slow inhale, I will the butterflies fluttering in my belly to abate and do my best to temper my enthusiasm. We've yet to have a conversation. For all I know, I may be alone in these feelings. But damn, that wasn't just sex. That was passion, power transference, and unabashed pleasure.

It was soul-stirring and life-affirming. The entire experience was right and real in a way nothing has ever been before.

But again, until we have a chance to talk, it's better if I put these feelings on hold. I don't want anyone getting hurt, so communication and clear expectations are key.

Later. There'll be time to talk and figure things out. Preferably when we're not at Greedy's family's cabin. And not while I'm desperately trying to keep my shit together knowing my mother is close by.

I'm already burned out on holiday rom-coms and spicy Santa novellas. This happens every year. The buildup that comes along with the holidays, the ads for Christmas romance stories and all things holiday cheer are so overdone that by the time it finally arrives, the actual day is lackluster.

Instead of forcing myself to work through my holiday TBR, I'm rereading my favorite hockey romance series. Maybe I'll revisit the holiday list next year.

I snag a plush blanket off the end of the bed, and for the first time since we arrived, I venture toward the library.

Despite how frustrated I am by my trepidation, my footsteps are tentative. Greedy made it clear that he doesn't care whether I use this room, as long as I stay out of his way. Yet it's still a struggle not to be wary of being in this space. As if my presence here without him is sacrilegious in a way.

I swear I can still smell him on the sheets in this room and picture him in the doorway, a version of him that's a little younger and far less angry.

He's everywhere. Inescapable.

It's one of the reasons I slept downstairs with Kabir last night. That, and I wasn't done basking in his affection. His brand of aftercare is sublime.

I push open the door to the library and am instantly hit with a blast of cold, stale air. Shivering, I peek into the familiar space, then find the light switch on the wall. It's drafty, and the space smells of old books. My olfactory response is automatic. The familiar scent alone instantly eases my anxiety.

As I make my way toward the chaise lounge situated in the middle of the room, recollections and memories consume me.

Holed up at this cabin with Greedy three years ago. Lazy summer days spent reading. Long nights snuggled up in his arms, getting lost in a book while he dozed. We came up here multiple times that summer, using this place as our personal retreat.

With a long breath out, I banish the memories.

What was can never be again.

It hurts. The memories. The choices I made. It all fucking hurts.

I bite down on the inside of my cheek to distract myself and keep the tears at bay. My period is about to start, too. That has to be why I'm so emotional today.

Spreading out the blanket and curling up on my side, I settle onto the lounger. Before I load up my e-book, I take another deep breath and scan the space I know so well. This room I still love.

For the most part, the library looks the same. The furniture and the decor haven't changed since I was last here. If I didn't know better, I would think the pillows are arranged exactly how I left them.

And yet, as I burrow deeper, searching for a comfortable position while trying to focus on my Kindle, I can't help but sense subtle differences.

The trees outside the window are taller and bare. I've never been here in the winter. That's got to be it. The room is cold, and the view is different.

I'm different now, too.

Sighing, I cue up the tried-and-true dark hockey romance.

Except I can't focus. After I've read the same sentence four times, I sit up and bury my head in my hands.

Why can't I get Greedy out of my mind? From what I can tell, he's stayed away from this room since we arrived. Heck, I don't think he's even in the house right now.

I should be taking advantage of this time alone. It may be all I get during this trip.

Silently admonishing myself, I flop over and lie on my other side, facing the built-in bookshelf instead of the window. Once I'm settled, I home in on the row of novels in front of me.

My heart stumbles. What the...?

Holding my breath, I push to my feet and stalk over to the shelf.

"No way," I mutter, tracing the spines with my fingertips. It's suddenly very clear what's changed in here since my last visit. This is why it feels foreign yet familiar.

The books are different. The books are... mine?

My throat constricts and tears prick at my eyes.

Some of the books are old and weathered, with broken spines and well-worn, well-loved covers. Others look to be brand new.

The shelves are full of hardbacks, paperbacks, and special editions with foil embossing on the letters and even sprayed edges.

"No way." Hand trembling, I bring it to my mouth as I step to one side and continue perusing.

These are titles I know. These are titles I *love*. Books I owned and treasured once upon a time.

Dropping my hand to my heart, I will the traitorous organ to calm. But it continues racing, aching, fissuring.

What was once Greedy's mom's library has been completely transformed. Gone are all the books she loved. They've been replaced by books I haven't seen in years. Books I cherish and adore. Books I assumed my mother threw out when we moved out of my childhood home.

A sob climbs up my throat, catching me by surprise. I press my lips closed, as if the action can keep the well of emotions from spilling out.

He saved my books.

Not only that. He's clearly purchased special editions of many of my favorites, so there are multiple versions of several titles.

Tears flood my eyes, but I swipe them away. Though it makes little sense, anger joins the mixture of emotions consuming me. He should have warned me.

A therapist once told me that anger is an easy default for many because it's a productive emotion. It builds, then peaks. It has a beginning, a middle, and an end. It's not an emotion that people often sit with, because it takes so much mental, emotional, and physical bandwidth to maintain.

Yet...

The anger creeping through me is set at a low boil. It's steady. Heated. I could sustain it forever.

And I might have to.

I'm not sure I can ever forgive myself for what I did and how I handled things when it comes to Greedy.

All he wanted was to hold on and love me.

I'm a monster for how I treated him. Back then, and now, too. I'm a monster, and I'll be angry with myself forever.

It's all I deserve.

Chapter 31

Greedy

NOW

Christmas Eve brunch was as awful and awkward as I anticipated.

I can't even blame Hunter's extra guests at what should have been a family meal. Spence was annoyingly polite, and Levi was his usual reserved, respectful self.

Magnolia's presence—at the table, in my family's cabin—is what truly made it an insufferable experience.

Nothing specifically terrible happened. In fact, the woman barely participated in the stilted conversation we engaged in. She wore this sort of vacant, far-off expression throughout the meal.

If her absenteeism hadn't been a much-needed break for Hunter, I would have been upset on my father's behalf.

Fuck. I shouldn't care.

Hunter isn't of any concern to me anymore.

It was easy enough to avoid her the first day, but then last night...

The dish I'm scrubbing clanks when it slips from my grip and sinks in the soapy water.

Clearly, none of them realize that the upper balcony has a straight-on view of the hot tub.

I brace my arms on either side of the counter, blowing out a long, pained breath.

Fucking hell. I can't think about it right now. Not again.

My mind has been plagued by the sights and sounds all day: the three of them in the hot tub. Together. Literally.

What I witnessed? I thought it would be us. Hunter and Levi and *me*. Maybe not right away, but for the briefest of moments, I got my hopes up, thinking that's where we were headed. The three of us. Together, despite the odds.

But with the unceremonious arrival of His Royal Highness, I've clearly been replaced. Not that I could have been with them after his revelation anyway. Levi and Hunter withheld information. They lied by omission.

I'm fucking livid about the bomb Sir Kabir What's-His-Ass dropped, but I'm even angrier at the way Hunter and Levi are going on with their lives as if they're completely unaffected.

I blow out another breath, my chest constricting painfully. At least the kitchen is benefiting from my hurt and frustration. My mom used to stress clean, too. The countertops and table are spotless, the entire kitchen pristine, save for the pile of dishes I'm still working on.

I dismissed the caterers half an hour ago so I could hand wash these on my own.

They were my mom's.

They weren't expensive, and they're not particularly fancy. Magnolia called them "garage-sale chic" when I was setting the table, whatever that's supposed to fucking mean.

They're simple white dishes, outlined in green with red berries. Holly, maybe? The set includes matching teacups and saucers, as well as silverware.

They belonged to my mom's mom. She loved using them during the holidays.

Once my temper settles, I reach for the plate on top of the stack.

Once each piece is clean, I lay it out on the kitchen island on long strips of paper towel so they can properly dry. That's how my mom used to do it.

My heart aches at the memory. God, I wish she was still around.

I'll put these away tonight. I can't stand the thought of Magnolia St. Clair-Ferguson commenting on them again.

The caterers can figure out the table settings for tomorrow. I'm already over this godforsaken trip. I need to be done. It's time for me to finally move on.

I'm laying out the last of the plates, ready to move on to silverware, when she enters the kitchen.

Before I see her, before I hear her, I sense her. Just like I always do.

That initial pang, the tugging sensation of my heartstrings. The physical, visceral pull toward her. My soul informs me Hunter is near before any of my senses have registered that I'm not alone.

With a centering breath, I turn around slowly.

Her marble-green eyes are wide, her mouth pink and pouty. *Fuck*. That mouth. She's got her bottom lip trapped between her teeth, and I bet she doesn't even realize it.

"Hey," she offers quietly. "Do you need help?"

I bite back a cutting remark and force my shoulders to lower. "No, I've got it."

With that, I turn my back on her and get started on the silverware.

"Are you sure?" she asks behind me, her voice more meek than I've ever heard it.

I glance over and track her movements as she approaches. She smooths one hand over the pristine countertop I just wiped down.

"I could dry?"

"I said I got it," I snap through gritted teeth.

The last thing I need is her in my vicinity. Her presence, her scent. I was abundantly clear when we got here that all I want for Christmas is for her to stay out of my fucking way. That desire is stronger than ever after the hot tub shenanigans last night.

I ignore her for several seconds, but she doesn't take the hint.

Finally, with my heart pounding against my ribcage, I turn to her and glower. "What?"

"Can I ask you something?" She's still worrying her bottom lip. She's going to make it bleed if she doesn't quit it. A vision of me biting into her swollen flesh infiltrates my brain.

With a shake of my head, I banish that thought from my mind.

I need her gone. I need her out.

"If I say no, will you leave me alone?"

She glares in response.

I turn back to the sink, but a second later, she takes a step closer. Then another. It's not until I turn and cross my arms over my chest that she halts.

"What do you want, Hunter?"

She grimaces at the use of her name.

Good.

It's rare I call her anything but Temi. That's an old habit I need to break, once and for all. That name had an important meaning to me. But no more. It's all been destroyed.

"What's up with the library?" she asks, planting one hand on her hip.

Now it's my turn to grimace.

Fucking hell.

It was stupid to hope she wouldn't go in there. That even if she did, she wouldn't notice the changes.

The library in its current state is my personal shame personified.

She left.

I waited.

She moved on.

I curated a whole goddamn library, filling the shelves with books she owned and special editions I worked like hell to track down for her over the last few years.

That library is an embarrassment. A trophy room honoring my stupidity. My naïve hope that she'd come back and still want me.

Scoffing at my own foolishness, I turn back to the sink, keeping my head low and scrubbing at a fork with a little too much force.

"Greedy, what happened to the library?" Her tone is terse this time. Like that'll make me open up to her.

I grit my teeth and shake my head. Fuck. Why won't she just take my silence as her cue to leave me the hell alone?

At the gentle caress to my shoulder, I flinch, pulling out of her hold like I'm dodging a linebacker who's got me cornered in the pocket.

"I don't know what you're talking about." I take a step back so there's space between us once more.

That's what does it. That's what finally makes her snap.

"My books, Greedy. Some of the books up there are *mine*."

All the books up there are hers. But I don't correct her. I can't. I'm not doing this with her. Not tonight. Not fucking ever.

With a glance at the dishes laid out on the bar, then the silverware still soaking in the sink, I toss the sponge into the soapy water. Then I stalk out of the kitchen.

I'm done.

I have to be.

Hunter clearly disagrees.

"Greedy!" she howls from behind me as I pick up speed and jog down the hall. "Don't pretend like this is nothing."

I stop in my tracks and spin on my heel. She lurches to a stop just inches away from plowing into me.

Head bowed, I get right up in her face and glower. "You're allowed to pretend, but I'm not?"

"No," she says, reeling back. "I just meant..." Her voice trails off as she reaches out. Before she can touch me, though, she drops her hand back down to her side. "I just don't understand," she whispers.

With a harried breath, I exhale.

"You left, Hunter."

Lips parted, she searches my face with sad, wide eyes.

"You left, and I was still here, planning out the life I thought we'd share."

Emotion clogs my throat, but I choke it back.

"I waited. I gave you time. I gave you space."

Shaking my head, I slam my eyes shut, itching to claw at my scalp. Yet another old habit I need to quit.

"I waited for you," I croak out, dropping my focus to a spot down the hall just over her shoulder. It hurts too damn much to look at her. "I waited, and I agonized about *everything*. Should I stay in North Carolina? Should I fly to London and find you? Every month, I'd sneak into my dad's office and go through his credit card statements, looking for clues."

"Greedy..." She reaches for me, but I yank my arm away with so much force I nearly stumble.

"I waited, and I was patient. I was even okay starting over, if that's what you needed. But I'm done waiting now." The words are quiet, jagged, my throat full of gravel. "Now that I know the truth—what you kept from me, and how easily you moved on—"

Her breath shudders out of her. "It wasn't like that, Greedy. I swear."

Every word is laced with a sincerity that nearly breaks me.

That sensation dries up quickly when I think of Kabir. When I think of the *years* she stayed away. What she was doing while she was gone and who she was doing it with.

I'm a fool. So fucking stupid. I wasted so much time holding out hope.

Anger coils in my chest, overtaking the sadness and sorrow that gripped me moments ago.

I turn away from Hunter once more and lengthen my stride until I reach the stairs.

"Don't follow me," I bark over my shoulder, only to discover that she's already on my tail.

I take the stairs two at a time, aiming for the second-floor guest room where I slept last night. Once I'm in the room, I pivot and reach for the handle. But before I can get the door shut, she slips in.

God fucking dammit.

"Can we please talk about this?"

Fire floods my veins, and I bark out a humorless laugh. "Are you for real right now? After three and a half years, you finally want to talk? Why? Because now that I know the truth, or at least some of it, you think—"

"You know the whole truth about what happened before I left," she snaps.

"Not because I heard it from you," I counter.

Her expression tightens with a mixture of indignation and guilt.

In the next moment, she's blinking rapidly, no doubt trying to keep tears at bay. She's an angry crier. Always has been. But she has no right to that emotion. If anyone deserves to be angry, it's me.

"Just talk to me," she tries, softer, her shoulders falling. "I want to know about the library."

Tough shit. She made her choices. She shut me out and lied by omission. Now it's my turn to do the same.

"Get out." I jab a finger at the door.

Rather than giving in, she steps closer, getting right up in my space.

"No."

Heart hammering, I grit my teeth. "I swear to god, Hunter, I'm only going to tell you once more. Get. Out."

Her chest brushes mine, sending a shock of electricity through me and pulling a hiss from my mouth.

"And if I don't?" she asks calmly.

Too calmly.

A switch has been flipped. She's not asking anymore. She's not looking for common ground. She's defying me.

She's gone into Brat Mode, and she thinks she's got me trapped. Little does she know that I won't back down. Not this time.

With a pointed glare directed at her, I inch forward, forcing her to step back. I do it again and again, creeping into her personal space.

She matches my steps one at a time, her chest heaving and her breaths coming quickly.

I don't stop until her back is flat against the door and the handle clicks in place.

"If you don't leave this room right now," I start, hovering close enough that her quickened breaths tickle the skin at the base of my throat. "I'll fuck the sass right out of you like His Royal Highness did that night in your room."

Her eyes widen, first in what looks like shock, then her pupils blow wide.

"Or maybe you'd rather I choke you with my cock the way he did in the hot tub last night while Levi railed you from behind. Is that it?"

Her mouth falls open and her eyes widen further, this time in horror.

A disgusted scoff escapes me. "Did you really think I didn't know? You thought you could get filled and fucked by other men in *my* house, and I wouldn't find out?"

"You're vile," she spits out, rolling her shoulders back.

"Are you fucking kidding me right now?" I bark out a laugh. "He called you a cum dumpster, Tem. And you ate that shit up. What sort of man—"

"The sort of man I need," she hisses.

I snap my mouth shut. Fucking hell. She can't be serious. But the resolute glare she gives me makes it clear she isn't joking.

It was one thing to hear it from Kabir, but for her to admit that she likes it? That she *needs* it?

"This isn't you," I whisper, dipping lower, desperate to get through to her. "For god's sake, Tem. I have half a mind to remind you of *exactly* what it is you need."

Chin lifted, she narrows her eyes. "Fuck you, Greedy."

Licking my lips, I lock gazes with her. "Fuck me, huh? Maybe that's what you need. What we *both* need to get this out of our systems and move on with our lives."

Her breath hitches, and she searches my face, those green eyes I still see in my dreams going glassy.

I tuck a few loose strands of hair behind her ear, then tug on them when the motion feels too soft. "What do you say, Tem? It wouldn't be the first dick you've taken in the last twenty-four hours. Not even the second, if my eyes weren't deceiving me last night."

With a disgusted huff, she splays both hands on my chest. "Fuck. You."

I swat her arms down and pin them to her sides, then crowd her space until our chests brush with every heaving breath. My body aches to push into her, to pin her against this door, to feel every inch of her writhing below me.

"You keep saying it, baby. Do you really mean it?"

Anger and disgust rise between us, twisting and transforming into something new. Her every exhale mingles with mine, and between one heartbeat and the next, my cheeks heat and arousal courses through my veins. We've always shared a connection, but now it's morphed into an ungrounded jolt of electricity, a live wire hissing and sparking.

We stand against the door for a breath. Then another.

My throat burns with emotion. My pulse hammers in my head.

Just when I think I can't take it a second longer, Hunter rises to her toes and smashes her lips into mine.

Chapter 32

Greedy

NOW

She kisses me so harshly I have to press a hand to the door at her back to stay upright.

Her tongue pushes into my mouth, needy and desperate. We're a clash of teeth and hands, stripping clothes off each other, and in my case, fighting like hell to remain in the present.

This girl I'm kissing isn't *my* Hunter. My girl is gone. She doesn't exist anymore.

The idea slams into me like a freight train. I grip Hunter's face and feed her my tongue, fueled by the anger and jealousy churning in my gut.

She's not mine. She won't be, ever again.

I'm going to fuck her out of my system, and once we leave here, I'll move out. Then I'll finally, fucking finally, be able to move on.

Our kisses turn even more savage—violent and brutal. She bites me, and I bite back. A coppery taste floods my mouth, but I have no idea whether it's her blood or mine.

She's intoxicatingly sweet—strawberries and sugar—just like I remembered.

Fuck.

I can't let myself remember. Not now. Not when all I need is to get her out of my goddamn system.

Fury ignites in my veins as I kick off my pants.

Hunter's shirt comes next. I whip it over her head, then I yank down her bra and trail bites and kisses from her neck down between her breasts. I drop to my knees before her, pull her panties down her legs, then peer up at her.

She's panting, her eyes hazy but focused on me.

Glaring, I run my nose through the little strip of hair along her pubic bone. Her scent is mostly familiar and intoxicating, though there's a hint of something new.

"Tell me something, Hunter. Whose cum would coat my tongue if I stuck it in your pussy right now?"

Her nostrils flare, her eyes heating with anger.

"Answer me," I command, slapping her clit lightly for emphasis.

"Fuck," she whimpers, dropping her head back against the door. "I need more."

More? More what? More of me? Or more of someone else?

She needs more, the same way I need to forget her. But her scent is too intoxicating, and the need to feel her writhing on my tongue is too strong to ignore. I lick her gently, and she groans, clawing into the door behind her.

I tease her, licking and kissing, sucking on her pussy lips and flicking my tongue against the sensitive bundle of nerves. That's all I give her, though. Just enough to have her panting and needy, but not enough to send her toward the release she craves.

Her body arches and shakes with every flick of my tongue. Her moans become more and more desperate. I keep at it, lapping at her folds and sucking her clit into my mouth.

God dammit. If I wasn't already on my knees, the noises she makes as she fucks my face would have brought me here. Her movements grow frantic, her arousal intensifying. The taste of her on my tongue is suddenly richer, deeper.

Trembling, begging for release, she shoves her hands into my hair, scraping my scalp with her nails. The sensation that rolls through me as she scratches over my hidden tattoo jolts me back to reality.

It's the reminder I need.

Slowing, I kiss her pussy lips. Then I run my nose through the soft blond pubic hair once more. I pepper her mound with kisses. When I shift to the side to nip and bite at her hip, she catches on and hisses.

"God dammit, Greedy."

With a dark chuckle, I rise to my feet.

"This is supposed to be a hate fuck."

I grip her shoulders and spin her around so her front is pinned against the wall, right next to the door. I rub my cock up and down her ass, teasing her as I taunt her.

"I don't give a shit if you come or not."

Lie.

"You have a boyfriend to take care of that."

Which I hate.

"And His Royal Highness."

Who I really fucking hate.

"I'm going to fuck you until I nut inside your well-used cunt, and if you don't get off, I'm sure you can find someone willing to finish the job."

I cringe at my own crassness, but I punctuate the statement with another thrust of my dick against her body.

This is what she likes? What she *needs*? To be degraded during sex? Every word is sour on my tongue. My every instinct is warring with me, telling me to apologize, urging me to swear that I'll never speak to her like this again.

I hate this.

Fucking hate it.

But by the way her breath hitches and her back arches toward me, like she's seeking my cock, I'm the only one.

Fuck. Fine.

I spit on my dick and smooth the saliva over the head before lining myself up.

"Just put it in already," Hunter sasses, pushing back until my tip is coated in her juices.

As a wave of pure ecstasy overwhelms me, I fumble between her legs, lining myself up with her drenched opening.

I thrust forward hard, and with that one fluid motion, I'm home.

Fucking. Home.

There's not an ounce of resistance. Her warmth and slickness welcome me as a thousand memories flood my consciousness and a dozen emotions spring to life in my mind and in my heart.

I'm all-in. She's all around me.

The familiarity of her hits like a punch to the solar plexus. I could stand here for hours or even fucking days, just soaking in the sensation of being connected like this. Committing this moment to memory.

I find her bare hips, cupping them reverently. When I pull out, I keep my gaze set on her round, pert ass, watching with rapture when my cock disappears past her peachy cheeks and slides deep inside her again.

The second time hits harder than the first.

Emotion clogs my throat, and tears sting the corners of my eyes as I hold myself inside her. My fingers ache to move, to run up and down her hips, to caress the delicate skin of her stomach, honoring the place where a life once grew.

Chin tucked, I rest my forehead on her shoulder, stilling inside her. Caressing her sides, I focus on memorizing every dip and curve, every inch of her skin.

If this is it—if this is the last time we ever—

Fucking hell. I can't do this.

I can't hate-fuck her or even pretend this is who I am or who I could be.

Fuck. Fuck. Fuck.

"Move, dammit," she hisses, pulling me from the torturous reverie of my own emotions.

Instead of moving like she demands, I stand stock-still, holding her, immersing myself in the way her body engulfs mine, tattooing this moment, when I'm buried deep inside her, on my heart, and—

"Greedy," she chokes out. Her tone is laced with the same desperation threatening to drown me. "Move," she begs. "Fuck me like you hate me."

No.

It's a singular thought, but a resounding, universal rejection.

No. It's my truth. It may also be my undoing.

I don't hate her. I can't. I love her. I've always loved her. I'm *in* love with her. Pathetic and fool-hearted, too. I'm such a sappy sucker. It doesn't matter that she doesn't love me or that she left, that she lied, that she came back and yet still didn't tell me the truth.

None of it matters. She's all I want.

If the ragged way she's breathing and her gravelly, desperate tone are any indication, then part of her still wants me, too.

"Tem." I brush her hair over one shoulder and place a soft kiss on her neck.

"Don't, Greedy," she whimpers. I swear her cunt spasms around my length. "Stop."

"Stop?" Painful regret claws at my insides. I move to pull out, but her pussy is choking my cock, keeping me firmly locked in place. "Stop what?" I demand, my tone harsher than I intend.

I try to pull out again, but she clenches around me so tightly I can't move. Nor do I want to.

Clearly, she doesn't want to stop the physical connection between us. Does that mean she's asking me to sever the emotional pull that's had me in a chokehold since the day we met?

"Stop feeling? Stop remembering? Stop loving you?"

I can't. Three fucking years, and I can't let her go.

"Greedy," she says on a sob.

"Shh," I soothe. I cocoon her body with mine, my cock still buried deep inside her, exactly where it belongs.

When moisture hits my lips, I bend low to kiss away the tears flowing freely down her cheeks.

"We aren't over," I whisper. "We were never over, Tem."

"Greedy," she says on a gasp. Her body shudders, and she releases a full-out sob.

I want to spin her around, hold her, promise to never let her go. But I have to say my piece.

"I loved you. I fucking loved you." The partial truth is hard to force out. I think she knows, but I need to be sure. Circling her shoulders and cradling her back against my chest, I confess into her hair, "Hunter, I still love you. I can't stop. I don't ever want to stop."

She sucks in a shuddering breath. "Greedy," she pleads again, her voice a whimper, as she tries to turn in my arms. She's lax now, limp and leaning back against me. Like she's out of fight. Or maybe she's just finally ready to stop fighting our connection.

Before I can turn her around and look her in the eye, the door flies open beside us.

His Royal Highness flies into the room, seething, seeking out Hunter. He freezes when he catches sight of her, then he shifts his focus to me, and his expression morphs into a glare.

Levi is two steps behind him. He freezes beside his new friend, his jaw dropping as he takes us in.

We're stripped down, still connected.

Hunter shifts in my arms, turning to look at her stupid European lover.

His ice-blue eyes double in size, and horror etches into the sharp angles of his stubbled jaw.

"Greedy," Hunter whispers once more, but this time to Kabir.

Between one blink and the next, he lunges in and rips her out of my arms. The move is packed with so much force that I stumble forward, arms swinging wildly to avoid smashing my face into the wall.

"Get the fuck off her!"

Chapter 33

Hunter

NOW

I'm as soft as a feather, as light as tissue paper, as iridescent and transparent as cling wrap. A chill washes over me as Kabir lowers me to the floor.

Without Greedy at my back, pinning me against the wall, there's nothing holding me in place.

I drift and sink and fall, my mind glazing over, losing sense of place. It isn't until the scents of teakwood and peaches envelop me that I have the wherewithal to look around.

Levi is crouched in front of me, holding me by the shoulders gently, like he's afraid I'll break. He takes his time adjusting my bra until it's in place again. Then he fetches a blanket off the bed and wraps me in it. Once I'm covered, I sit back against the wall and suck in a heaving breath.

My lungs expand fully for the first time in several minutes. I exhale, but on the next inhale, my lungs seize, and I can't get the oxygen I need.

I suck in a short breath, then another, until I'm gasping.

Gasping.

Sobbing.

Crumbling.

"Hunter," Levi says, his face a mask of pain, his denim-blue eyes flitting back and forth, searching.

"Hunter," he repeats, shaking my shoulders as if I can't hear him.

I can. Though I can't tell him. I can't form a single word, and I can't stop sobbing.

"What's wrong with her?" he asks.

What *is* wrong with me?

I blink once, and then again. Then I snicker. My sobs transform into belly laughs that rock through my whole body. Crossing my arms on my propped-up knees, I bury my head and curl in on myself. Back and forth, I rock, my bare bottom brushing against the floor with each pass.

"What did you do? What's wrong with her?" Levi barks out, his voice aching and desperate.

I peek between my arms, avoiding Levi's searching gaze. He's trembling with rage, his sights set on a fuming, shirtless Greedy.

Kabir, wearing a murderous scowl, holds Greedy's arms behind his back.

Greedy's cheeks are red, his mossy-green eyes ablaze. His bare chest rises and falls with an effort that matches my own. His muscles are slick with a sheen of sweat and taut with tension. I survey his torso, scanning the dips and valleys of his perfect cut form. My focus snags on the soft tuft of hair leading from his navel down lower.

His pants are still shoved down past his hips, his hard length hastily stuffed back into his boxer briefs.

"What happened," Kabir demands.

"Nothing happened that—" Greedy tries.

"No," Kabir growls. "I don't want to hear a word from you. Not yet." Then, turning to me while still restraining Greedy, he asks, "Hunter, did he—"

My heart sinks at the same moment my eyes flit to Greedy's. "No. He didn't do anything I didn't want him to do. I—it wasn't—" I stumble over my words. How the hell do I make this make sense?

Greedy didn't force himself on me. I told him to fuck me. I wanted to feel his wrath. I was a willing participant in the twisted encounter they walked in on. But I don't understand how a hate fuck turned into... whatever the hell just happened between us.

Spence cocks a brow at me, then leans in close to Greedy. "Why were you just standing there?" he demands. He's still got a firm grip on Greedy. "What did she say?"

"She didn't fucking say anything!" Greedy bites back, shooting daggers at the man holding him back, then turning haughtily to scowl at Levi.

Greedy.

His name... in that context...

Groaning, I drive the heels of my hands into my eyes, then look to Spence. "I said Greedy," I admit, the memory hazy and heavy at the same time. Not that my first love knows what that means in that context.

Shoving Greedy out of his way, Spence takes three long strides across the room, then drops to his knees in front of me.

Without a word, Levi shifts, making room for the other man beside him.

Gingerly, Spence cups my cheek with one hand. He inspects me, turning my face from side to side. "You said greedy," he confirms, his tone low, but not so low that the other boys don't hear him.

Tears well in my eyes as recollection of the last few minutes floods my system. It's amazing what the human mind will do to protect itself. Moments ago, I couldn't recall what happened.

Now, those thirty seconds play on repeat in my mind. How Greedy sank into me but didn't make any moves to fuck me, as promised.

The energy that surged between us, emotions and heartbreak rising until they peaked.

The way he stilled inside me. Kissed me softly. The words that poured out of his mouth.

We went from hate-fucking to something so intense and vulnerable in the blink of an eye.

Greedy's lips on the back of my neck.

The softness with which he caressed my hips.

The way the tips of his fingers brushed my low stomach.

"What the fuck is happening? What's wrong with her?" Greedy demands, pulling me from my thoughts.

Spence glares over his shoulder. "She said 'greedy' during sex,"

"Yeah. So?" Greedy grits out. "That's my fucking name."

"That's her fucking safe word," Spence booms, his anger rising along with Greedy's.

I hang my head in shame. Not because I used my safe word, but because I didn't communicate my needs or my boundaries to my partner. Not only that, but I was having sex with someone who's not my boyfriend, nor my lover...

"Get out," Spence says flatly, rising to his feet and turning. He crosses his arms over his chest like he's standing guard, protecting me from a threat.

"No. I need to talk to—"

"Your needs are of no concern to me at a time like this, Garrett Reed."

My heart sinks. Spence rarely loses his cool.

Levi reaches for me, tipping my chin up with two fingers. "You want him gone?" he murmurs softly. "It's your call, Daisycakes."

I smile meekly at the nickname. "I just need a little space."

With a single nod, he hops to his feet. He offers me a hand and helps me stand up. Once he's sure I'm steady on my feet, he turns to stand shoulder to shoulder with Spence.

"Get out, G."

"You can't be serious," Greedy protests, fisting his hands at his sides. "Tem, if we can just—"

"Out!" Spence hollers.

At the same time, Levi steps forward and grabs Greedy by the arm, guiding him out of the room before he can utter another word.

Chapter 34

Greedy

NOW

I'm sitting in the basement, feeling like an absolute bag of shit, when the doorbell rings upstairs.

Assuming it's the caterers, I ignore it.

When the pounding begins, I throw my head back and curse.

Fucking hell.

Last time someone came pounding on my door, my whole world flipped on its axis. Who the hell is here now, and what do they want?

I stalk up the stairs, my anxiety rising with each step. The pounding is relentless, like it was the morning His Royal Highness first made his appearance. But Kabir is already here. He's still upstairs taking care of Hunter.

"Fuck." I jog the length of the hall, desperate for the echoing sound to stop.

Carelessly, I swing the door wide open without looking out the window on either side of the entry.

Three people stand on my doorstep.

"Is Hunter here?" Josephine Crusade asks, though the question is more of a demand.

She has both hands planted on her hips.

One of her boyfriends, Kendrick Taylor, stands to her right, lowering his fist.

Another man, Kylian Walsh, is standing on her other side. He's not looking at Josephine, though, or even at me. His gaze is fixed on a device in his hand.

"Hey to you too, Joze," I mumble.

"Can we come in?"

Fucking hell. Did Hunter call her? Shame and dread swirl up in a cyclone inside me. Rightfully so.

Every time I think about the look on Hunter's face—the fear I caused, the panic I created—*Fuck*. It wasn't intentional. I would fucking never... but the way she looked at me, and then the way her demeanor shifted once she made contact with Kabir...

"Greedy?"

"Yeah, come in." I move out of the doorway to make room for the trio. "Did Hunter call you?" I ask as they pull off gloves, boots, and winter coats.

"What?" Josephine asks, pulling the hat from her head. "No. I'm here because I can't get ahold of her."

Kendrick helps her out of her coat, then takes a knee to untie her boots for her, too.

"She hasn't returned any of my calls or texts for the last few days."

I wince and give her an apologetic smile. "The reception sucks out here sometimes."

Kylian lifts his head, taking his eyes off his phone. "I could fix that."

Joze wraps her arms around Kylian's waist. "We're heading out of town the day after tomorrow," she says to me. "I just wanted to see Hunter before we left."

My heart softens at that. As uncomfortable as things have been between Hunter and me since she returned, I couldn't be more thankful that she's got a friend like Joze.

"Come on in," I tell them, guiding them deeper into the cabin. "Kitchen is that way, and there's a bathroom down that hall."

The guests follow me to the staircase, where I pause. "Hunter's upstairs," I tell them, nodding to the landing above. "All the way up, then take the narrow set of stairs up to the primary."

Kendrick searches my face, and Josephine knits her brows together in a clear show of confusion. Before she can question me, I shake my head.

"I have a few things to take care of," I offer casually. "Good to see you guys. Merry Christmas if I don't see you again before you leave."

With a dip of my chin, I turn away and leave them at the base of the staircase.

I need out. Out of this house. Out of this whole situation.

I'm glad Joze is here. Hunter needs her, especially now.

It wouldn't surprise me if her perception of me changes by the time they leave today. Either way, I'm not interested in sticking around to find out.

Chapter 35

Hunter

NOW

"So… I didn't realize we'd have an audience." Joey raises both eyebrows and scans the room.

I fight back a smirk, my first genuine smile in hours.

God, I'm so glad she's here.

I take in the four sentries stationed around us. Her guys—Kendrick and Kylian—are positioned against the far wall, gazes fixed on their girl. Levi and Spence are hovering near the door, their focus shifting from me to our guests.

I've been to Decker's cabin here on Beech Mountain a couple of times, but Joey's never been up here with me. It was like a piece of myself clicked back into place the second she walked through the door.

My first question was one loaded with false hope.

"Did Greedy call you?" I blurted out when Spence opened the bedroom door.

He didn't. Joey showed up on her own, because she and her guys are heading out of town the day after tomorrow for her honeymoon. Decker won't tell her where they're going—which sounds very on brand for Decker Crusade—so she's been trying to get in touch to update me.

We're lounging in the middle of the king-size bed in the room Kabir and I slept in last night, lying on our sides with our heads propped on our hands. It's sort of funny that we always end up hanging out in someone's bed. But a warmth grows inside me at the familiarity of the scene.

Well, at least the part with Joey. I'm not used to having four additional sets of eyes on us.

"Um, yeah. About that…"

I survey my guys, taking in the way Spence and Levi are standing shoulder to shoulder.

"Could you give us some privacy?" I ask.

Spence cocks a brow, the look alone telling me exactly how much he dislikes my request.

"I have no intention of leaving you with virtual strangers," Spence states, lifting his chin.

Kylian peers up over his glasses. "Likewise," he adds, nodding toward Joey.

I'd roll my eyes if I had any strength left. After the incident earlier, my body is all out of fight.

Sighing, I turn back to my best friend. I'm so glad she's here. I don't care what the circumstances are or who thinks they need to stand guard.

"What if all four of you go find something to do?" Joey suggests. "Then neither of us will be amongst strangers."

Spence scoffs. "We don't know you either, Josephine Crusade."

I fight back an eye roll, taking in the assumed expressions on Kylian's and Kendrick's faces. I grew up with them. I've known them longer than Joey has, so they have no issue with the suggestion. Clearly, this is my battle to fight.

"Joey's my best friend," I say firmly.

It's Levi's turn to scoff. "You've never mentioned her to me," he insists as he crosses his arms over his chest.

Flovely.

Now Levi and Spence are ganging up on me?

"I met her at the start of this semester," I offer. "She really is my bestie, though. Greedy—" I clear my throat, forcing myself not to get hung up on the word. "Greedy knows her and can vouch for her, too."

Spence's eyes go wide, as if he's prepared to argue, but before he can, I hop off the bed, stride across the room, and circle my arms around his neck.

"I'm okay," I whisper. "I promise."

Gaze softening, he grasps my waist.

I turn my head and rest my cheek against his chest, focusing on Levi. "Why don't you guys head down to the basement and shoot some pool?"

"What do you say, boys?" Spence asks, regarding Kylian and Kendrick. "Care to join us for a round of billiards?"

Levi snorts at his formality, then leans over to kiss me quickly.

"Thank you," I whisper before he pulls away and heads for the door.

Kendrick and Kylian both speak with Joey briefly, then follow Levi to the door.

Spence still has his arms around me when they file out.

"I'll have my phone on me. Call me immediately if you need me."

"I'm okay," I assure him, but nod my agreement all the same.

"Follow me to the door. Lock yourselves in," he instructs.

I fight back the urge to argue. I can't imagine Greedy will come back up here anytime soon, and my mother and Dr. F ventured out today for last-minute shopping in town.

I usher him out and give him a quick kiss before closing and locking the door.

Turning back to the bed, I meet Joey's gaze and burst out laughing.

Her eyes are wide, her brows up in her hairline.

"Hunter... what was that?" she asks, waving a hand toward the now closed and locked door.

Groaning, I make my way over to her, then dramatically flop onto the bed.

"*That* was Kabir," I say.

"He's British?" Joey asks, her tone reverent.

"Yep."

"And he's super protective of you."

"Uh-huh," I confirm, face buried in the comforter.

"Okay. Real talk. Are you with him, and does he make you call him Daddy?"

I snort at the amusement in her tone.

"I'm—" How the hell do I categorize my relationship with Kabir? "I'm not sure what we are, exactly," I admit. "But," I say, determined to lighten the mood, "he prefers I call him Sir."

Joey bursts into a fit of giggles, circling her arms around me and forcing me to face her.

"We've got some major catching up to do," she tells me pointedly.

We do.

For months, I've avoided telling her my story, but now I'm desperate to get it out. To tell her everything. Now that the truth of what happened that summer is out in the open, the idea of sharing my story gives me a sense of peace. I'm not proud of what I did, but it's time to come to terms with the decisions I made and how I ended up here.

So that's what I do.

For nearly an hour, I give her all the details. I tell her about falling in love with Greedy. About that magical summer. My trip to the hospital and how I found out I was pregnant while suffering a miscarriage.

I tell her about Levi. How he helped me then, and the feelings I have for him now.

Then I relay the details of my time in London. From the fake smiles and flaky roommate to the mental health crisis and my diagnosis.

I go as far as to tell her what happened between Levi, Greedy, and me on the night my mom appeared. I even share what happened the other night in the hot tub, then this afternoon with Greedy.

Joey takes it all in, gripping my hand at the right times, then giving me space when it's clear I'm struggling to get through a story or an explanation.

By the end, we're both crying, but for the first time in a very long time, the tears that fall are cathartic.

"What do you want to happen next?" Joey asks.

We're sitting up in bed now, facing each other, both puffy-eyed and sniffling. The entire bed is covered with crumpled tissue.

"Honestly? I don't know." Dipping my chin, I pluck at the corner of a tissue. "Things with Greedy are getting worse every day," I admit, defeated.

"But you still want him." She gives me a small, sympathetic smile.

Sheepish, I peer up at her and nod. I do. I don't know how; I don't know that it's even possible, given his mutual hatred of Spence and the dismal events of the last twenty-four hours, but in my heart of hearts, I want Greedy. And Levi. And Spence.

I want them all. And if I can't have them, I don't know how I'll survive having to choose.

Chapter 36

Kabir

NOW

I do not appreciate being relegated to the basement, particularly alongside strangers and with no indication of where Garrett Reed has gotten off to.

I palm my phone where it's nestled in the front pocket of my trousers, knowing damn well she won't text me but craving the connection, nonetheless.

"Are we shooting pool or are we just gonna stand around looking at each other?" one of the newcomers asks. Hunter introduced him as one of her friend's boyfriends—Kendrick.

A quick Google search didn't produce anything more than his sports stats, a few articles regarding his prospects with the National Football League, and two deeply buried references to an arrest earlier this year.

The arrest gave me pause, but based on what I could find and the vibe he's throwing down, he's no threat to our girl. The familiarity between him and Levi makes it clear they've met before, as well.

"Let's play." Levi springs into action, setting up the game.

He deftly racks the balls, then places the cue ball on its mark and steps back. "Be our guests," he tells the others.

Kendrick is holding a billiard stick, but the other man is propped up against a wall, staring at his phone.

He's a harder nut to crack. Quiet but calculating. Observant but not in a way that makes me question his intentions. It's like he is analyzing each move we make strategically.

I circle the table, stick in hand. "Are you playing, mate?"

The man doesn't look up, nor does he answer my question. Instead, he replies with an unsettling statement.

"I recognize you."

"Is that so?" I ask, standing a bit taller, curious as to which of my business dealings he may be familiar with.

"You're the founder of Project Nemesis," he states.

Color me shocked. Out of the many forward-facing business endeavors in which I lead the charge, Project Nemesis receives the least amount of attention from the general public.

Lips pressed together, I give him a longer assessment.

"I am." I take pride in the not-for-profit training agency I founded years ago. Project Nemesis combines the latest biometric innovations, forensic research, and surveillance technology in an open-source environment only accessible to vetted and trained program participants. The program is used to track and obliterate sexual predators around the globe.

Intrigued, I rest my back against the wall beside him. "What did you say your name was?"

He arches his brows and taps at his phone's screen. "I didn't."

Rude.

"What's your name, then?"

"Kylian Walsh."

Now we're getting somewhere. He likes directness. Noted.

"All right, Kylian Walsh. What agency are you with?" I keep my voice low. If he's involved with Project Nemesis, then there's a good chance his friend doesn't know the details of his line of work.

"No agency or government affiliation," Kylian states. "I completed the Project Nemesis training independently. For a personal project."

Bloody hell. The training is emotionally and mentally taxing, and it's typically only accessible to government hunter agencies deemed worthy of the program. If he completed it on his own—for a "personal project," no less—I'm even more intrigued.

"I took your turn for you, Kyller. The Brit is up."

Straightening, I survey Kendrick, then Levi, who are both watching us.

A quick scan of the table shows me exactly what sort of position Levi has set us up for.

"Well done, you," I murmur as I circle to where he stands.

Analyzing my options, I shift to move behind him, smoothing a hand over his low back as I travel around the table. The move is slow and languid, allowing me to revel in his personal space for a few breaths longer than what's truly necessary.

"You met Kylian?" he asks quietly.

"I did. Peculiar fellow, but I like him."

Levi frowns, his brows knit together in concern. "Kylian is with Joey."

A thrill shoots through me, but I keep my expression neutral. "Yes. I'm aware he journeyed here with Hunter's friend."

His brows pull together even tighter. "No, I mean he's *with* Joey. He's one of Joey's boyfriends."

"Are you jealous, champ?" I ask, fighting back a grin.

"Jealous?" His lips part in shock. "What? No."

"So then you assume that since I'm pansexual, I want to fuck every person I meet?"

Panic flares in his bright blue eyes. He pulls his backward ball cap off his head to run a hand through his hair. It's a nervous tic. One I quite like eliciting from him, if I'm honest.

"No, that's not it at all—"

I slip a finger through the belt loop of his jeans at the small of his back where the other guys can't see and tug.

Dipping in close to his ear, I let my chin brush his shoulder. This close, my senses are flooded with the sweet scent of peaches and sharp notes of mahogany teakwood.

It takes more strength than I'd like to admit to fight back a groan. "Just so we're clear," I whisper. "I understand all the dynamics currently at play. Kendrick is with Joey. Kylian is with Joey. You are with Hunter. I am with Hunter. And you are also with me."

A sharp intake of breath tells me I've hit the mark.

But Captain America knows the game already. After all, he learned from the best.

Taking a play right out of Hunter's book, he careens back and raises one eyebrow. "Am I?"

He holds my gaze in challenge, very much aware of what he's doing. Now it's my turn to put him in his place.

"You're with me if you wish," I tell him, leaving the actual declaration to him.

I release my hold on his belt loop and slip my hand into the back pocket of his jeans. The stiff fabric makes it impossible to really feel him, yet I can still appreciate the tautness of his ass.

Suddenly, it's not the only thing stiff. I give him a sharp squeeze. "Is that what you want, brat?"

Levi's tongue darts out, and he wets his lips before turning to look me in the eye.

"Yes, sir," he murmurs.

There's a sarcastic hint to his tone, but I can't fight the grin that takes over my face at the confirmation that he wants me, too.

"Do we need to set a timer for you two?" Kendrick rumbles.

I glance up. "Cute," I remark, then line up my shot, sink one ball, and then another.

Sink. Sank. Sunk.

I go for three and miss, but barely. When I right myself, I turn and catch Levi studying me, his gaze full of desire.

Fuck yes. He undoubtedly wants me, too.

Chapter 37

Levi

NOW

"What the hell, G?"

A blast of cold air hits me, followed by an even colder glare.

I've been looking for Greedy for nearly an hour. I've been through the house more than once, searching every room. I was ready to give up for the night and go check on Hunter when I popped into the primary bedroom one more time.

Honestly, I didn't even know this was a balcony, but when I caught sight of the door, I gave the handle a tug, even though I'd all but given up on actually finding him.

Color me shocked when it swung open to reveal my best friend standing outside in the bitter cold.

"How long have you been out here?" I step out onto the small landing—a Juliet balcony, I think it's called?—then instantly question my life choices.

There's barely enough room for Greedy to be out here alone. I have to crowd his space and position my feet wider than his in order to even shut the door behind me.

His focus is set on the view around us—mountains and valleys, night sky and wisps of clouds that travel across the horizon and hide the brightest stars. From this angle, there's even a clear view of the lower balcony. Where the hot tub is. Because of course there fucking is.

He doesn't look at me. Doesn't even acknowledge my presence, despite how I'm all up in his personal space.

"G," I say again.

What the hell do I do now? My goal was to make sure he's okay after what Kabir and I walked in on and how Hunter reacted. But he's stone still, his face an expressionless mask.

I reach out to get his attention. But when my fingers brush the hand he has braced on the railing of the balcony, I hiss and recoil. "Dude, you're fucking freezing."

He doesn't react. Doesn't say a damn word.

Shit. Shuffling back as far as I can, I pull my hoodie off.

He watches me, his face emotionless as I work, but he doesn't move or react as I awkwardly try to pull the layer over his head.

I've struggled for several seconds before he grumbles something unintelligible and finally puts a little effort into working his arms through the sleeves.

"Why are you out here?" I ask, gritting my teeth as the cool night air passes through the thin fabric of my T-shirt.

"Why are *you* out here?" he fires back like a petulant child.

"So it's going to be like that?" I straighten and level him with a glare. When he doesn't reply, I change tack. "I was looking for you. I wanted to... check on you. Make sure you're okay."

"Does it look like I'm fucking okay?" he seethes. He balls his hand into a fist and slams it into the balcony railing. "Fuck!"

I snatch up his hand, fighting the urge to recoil at the frigid sensation. It's like an icicle. His skin is tinged blue. I can't imagine pounding the railing helped matters.

"Come here," I huff out, frustrated. I take his hands in mine, then suck in a sharp inhale and brace myself.

Stepping closer so our feet are practically touching and our thighs are woven between one another, I slip his hands under my shirt.

I hiss as I press them to the still warm skin of my torso and clench my abs, powering through the sensations as I work to get him to unfist his hands and splay them along my stomach.

Eventually, he exhales, flexing his fingers ever so slightly against my torso, as if he's checking to make sure he still has feeling in each digit.

"Better?" I ask, my words choppy as my own body temperature plummets.

He's standing out here, fucking freezing, no doubt punishing himself for an incident he didn't even understand. But as heat transfers from my body to his, he physically relaxes.

"Yeah," he says thickly, his breath skating over the skin of my neck. "Thanks, man."

As the seconds pass and he allows me to hold him, I yearn to comfort him, to take away the pain. At least some of it. It's honestly too much for one person to bear.

Why the hell either of them thought they could, what, bang each other out of their systems? It was ludicrous. The idea was doomed from the start. According to Hunter, the encounter was completely consensual, but then it all started to feel like too much.

"Hunter takes responsibility for what happened," I tell him. "She knows you didn't know."

"But I fucking should have," he bites out, digging his fingers into my skin with so much force I have to fight back a wince. "I should have known, Leev. All of it. Everything." A choked sob escapes him then. "I should have fucking known."

He collapses into my arms, and I'm so shocked I don't immediately react.

Eventually, I come to my senses. I wrap my arms around his torso and smooth one hand up and down his back, hoping to imbue him with at least a small sense of comfort.

He slips his palms over the planes of my abs and around my obliques and upper back until he's cupping my shoulder blades.

"I should have known," he repeats, the words gritty and broken as he continues to cry.

Emotion overwhelms me. *Fuck*. He's right. He should have known. Hunter lied. I lied. We kept secrets, and we cut him out in the name of self-preservation.

Even as recently as last week—when my fake dating arrangement with Hunter evolved into something so much more—he should have known.

"I'm sorry." I stroke his back through the thick fabric of my sweatshirt as he clings to me. "I'm so fucking sorry for not being a better friend, G. For not telling you what I knew back then. For not being up-front about what's going on now."

He shakes his head in the crook of my shoulder. "Back then?" he croaks. "Yeah. You should have fucking told me. But now..."

He sniffles and pulls away, using the sleeve of my hoodie to wipe his nose.

"Dude," I deadpan. "Gross. You better wash that before you give it back to me."

Greedy snickers. "It smells like you." He pulls the neck of the hoodie up to his nose and takes a long whiff. "It's fucking delicious. You're not getting it back."

I fix my expression into something like a glare, but I crack. I turn away quickly, but not before he catches my smile.

"I don't blame you for anything with Hunter now," he tells me, lowering his head and roughing a hand over the back of his neck. "She's... incredible. If you're what she wants—"

I shake my head and pull my shoulders back. "I don't think I'm the only one she wants."

Greedy presses his lips together and pushes his tongue out to wet them. "I don't know how we come back from this."

"Don't," I suggest. "Don't try to come back. Don't keep going back and dredging up the past. Start fresh with her, man. Let go of then and focus on now."

"What if she doesn't want who I am now?" he asks in a hushed tone.

That's an impossibility. Greedy's incredible. He's gorgeous. Brilliant. Exceptional on the field. Amazing to his family and friends. He's the best friend I've ever had. Anyone would be lucky to be loved by him. So fucking lucky.

"She does," I tell him. In my heart, I believe that. Hunter loved Greedy. Hunter loves him still. "But I said it before, and I mean it even more now. I'm not giving her up for anything."

"She's what you want," he says, nodding, as if he's accepting the truth of the situation for the first time. Finally.

Teeth chattering, I find the hem of the sweatshirt and plant my hands against Greedy's now-warm back.

He goes rigid and sucks in a sharp breath. "Jesus, Leev!"

For a second, I think he might pull away, but when he settles again, moving his hands higher up my back, I pull him closer and line up our bodies so we're standing chest to chest, cold hands seeking warmth on one another's bare back.

"She's not the only one I want," I admit. I swallow past the lump of anxiety rising up inside me and force the words out. "I'm sorry I haven't been a better friend since I've been back." Licking my lips, I gently rest my forehead on his, willing him to feel my sincerity. "And I'm sorry I didn't tell you why she left and what I knew back then."

I hold him. He lets me hold him.

If my instincts are correct, I think he's holding me just as tightly.

Pressing my fingertips into the taut muscles of his low back, I garner all my courage, exhale, then say, "G... maybe you and I could start fresh, too?"

He pulls back a fraction and locks eyes with me. It takes every fucking ounce of self-restraint to not smash my mouth against his. Instead, I hold my breath and search his face.

"Yeah," he says, his shoulders loosening. "I'd like that."

Finally, I exhale, sinking into the peace that those simple words have created.

He nods once, looking out over the mountains, before eventually pulling away. "I need to talk to Hunter first, though."

Chest tightening, I nod. Knowing him, he won't rest until he knows that she's okay—that they're okay.

I just hope like hell they really can start fresh, and that once they're in a good place, there'll be room for me, too.

Chapter 38

Hunter

NOW

After a few hours, I convinced Spence that I really was okay, and he finally let me leave his room.

Now I'm trying to find Greedy, and the primary bedroom is the only place I haven't yet searched. Begrudgingly, Spence is stationed outside the door, looking completely out of place as he sits cross-legged on the hardwood floor.

I appreciate his concern—the hovering and the check-ins. His need to stay close, to ensure I'm well. Typically, I revel in his particular brand of love and care. But I need to do this on my own.

Something inside me broke earlier. Spence knows that. I know it, too. It's not the first time he's witnessed me breaking.

But Greedy wasn't the cause, and I'm determined to stand on my own two feet and apologize to him for how I reacted.

I head for the library first but stop at the sound of a low, harmonious laugh in the distance.

Heart beating in anticipation and a little fear, I open the door to the Juliet balcony. I'm not surprised to find him here, but I didn't expect Levi to be here too.

"Hi," I greet them quietly, looking from man to man to try and gauge the mood. Upon closer inspection, my eyes practically bug out of my head. "Duke! Why don't you have a coat? You must be freezing!"

"I am," he grits out between chattering teeth.

Greedy cringes, his expression going sheepish. That's when I realize that he's wearing Levi's favorite hoodie. It looks good on him—everything does—and he's surely warmer than Levi, but it's still impractical against the frigid night air.

"Can I talk to you?" I ask.

Before Greedy can reply, Levi gently guides me back into the room and brushes past me. "I'll give you two some privacy." With a kiss to the crown of my head, he whispers, "I'll be in the hall if you need me."

I don't bother telling him Spence is already out there. He'll figure that out soon enough. "Thank you," I murmur as he exits the room with a glance back at me.

Once the door clicks shut, I turn back to the balcony, only to find that Greedy has widened his stance and turned his back to me completely.

"Hey." I place my hand on his low back. "Can I join you?"

He pulls in a sharp breath, then lets out a shuddering exhale.

"Stay inside. It's too cold out here for you."

My stomach twists at the rejection in his tone.

It wasn't too cold for Levi, but pointing that out will only cause more strife. If he needs space, I want to give him that. He deserves to work through the anger and frustration he's feeling in whatever way he sees fit.

"Can I stand in here and talk to you, then?" I hold my breath, waiting for a response that never comes. Cold air bites through my fuzzy pajamas, the chill settling deep in my bones.

Eventually, I step out of the doorframe to shield myself from the elements. Resting my back against the wall, I close my eyes and blow out a long, centering breath.

"Tem—" he starts, his voice panicked.

Dammit. He thinks I've left. Again. Like I always do.

"I'm right here," I tell him softly. Rather than peek around the doorframe and confront the bitter cold again, I reach out, following the rough grain of the wooden doorframe with my fingertips. I search until I find my target, then I brush my hand with his. "I'm right here."

Emotion clogs my throat when his fingers twitch, acknowledging my presence. Despite the fear rippling through me, I force out the words I've held back for so long—the words he needs and deserves to hear.

"I'm sorry."

Another twitch of his fingertips against mine.

"I'm so sorry, Greedy. I panicked, and it just came out. That wasn't fair to you. I take full responsibility for earlier. I never meant for you to even find out—"

"Can I ask you something?" he interjects before I can babble on. His voice is low and gravelly, the familiar timbre carried in on the cold night air.

I nod, even though he can't see me.

He waits several seconds, then clears his throat. "Why is my name your safe word?"

Heart pinching, I close my eyes. Now I have to tell him. He deserves an explanation. He deserves so much more than the way I've treated him.

"It just... is. The first time Spence and I were together, we set safe words. I still don't understand why I said your name. Maybe because you were the one thing I didn't want to think about when I..." I hesitate, pulling my lip between my teeth as my stomach sinks.

Greedy is silent, but his fingers catch mine, giving me the courage I need to continue.

"I didn't want to think about you when I was with another person. Intimately, I mean." Then, with a desperation and sincerity I hope he believes, I add, "I can't really explain it. It seems stupid now. But I was hurting and doing everything I could to lock away all my emotions back then. I did everything I could possibly do to forget you. I thought if I could just move on... make myself forget... that in the end, we'd both be better off."

That's the truth, whether he wants to believe it or not.

"I was sick," I admit on a whisper. "I didn't cope well. I hated myself. The sadness I carried each and every day was crushing me. Suffocating me. I tried to ignore it, pretend that I was okay. But I wasn't good at playing pretend, either. Soon after I met Spence... I broke."

I close my eyes, fighting back the tears that ride on the waves of self-loathing.

According to my therapist, there's nothing I could have done to block out the intrusive thoughts or to fight off the suicidal ideations that plagued me at that time. I was always destined to be diagnosed with PMDD. Yet I still hold on to so much shame.

His voice is a gravelly whisper when he finally responds. "I wish you would have let me be there for you. Back then. More recently, too."

The simplicity of the confession takes my breath away. Gasping, I will the fresh wave of tears that crests to abate. I sniffle quietly.

A second later, Greedy clasps my hand.

We've endured a lifetime of sorrow because of my choices. I may never be able to communicate the gravity of my guilt and anguish over what I did—over what I'm still doing. My default setting is self-sabotage: if I wreck it first, no one else has the power to ruin me.

I don't deserve his understanding or his forgiveness. At bare minimum, I need him to get that the misunderstanding earlier was my fault.

"I'm sorry," I say again. "For what happened downstairs. I was out of my head, and as soon as it felt too real, I panicked. It's on me for safe-wording when we hadn't discussed it prior."

Greedy's hand flexes in mine, his fingers tightening, as if he's fighting the urge to ball his hand into a fist.

"You wanted me to stop, and I didn't." Self-loathing drips from his every word.

"But I'm the one who didn't communicate that," I huff out. Why doesn't he get it? He's not to blame. For any of it. Not now, and not then. It's all me. "I'm the one who applied rules you didn't even know existed until it was too late."

A choked sob escapes me. I try to pull back—turn in on myself—but Greedy doesn't let me remove my hand from his grasp.

"I'm sorry, Greedy," I whisper again. "I'm so fucking sorry."

My shoulder aches as I strain against the wall, my hand still firmly in my first love's grasp. My head—and honestly, my heart, too—are screaming for me to run. To retreat. To remove myself from the equation and give Greedy the peace he deserves.

But as I pull away, he clings to my hand tighter. I can't see him. He can't see me. We're both hurting, and there's no easy path from here.

"I'm right here, Tem," he whispers from his position outside on the balcony.

The sincerity in his tone prods at the deepest, most vulnerable part of my soul.

"I'm right here, and I'm not going anywhere."

Chapter 39

Greedy

NOW

It took a solid forty minutes in the hot tub before the chill in my bones subsided. I texted Levi so he'd know where I went and to let him know that the primary bedroom was available.

Now that I've regained feeling in my extremities, I want to check on Hunter. I need to see with my own eyes that she's still okay.

Our moment on the balcony felt like a reset. As much as it hurts to think about what happened when she left for London, I'm starting to garner hope that there's still a chance for us. It's time to lay down our defenses and move past all the pain we've inflicted on ourselves and on each other over the last three years.

I may not be who she needs anymore, but at the very least, I can offer her peace.

I hover at the door to the primary bedroom for several breaths. By the time I find the courage to actually knock, my hand aches from clenching it into a fist.

Heart pounding in my ears, I softly rap my knuckles against the door.

It swings open two seconds later.

I stand tall and take a deep breath as Kabir hovers in the doorframe. Physically, I've got a few inches on him, but his presence is larger than life.

At this moment, with the way he's looking at me? I have to fight the compulsion to cower.

"Can I help you?" he asks, looking down his nose at me as if he has no idea why I'd be here.

"I need to talk to Hunter."

Mirth sparks behind his blue-gray eyes. "Haven't the two of you already said your piece?"

"Spence," she scolds from somewhere inside the room.

Kabir snaps his mouth shut, but he eyes me warily for a few more beats before he takes a step back and pulls the door open wider.

He positions himself so that I can't get in without brushing past him. I take that as my invitation to shoulder-check him. He makes a satisfying *umph*, then smooths the front of his Oxford shirt.

Inside, Hunter is sitting cross-legged in the middle of the bed, wrapped up in light pink fuzzy pajamas with her hair twisted up in a messy bun on the top of her head.

When our eyes connect, a lifetime of sorrow zings between us.

I didn't have a chance to look at her earlier when I was on the balcony. Regret and remorse churn low in my gut, even though she harbors all the blame for what happened between us earlier.

I didn't know.

She knows I didn't know. That I would never...

Even so, the urge to sink to my knees and apologize over and over again consumes me. I'm stuck in a mind warp of indecision as I stand before her, at a fucking loss as to what to do, what to say.

A throat clears, snapping me out of my mental anguish.

Shit. I have to get my head on straight.

Swallowing down the anxiety clawing up my throat, I ask, "Can I talk to you? Alone?"

Behind me, Kabir scoffs, but she's already nodding and scooting to the edge of the bed.

"Spence," Hunter admonishes. She rises from the bed and stretches her arms overhead, revealing the smooth expanse of her lower stomach.

I home in on it. Her pale, creamy skin. The toned area between her navel and the waistband of her sleep shorts.

My mind spirals, and my heart aches so acutely that I rub at my sternum to ease the pain. I can't help but think about what could have been. What should have been.

She was pregnant. Her stomach should have grown round and heavy with my child. *Our* child. Her belly should be softer. She deserves comfort, care, softness in her world. She's had to be so tough for so long, just trying to survive on her own. She should be allowed to be softer.

The ache that's lived inside me from the second I found out is still there.

But now, it doesn't throb with anger; it no longer feels like betrayal. It's a layered emotion that stems from sadness and roots in melancholy. It's speckled with grief, but it's also flickering with hope for what comes next.

We're here. Together.

We've hurt each other in ways neither of us expected. The position we've landed ourselves in is riddled with nuance and complexity. At the end of the day, though, when I step back, when I think about my life and consider what's most important?

It's her.

It's always been her.

Hunter clears her throat, snagging my attention. I've been silently, awkwardly standing here for who knows how long. I meet her eyes and offer a soft, apologetic smile.

She approaches, her bare feet slapping the wooden floor lightly with each step. When she reaches me, she takes my hand.

"Let's go sit in the library."

I nod eagerly, not daring to look back at His Royal Highness.

Turning to Kabir, she says, "We'll be right in there. You can stay here."

I fight back a smirk as she guides me into the room that holds so much significance to both of us, individually and as a couple.

"I'll be out here the entire time," Spence announces, his voice loud enough to carry.

I pull the door mostly closed, and when Hunter doesn't object, relief and satisfaction sink into my bones.

She pads over to the chaise lounge. Seeing her in this room, sharing space with her in this way, makes me want to hit rewind. Or refresh.

I'd give anything to take away her worries and doubts about me. I just want to start again.

She sits down and adjusts herself. When she's comfortable, she peers up at me.

"Thank you for coming to find me earlier," I start, my voice already cracking with emotion. "For apologizing. For being patient with me."

Hunter tucks her legs under her body, shifting to make room. "Sit with me?" She side-eyes the cushion of the chaise beside her in invitation.

Flooded with a wave of relief, I sit as close as I can without touching her. I want to give her space. I want to give her peace.

What happened earlier... *fuck*. I stupidly thought hate sex would force all the anger and frustration out of my system. I wanted to punish her—for running, for lying. For continuously pushing me away.

But now it's clear: that role has already been filled. She's been punishing herself for years, and she even made jaded and misguided attempts to protect me in the process.

She deserves soft. She deserves sweet. That look in her eye as she cowered and said my name over and over again will haunt me until the end of my days.

It hits me then.

"When you said my name the other day, on the drive up here..." I scan her face, searching for the truth.

She grimaces but nods. "I needed him to stop," she explains. "I'm not trying to hurt you, Greedy." Her voice wavers, and she sniffles. "Even though it seems like hurting you is all I ever do. I hate myself, honestly… for what I did, and for what I keep doing."

"Tem." I wrap my arms around her without thinking.

Immediately, she goes stiff, and I freeze. Before I can pull away, though, she softens, sinking into the embrace and nuzzling her face into the crook of my neck, returning the hug just as tightly.

She blows out a long breath. One of the little tendrils that's fallen out of her bun flutters in front of her face. I can't resist reaching out and tucking it behind her ear.

Instead of sitting up and pulling away like I expect, she scoots closer so our thighs press together and rests her head on my shoulder.

I drape an arm around her back as she sinks farther into my hold. Instinctively, I kiss the top of her head.

We sit like that for a few minutes, quiet and contemplative.

"I'm sorry I pushed you," she eventually says, tilting her head back and focusing on my face. "About the books. About the library."

It seems juvenile now, losing my temper over her questions about a topic she has every right to know the details of.

It's then that it clicks.

I can spend the next days, weeks, months, or even years hurting her the way she's hurt me. Though if I choose that path, we'll never move forward. We'll never be anything other than bitter exes and stepsiblings.

I shutter my eyes closed. Fuck. I don't want to fight. I don't want to punish her or seek retribution. For the secret she kept. For decisions she made years ago.

Life is messy and complicated.

We're guaranteed nothing.

If we have any chance left at all, this is it.

I kiss the top of her head once more. "I overreacted. I was angry—"

"You had every right to be," she insists, turning in my arms to gaze up at me.

I shake my head. The blame isn't all hers. We could sit here all night, hashing things out, apologizing, trying to untangle the hurt and the pain.

"Let's start over," I suggest, clinging to the very idea Levi suggested a few hours ago.

She holds her breath, wide-eyed, silent.

I keep my expression flat. "I mean it, Tem. Let's start fresh. Ask me again what you asked me in the kitchen."

Her tongue darts out to wet her lips.

She looks from shelf to shelf. Then she sniffles, searches my gaze, and asks, "Why are the books in here different?"

Closing my eyes, I inhale deeply and will my heart to keep on beating as I dive into the truth.

"A few days after you left for London, I went to your house. Your—Magnolia," I correct, "had been bringing carloads of belongings over for days. She had yet to bring any of your stuff, though.

"Your room—" I blow out another breath as memories flood my vision.

I spent an embarrassing amount of time in Hunter's empty room. I wanted to be wherever she was, and if I couldn't be there, then I needed to be in a place she had recently been.

"Your room wasn't packed."

She ducks her head and smooths a hand over the cushion on her far side. "I only took what I needed to London. I wanted a fresh start."

"I figured as much. I packed up all of your books. Your notebooks, and diaries, too."

Hunter's eyes widen, and her lips part.

"I didn't read any of them," I assure her. Although I was tempted to. In those early days, right after she left town, I was desperate for any connection I could cling to.

"Most everything is here." I point to a lower shelf that holds her notebooks, yearbooks, and other bits of memorabilia I thought might be important to her.

I even wedged the salvageable paper airplanes from her yard between her yearbooks. But that's probably too much to reveal tonight. Or maybe ever.

"Somewhere along the way, I got into special editions." The back of my neck heats at that confession. It's a secret I haven't shared with anyone, ever. Just me, my credit card, and our mail lady know the true depth of my book-buying habit. Let's just say I'm glad my dad never asked me to justify my credit card purchases. "I signed up for email newsletters, and I followed authors whose books you had several of. I figured those were your favorites. I kept up with their new releases. I even bought backup paperbacks of the books that you had annotated and dog-eared to death."

She smiles at that, even as tears track down her cheeks.

"I just wanted you to have a place that felt like yours when you came back to me," I confess.

A soft sob escapes her as she buries her head into my side.

"I didn't want this. For either of us," she admits with a sniffle. "I honestly didn't mean to stay gone that long."

My entire body sags. It's a truth I'd hoped for and a confession I needed to hear.

"I don't want to fight with you anymore, Tem." I twirl a loose strand of her hair around one finger as she nestles into my side.

"I don't either." She places one hand in the center of my chest, then glides it over so that her palm is resting over my heart.

My pulse picks up, hammering double-time, my emotions coiling tight in my chest. I have to cool it, temper my enthusiasm, see what progresses naturally, rather than try to force her into something she's not ready for.

So instead of leaning over and kissing her like I'm desperate to do, I simply say, "Let's get through tomorrow. Then we'll see what comes next."

"Deal." She sighs softly, melting into my side, and for the first time in years, genuine hope fills me.

Chapter 40

Hunter

NOW

"What's going on?" I ask through a yawn, trudging into the kitchen. As I cross the space, a shiver racks through me. I should have grabbed slippers or socks before coming down.

The table is already mostly full, and it's quite the spectacle already.

Dr. F and my mother are sipping coffee, and if I'm not mistaken, they're wearing matching red-and-black buffalo-plaid pajamas. There also appears to be a stack of coordinating pajamas on the table for the rest of us.

Flovely.

"Nice of you to finally join us, sleepyhead." My mother's words are lighthearted, but the delivery is a little too rehearsed to have me convinced.

Hackles raised, I fill the kettle and set it on the stove to heat, then turn back to the group to regard them.

Along with Dr. F and my mother, Greedy and Levi are here, both sipping from steaming mugs.

"Good morning," I murmur, taking the empty seat between them and nudging Levi's knee with mine.

"Morning, Daisy. Merry Christmas."

"Merry Christmas."

With my heart in my throat, I turn to Greedy.

We called a truce last night. Agreed to muddle through today and let our animosity rest. After what we've both endured, though, it's hard to trust the sanctity of any truce or agreement.

"Merry Christmas, Greedy."

His smile is genuine and warm.

He reaches under the table and rests a hand above my knee, squeezing. "Merry Christmas, Tem."

Relief washes over me and quiets my anxiety.

The tea kettle starts to sing, and as if on cue, Spence appears.

He kisses the top of my head in passing—a move I'm sure everyone caught, but no one comments on, thankfully—then moves on to fix tea for the both of us.

Standing, my mother fiddles with the buttons of her plaid PJs. She looks wholly uncomfortable in the getup. I fight back a laugh and clear my throat instead.

"Okay. Right. Now that you're all here," she says, her tone matter-of-fact, "we can get started."

Levi grasps my hand, but it's Greedy I look to first.

What are we starting, and why does she look so eager?

He voices the question lodged in my throat. "What are we starting, exactly?"

Dr. F tsks teasingly as he stands. "Come on, my boy," he encourages, offering a hand to Greedy and helping him to his feet. "It's Christmas morning. Let's open presents."

Presents was an understatement. Devices, clothes, gift cards galore. There were even a few things for Levi and Spence under the tree.

It was the material version of love-bombing. So many gifts. So much excess. I hadn't thought to buy a single thing, which makes me feel like shit. I was honestly too wrapped up in the end-of-semester hustle with school, and then Spence came into town and significantly distracted me in other ways.

Now we're all seated around the table, having just finished a delicious catered meal. Greedy's mom's Christmas dishes are notably absent from tonight's feast.

After he explained their importance, I don't blame him for not wanting to risk them being damaged or listen to my mother criticize them.

I'm counting down the hours until she and Dr. Ferguson leave tomorrow morning.

The anticipatory relief is palpable. We just have to get through tonight—dessert, coffee, maybe a bit of small talk—first.

With my mother heading back to the house, I'm in no rush to return to South Chapel.

But is staying here a few more days with all three men without a fight breaking out even possible?

Kabir is sitting at the table, dressed formally, sipping the after-dinner coffee that was served along with the yule log and the cheesecake.

Levi is to his right, closest to me. He's still wearing the buffalo-plaid pajama pants from this morning, along with a crisp white T-shirt.

I'm at one end of the table, and my mother is at the other. Greedy is by my side, dressed in sweatpants and a South Chapel U long-sleeve tech shirt, with his dad seated next to him.

Dr. Ferguson is leaning back in his chair, grinning as he finishes up another story about Christmas past. Apparently, Greedy loved to set traps, hoping to catch Santa, and his efforts got increasingly sophisticated and complex year after year.

Dr. Ferguson, in an effort to avoid a catch Greedy left out one year, actually fell down the stairs and dislocated his shoulder.

We're all laughing by the end, even my mother.

It's been an okay day. Pleasant, even. It's the first day in a long time that hasn't felt heavy.

When the laughter dies down, Dr. Ferguson clears his throat. Assuming he's ready to launch into another story, I sit back and scan the room as I sip my tea.

Spence shifts in his chair, causing the feet to scrape against the wood floor, catching my attention. When I focus on the group again, Dr. F is on his feet at the other end of the table.

He stands behind my mother, his hands cupping her shoulders. Clearing his throat once more, he zeroes in on me.

"Now that all the presents have been opened and dinner and dessert are done, there's something Magnolia and I need to discuss with you kids."

As he shifts his attention to Greedy, my heart hammers double-time, triple-time even, and a tidal wave of anxiety barrels into me.

Levi catches my knee under the table.

Greedy shifts his chair ever so slightly, clearly on alert as well.

Spence appears unfazed, though I've never known a person with a better poker face than him.

Dr. Ferguson lowers his gaze to my mother, then looks back at me.

Why the hell does he keep looking at me?

Are they breaking up? No. Surely she wouldn't travel all the way back here and go through all this just to break up with him.

They're both far too calm for that anyway, and she's been sticky sweet to him since she returned.

I look at her again, noting the sallowness around her eyes, her subdued expression.

Some of it is age, I'm sure. Some can be attributed to her lifestyle choices. She always has loved her wine.

Shit.

There's no way she could be pregnant, is there?

Greedy catches my gaze just as the thought registers.

The look of panic on his face tells me he doesn't like where any of this is headed either.

"There's no easy way to say this," Dr. F. starts. For a long moment, he doesn't continue, causing the tension in the room to thicken so drastically it's hard to breathe.

"Go on with it, then," Spence eventually urges, breaking Dr. Ferguson out of his dramatic spell.

"Your mother," he looks to me.

"Magnolia," Greedy corrects under his breath.

"She's sick. She needs a liver transplant."

Confusion swirls in my gut as I study my mom.

Rather than looking at me, she's focused squarely on her lap as she lets her husband speak for her.

"She doesn't look sick," I assert, aiming the accusation at Dr. F.

She doesn't look particularly well, either, but I keep that line of thinking to myself.

"We've been treating the symptoms," he supplies, smoothing his hands over my mom's shoulders. "It was likely caused by some kind of virus—Epstein-Barr or something similar. Some people are more susceptible to autoimmune diseases," he explains. "But there's hope, in this case. It's very likely that a partial liver transplant will save Magnolia's life."

The room is silent, yet the buzzing in my ears is incessant. I should be concerned about my mother's health, her emotional well-being. Instead, I'm more concerned about Dr. Ferguson.

This will hurt him. Having another sick wife—another person he loves battling for her life. And then there's Greedy. This isn't fair to him either. His dad's time and attention should be focused on him, not on my sick mother.

Honestly, my emotions surrounding my mother's health are almost nonexistent. The people around her, though, our shared family? I care deeply about how this will affect them.

"Hunter," Dr. Ferguson says, pulling me from my spiraling thoughts.

Clutching my hands in my lap, I assess him. The dark circles under his eyes I'm only now noticing. The way his lips are turned down and his shoulders are slumped.

"There's a strong possibility you would be a donor match for your mother."

"Bloody hell," Spence curses.

At the same time, Levi's grip tightens with bone-crushing intensity on my knee.

"Me?" I ask with a laugh. "I'm pretty sure I need my liver, Dr. F."

His answering nod fills me with dread.

"You would keep your liver. Most of it, at least. The liver is a regenerating organ. If you're a match, and a healthy candidate, you would undergo a partial transplant, giving a small piece to your mother, which would hopefully grow inside her and fully restore her health. It's called a living donor transplant."

I—I...

Confusion and fear and anger roil in my stomach. I don't even know what to think. What are the risks? What if it doesn't work?

"A living transplant," Dr. F continues, "is a very solid option in this type of scenario. It's the best-case scenario for both of you."

"Is this a joke?" Greedy demands, his spine snapping straight.

Dr. F rears back, his eyes widening. "I assure you, son, it's not."

"Then how the hell do you figure that a living transplant is the best-case scenario for Hunter?"

Dr. Ferguson's gaze softens. "I can't imagine Hunter wouldn't want to help her mother, Garrett."

Right. Most children would do anything in their power to help or heal an ailing parent. Except...

"Why does she need a partial liver transplant?" Greedy asks, his tone full of accusation.

Dr. Ferguson appears unfazed, but my mother sits up a bit straighter and glares in Greedy's direction.

"Magnolia has autoimmune hepatitis. She isn't in acute liver failure yet, but it's likely she's heading that way."

"Is it from drinking?" Greedy accuses, attention locked on my mother.

It isn't lost on me that he and Dr. Ferguson are the only ones engaging in conversation. I'm... hollow. My mother is silent. I don't dare look at Spence or Levi.

If I do, I'll break.

"Garrett," Dr. Ferguson scolds, wearing a disapproving frown. "You know there are multiple causes of hepatitis—"

"I do," Greedy replies, cutting his dad off at the pass. "It can also be hereditary. Are you really going to let Hunter go forward with compromising her own liver, knowing she may suffer the same autoimmune disease in the future?"

"We've got a lot of testing to do before a final decision is made," Dr. F says, avoiding Greedy's question. "We knew this would be a shock. That's why we waited until after the festivities to share the news."

He grasps my mother's shoulders again. In response, she curls her fingers around one of his hands. Only then does she finally look up and lock eyes with me.

I know this play. She's using him. Based on the hardness in her eyes, she's been planning this for a very long time.

"I just got this family back together," Dr. F laments. "I can't lose her now. I won't."

There it is.

A plea from the only parental figure who supported me when things got hard. On the surface, the request is reasonable. A small sacrifice on my part to save my mother.

But what if I just flat-out don't want to do it? What if I don't want to make a sacrifice for her?

I sit silently, clamping my mouth shut. If I open it, I can't guarantee that what comes out won't be a ground-shaking scream.

My mother continues to stare at me. Silently challenging me until my eyes burn and tears well along my lower lashes.

Eventually, Dr. Ferguson addresses me again. "Take a few days to think about it, kiddo. It's a big ask, but we know you'll make the right call. I can talk you through the medical components. Nothing has to happen immediately, but we should get the ball rolling soon."

"Hunter."

Greedy's voice breaks through the deluge of emotions that have swamped me and are holding me hostage. If I can just seek him out... follow the sound of his voice...

"*Hunter.*"

He calls my name again and again. It takes all my strength to turn toward him. To focus on his face. He's no longer in the chair at my side, but crouched at my hip.

I blink once, twice, and scan the table. Only then do I realize that Dr. Ferguson and my mother are already gone.

It's just Greedy, Levi, and Spence gathered around, staring at me, wearing expressions filled with pain and concern.

"Hunter." Greedy takes my hand and brings it to his lips. "You don't have to do this."

I open my mouth to reply, but I'm at a total loss.

All logical thought has evaporated.

How is she always three moves ahead of me?

"I can see your wheels spinning, Firecracker." Kabir takes my other hand, then guides me to my feet. "It's been a long day. You need rest."

I nod mindlessly. That's all I've got.

"Come," Spence tells me. "Let me run you a bath and then tuck you in and end this godforsaken day."

I nod again, offering apologetic glances to Levi and Greedy.

Neither man looks upset. At least not with me. They look as shell-shocked as I feel. Like a massive, major, life-changing bomb has just been dropped, all wrapped up in a pretty red bow.

Merry fucking Christmas, indeed.

Chapter 41

Hunter

NOW

I'm mindlessly scrolling, despite none of my socials properly refreshing. Reception really is shit here in the mountains.

I have a check-in text from The One and Only. He wished me happy holidays and asked that I call when I can. I don't know when he actually sent the text, though, since the reception is so spotty.

I start three separate versions of a message to Joey, then delete each one when I can't put into words what just happened.

How do I explain that my wretched mother is sick, maybe even dying, and that her fate lies in my hands, yet I can't bring myself to care?

The primary bedroom door opens and closes. Kabir again, I'm sure. He ran me a bath, then took off to make a cup of tea for me.

I glance up, trying and failing to smile. When the scene in front of me registers, though, I nearly drop my phone in the tub.

My mother strides into the room, chin lifted high. "There you are," she says breathily, waltzing past me toward the vanity. "I've been looking all over for you, darling."

I carefully set my phone off to the side, then sit up straighter in the water.

I'm always on high alert with her, but after tonight's conversation, I'm a ball of anxiety and a bundle of nerves.

"Hunter," she says, her tone dripping with disgust. "Aren't you going to ask how I feel?"

The. Audacity.

Rage ignites, engulfing the emptiness. I prefer it, really. Shuttering my eyes, I steel myself for the confrontation. It's the absolute last thing I need, but she's got me trapped. I'm naked and in the tub. I couldn't run if I tried.

I'm tired of running anyway. Tired of worrying about her reactions and the way her actions affect me. I take a deep, cleansing breath and lock eyes with her in the mirror. "That was a low blow," I state. "Using Dr. F to manipulate me."

"Hunter!" she cries in mock outrage.

She's such a phony. A liar and a fake.

"I was afraid if I told you myself, I wouldn't be able to get through it."

It would be a fair concern if we had any semblance of a normal mother-daughter relationship. Though we're both still looking in the mirror, she's no longer fixated on me. She's looking at herself, pulling at the skin around her eyes.

"What you're asking—it isn't fair," I tell her calmly.

She scoffs. "Don't talk to me about fair, Hunter. I'm so sick I can't travel any longer. I can't go anywhere on my own, and I can't stay awake for more than a few hours at a time. I'm sorry if my illness is an inconvenience to *you*."

"I'm registered for twenty-one credit hours this spring," I tell her. "Classes start in two weeks."

She turns then, her eyes hard as she sweeps them over me in the tub.

"I'm sure they make exceptions for medical leave."

I'm sure they do, but I have no interest in allowing anything to distract me from my goals, especially now that I know I can handle such a heavy course load.

"Why me?" I ask, fighting back angry tears. I will not cry. I will not cry. I can't let her see me cry.

Kitten heels clip across the tile floor as she approaches. Slowly, she squats until we're eye to eye.

"Darling, I gave you life. Brought you into this world." She reaches out as if she's going to caress my cheek.

I rear back on instinct, barely avoiding her touch, the warm water sloshing around me.

She scowls. Her beautiful features have never looked so ugly. "You're my daughter, my blood. You're the most likely match for this type of transplant, and you owe it to me."

"I *owe* it to you? Why?" I challenge. Because she birthed me? Because she weaponizes her position as my mother against me when it's convenient? She's never been there for me. Not for one single day in my life. She neglected and abused me. I owe her *nothing*. I don't want to give her anything.

A shrill laugh escapes her. "Why? Did you really just ask me *why*?"

A sharp knock pulls us both out of the moment, startling me and sending her shooting upright and spinning around.

The door eases open, and Greedy is there, filling the opening.

"Garrett," my mother chirps, her tone and demeanor morphing completely in an instant.

She shifts, blocking me from view.

"What are you—"

"I was looking for you," he supplies evenly. "My dad asked me to find you. Says he has one more Christmas surprise."

"Oh! Really?"

"Bible," Greedy supplies flatly, giving her a single nod.

My mother scurries back to the mirror, inspects her reflection, and then beelines out the door. She doesn't look back at me. She doesn't even have the courtesy to excuse herself or say goodbye.

Greedy guides her out of the room, pulling the door mostly closed behind him.

Instantly, the boulder pressing down on my chest is lifted.

And yet...

"I know you're still out there," I say, my voice loud enough to carry.

He peeks around the corner, a deep scowl of concern etched into his features. "I'll go. I just wanted to make sure she was gone for good before I left you alone." He backs out, his hand on the knob.

"No—Greedy. Wait."

He appears again, bracing his arms on either side of the doorframe.

"Please stay," I quietly request.

He meets my gaze, searching my face for a moment, and nods. "Want me to lock the door?"

"Yes," I reply automatically. "I'll text the guys so they don't worry."

I shoot off a text to Levi and Kabir, telling them where I am and who I'm with. Then, in no uncertain terms, I make sure they understand that they should not come in or worry about me.

Greedy and I, we're okay. We're more than okay.

At this exact moment? I'm craving more of him, more for us.

He approaches, his footsteps growing louder as I rearrange the bubbles in the tub. We've been here before, Greedy and me. In this bathroom. In this tub together, even. I gulp past the lump that threatens to cut off my airflow at the memories.

"I get it now." He stops beside the tub, lowering to the tiles and resting his arms on the side.

I search his face, unable to read into the neutral expression he wears. "Get what?"

"The self-preservation. What you've been running from."

Tears well in my eyes. Yes. It's so much easier to run, to keep my distance, than it is to go to battle with her day in and day out, in big and little ways.

"Baby..." he whispers, angling in even closer. "When you left for London... it was because of her, wasn't it?"

I bite down on my bottom lip and nod.

It's more complex than that, though. My reasons were multi-faceted. I ran from the pain of the miscarriage. I hid from the reality of what we discovered that day at the country club—that my boyfriend was about to become my stepbrother. Ultimately, I needed to get away from her. To start fresh. To create a life for myself that she couldn't touch.

So much for that brilliant plan.

"Tem," he pleads, pulling me from my racing thoughts. "We need to talk to my dad."

"And say what?" I ask, batting at the tears on my cheeks. "That his second wife is toxic, manipulative, and playing us all?"

Greedy clenches his jaw in response, eyes blazing with fury, but not at me.

I reach out a wet, bubbly hand, and for the first time in a very long time, I smooth my palm against his cheek.

He freezes, his jaw instantly going slack and the green of his irises softening. He nuzzles into my hand, giving more of his weight.

When he lifts his head, he kisses the center of my palm, then he releases it.

"It just clicked for you, didn't it?" I ask. "You heard the way she speaks to me in private. She's a mastermind. She hides that side of herself well. You've only now seen it. Why would your dad believe us?"

"He needs to know."

"There's nothing we could say..." I trail off. The last thing I want to do is fight with him. Not after the last few days. The last several months.

"He deserves to know, Tem."

"Maybe, but you shouldn't be the one who has to bear the burden of breaking his heart."

With a scoff, he hangs his head between his arms.

I reach out, tentatively at first, not wanting to startle him, and scratch his scalp. "Let me deal with Magnolia," I tell him.

Lifting his head, he hits me with a glare. "No. Not alone."

Sighing, I drop my hand.

We're at an impasse, and we both know it. Neither of us will convince the other tonight. We sit in silence as the water grows tepid. I'm considering adding more hot water when he speaks again.

"Do you want me to go?" Greedy tips my chin back, gently urging me to look him in the eye.

I shake my head. "Do you trust me?"

His expression falters for a millisecond—but then he nods. Sitting up slightly, I make space, then tell him, "Get in."

His eyebrows shoot up into his hairline, and his jaw starts ticking as he works his molars back and forth.

"I want to feel close to you," I tell him softly, letting the invitation linger between us.

Something must click, because a second later he rises to his feet, then pulls off his tech shirt and shucks off his sweatpants.

I scoot forward and add more hot water as he slips in behind me. When I peer back, I notice that he's still wearing his boxer briefs. When he's settled, I slide back against his chest, soaking in his warmth.

"Is this okay?" he asks, arranging his legs on the outsides of mine and holding me like he used to when we'd come up to the cabin together.

I rest my head on his shoulder and let it roll to the side so I can meet his gaze.

"More than okay," I whisper. For a moment, I study him, relishing the way his steady heartbeat thumps against my back and the warmth of the water surrounding us, cocooning us in a bubble of tranquility. In this moment, with Greedy's arms around me, all the bullshit with Magnolia dissipates from my mind.

I close my eyes and breathe in his familiar scent, for the first time in a long time willing memories of our time together to flood back.

The laughter, the shared secrets, the unspoken bond that has existed between us since the day we met in that parking lot. It takes effort to fight the knee-jerk response I've developed, but I refrain from burying my longing. He's here. With me. In this moment, we're together.

As I sink into his embrace, a sense of peace washes over me.

Except the tranquility doesn't keep, because on his next breath, Greedy asks, "When you say you didn't cope well in London... What does that mean?"

Trepidation creeps up my spine. Anxiety riots against my ribcage. I want to tell him, and yet...

"If I tell you, I need you to understand that where I was back then is not where I am now."

"What does that mean?" he asks, his tone gravelly. He sits up a bit straighter, realigning our bodies until he's holding me as tightly as he can.

"Just... let me get this out. I want to tell you, but I need you to let me explain before you react."

His throat works as he swallows, his focus intent, but eventually, he nods.

So I dive in.

I tell him about leaving for London. About crying every day and working at Splice late into the night.

I tell him about meeting Spence. About what I thought I was getting into—and how I sincerely never intended to have anything but a casual fling with him.

The harrowing truth about my breakdown is hard to force out, but I get through it, explaining the suicidal ideations that entered my mind and couldn't be tamed. The moments where I wasn't even lucid. The missing details that remain.

I recount how, when I started my period for the first time after the miscarriage, it was so eerily similar that it took me right back to that moment.

Then I tell him about staying in bed for a week. How Spence cared for me. How he got me the mental health support I so desperately needed.

"My official diagnosis is Premenstrual Dysphoric Disorder—PMDD."

He nods thoughtfully, as if he's trying to recall the information he knows about my illness. For his part, Greedy has held it together beautifully. He's barely reacted, and he hasn't interrupted me once.

Finally, when I've been quiet for nearly a minute, he speaks.

"Those nights... when you would come to me..."

I nod. "I still get low—I always have dark nights. It's worse when I ovulate, and then a day or two before my period starts."

"Fuck. I'm so fucking sorry you've had to deal with all this."

I sit up, prepared to brush it off like I usually do. I'll have to deal with PMDD for decades. There's no sense wallowing in self-pity over it.

"Don't." Greedy's voice is rough, low, and threatening.

"Don't what?" I sass, a spark of annoyance flaring up inside me.

"Don't act like this isn't a big deal. Like it's not a huge burden you've been carrying on your own for way too fucking long."

"It's not," I insist. "Spence has been there for me. Other friends, too."

He drops his head so his face is buried in my neck. "I wasn't."

The agony in his tone is palpable.

"Because I left," I remind him gently. Then, because I've been desperate to tell him for years, I add, "I always intended to tell you about the baby. About the miscarriage. About all of it. You're all I wanted that day, Greedy. It just..." I trail off, at a loss for how I can possibly justify the way I shut down that day at the country club when our parents told us they were engaged.

"Running felt like the logical solution back then," I admit. "It also felt like the kindest option."

With a shake of his head, he hooks his arms under mine and holds me tighter against his chest. "I get it. I fucking hate it... but I get it." He kisses the side of my head, right above my ear, cradling me to his chest as best as he can in the water. "We're both here now."

He brushes a few strands of hair away from my face, then ever so lightly kisses my temple.

"Let me hold you now, Tem. Let me back in. Not because you're unwell or feeling desperate. Let me hold you because I want to, and because you want me, too."

"Okay." The word escapes so easily, and with it, a little of the tension that's plagued me for years evaporates. With a calming breath, I relax in his arms and let him hold me.

"I'm sleeping in here with you tonight," he declares.

I smile, but I don't argue. "Okay," I say again.

Chapter 42

Hunter

THEN

"Our time is nearly up, but we'll talk again on Thursday."

Nodding, I thank Veronica, then sign off the video call. I've been in intensive talk therapy for weeks. It was every day at first, and in person. Since then, I've tapered down to twice a week.

London has grown cold over the last month, so the option to attend online sessions now is ideal.

For days, it's been drizzling and frigid. I miss the sun, but I don't hate being snuggled up inside. I stare out the window wistfully, grateful that I don't have to trek through the rain.

Moving through the penthouse, I consider dinner options. Spence started going back to his office on a more consistent basis last month, and since then, I've rediscovered my love for cooking.

I even got up the courage to FaceTime my dad the other day when I was making beef bourguignon. The call was short because his wife needed him to go pick up something for one of the kids. Even so, I got a little time with him.

We agreed to FaceTime again soon.

I kept most of the details about why I'm here in London to myself. Honestly, it still feels surreal.

Given the shock and trauma surrounding my pregnancy, followed by the miscarriage and finding out that my mother was set to marry the father of the man I was dating at the time, Veronica says PMDD was practically inevitable.

The disease wasn't caused by the trauma I endured, but that distress paved the way for the total breakdown that resulted in my mental health crisis. I have very little memory from that time—Spence had to fill in so many blanks for me. All I know is that I never, ever want to feel like that again.

PMDD is technically an endocrine disease. It can be managed with hormones, but the psychiatrist from NHS suggested we try SSRIs first.

Onboarding was a bitch. I was tired for days. But before long, I felt lighter. The world felt brighter.

The darkness returned with my next menstrual cycle, but it was more of a shadowy storm than an all-consuming eclipse. I've adjusted my meds twice since then, tweaking the dosage and the time of day I take it to smooth out some of the bumps.

Unfortunately, I'll spend the next several decades managing this disorder. The lows I experience seem to occur on the days I ovulate and the few days leading up to my period, so from now until menopause, this is my reality.

I've learned more about myself in the last few months than I have over the last nineteen years. The growth has felt overwhelming at times, like when I had to call Louie and tell her she can't be in my life any longer.

Turns out, the guy I found passed out in my bed that day was her drug dealer. Spence had all my belongings packed up and moved into his place immediately. He also had her fired. I harbor some guilt there, but there was no changing his mind.

I don't work at Splice any longer either.

Spence insists that he wants me to rest and take care of myself. As relaxing as it sounds, the reality is the opposite. Learning how to be gentle with myself and adapt my expectations to my menstrual cycle has been an uphill battle that I feel like I'm losing more days than not.

I'm constantly worrying about my water intake, and I'm a little obsessive about whether I've taken the proper dosage of meds at the proper time. Trying and settling on supplements, because if I skip a dose, then it's guaranteed I'll experience a shift in my mood. The same applies if I don't get out for fresh air or make it down to the gym for a workout.

How the hell do people with full-time jobs manage any sort of mental health struggles or chronic illnesses? So much of my healing and recovery is rooted in the deep privilege of having unlimited resources and time. That's all thanks to Spence.

Everything has a reason, and for everything, there's a season.

He says it all the time. After this experience, I truly believe it. Coming to London. The job at Splice. Even meeting Spence. Each moment was a serendipitous gift from the universe when I needed it most.

Spence's devotion to me is unlike any sort of love I've ever experienced. I certainly never encountered this kind of affection from my parents. Although I wouldn't go as far as to say Spence knows me better or loves me better than the first boy I gave my heart to, there's a significance to our connection that's different. He met me before my diagnosis, yet he still cares for me deeply now.

The girl I used to be would be ashamed to let another person see her at her lowest low.

Spence saw it, and he stayed.

He's all that's tethering me to London these days.

I don't know where our relationship is going or how long it'll last, but like my therapist says, it's no use foreboding joy. I can focus on the now. I can be present. I can embody calm.

I've survived every other thing life has thrown at me thus far.

Brighter days are always on the horizon.

The elevator dings, notifying me that Spence is home. I peek into the foyer from the kitchen, watching as he sets his briefcase down, then shrugs out of his coat and scarf. He's still talking on the phone as his shoes tap against the marble tile. Though as soon as he sees me, he tells the person on the other line that he has to go. That "an urgent matter has just presented itself."

Grinning, I rush to greet him, and when he wraps his arms around me and kisses me deeply, I melt into him.

"An urgent matter, huh?"

"Always. The most important thing in my life." He runs his nose along my jaw, kissing me below the ear. "Hello, love," he murmurs. "Are you well?"

Grinning, I answer honestly. "I am."

His eyes sparkle as he stands tall and gives me a salacious once-over that sends shivers through my core. "That's exactly what I was hoping to hear."

"Is it?" I tease. Spinning, I head back into the kitchen, knowing damn well he'll follow.

I stop by the island, and he sidles up behind me, caging me in as he brushes my hair to one side and resumes kissing along my neck.

"Months have passed, but I haven't forgotten. You owe me a date, Firecracker."

I rest my head on his shoulder and loop my arms around his neck, savoring the way his warm hands travel up my sides, over my hips, and up along my rib cage.

"And here I thought we were just supposed to be dinner and sex."

He swats at my ass and nips at my ear. We both know we're so much more than just sex these days.

"I'll show you dinner and sex," he says huskily into my ear. "Get dressed. We leave in an hour."

"We're going tonight?" I ask, unable to temper the smile that splits my face.

He presses his lips together and studies my face. "Are you up for it?"

Wide-eyed and practically bouncing on my toes, I nod. Then I'm off, headed to the bedroom to change.

"Wear something slutty," he hollers after me.

"Yes, Sir," I call back over my shoulder.

Chapter 43

Hunter

THEN

Dinner at Table 26 requires reservations made months in advance. Though clearly, that rule doesn't apply to Kabir Spencer.

My black dress has a neckline that plunges to my navel. Diamond hoop earrings and a matching tennis bracelet complete the look.

The jewelry was a gift from Spence, given to me after I experienced my first full cycle on SSRIs. I told him celebrating *not* having a mental breakdown seemed a bit ridiculous.

He told me he wanted to celebrate it all.

That's the day I realized I'm in love with him. He's reaffirmed the depth of my feelings for him time and again over the last few months.

We haven't exchanged the words, but the truth is always there. There's no denying the intensity of our connection or the layers of trust and care that came together to form the foundation of our relationship.

I love him. I'm almost certain he loves me, too.

He ordered wine with our meal, but I've only had a few sips. I'm hesitant to drink too much on my meds. Besides, alcohol isn't necessary. Tonight, I'm drunk on him.

We're sharing dessert now: crème brûlée and fresh berries.

He holds a spoonful to my mouth.

"Spence." I laugh, clamping my lips shut and shaking my head. I'm far too full, but he continues to feed me, despite my protests.

I slip one heel off and run my bare foot up his inner thigh in hopes of distracting him.

It works.

Discreetly, he captures my foot, kneading his thumb into the arch in a way that feels absolutely divine.

"You're feisty tonight." He picks up a strawberry and teases my lips with it.

I bite into the berry, and as the sweet juices hit my tongue, I close my eyes and moan dramatically. Then, when he doesn't feed me another bite fast enough, I nip at his thumb.

"Little brat," he scolds, popping it into his own mouth instead.

I lean forward, bringing my lips to his ear. "More like your little slut." When I sit back, his eyes have narrowed and darkened to a stormy blue-gray. He's watching me, calculating.

We've been intimate dozens of times over the last few months, but we haven't engaged in any degradation or depravity since my breakdown.

He's been treading lightly, and I appreciate his concern, but tonight? Tonight I know exactly what I want.

"Would you like that?" he asks, angling in close so his lips graze my ear. "Would you like it if I took my little slut into the bathroom of this Michelin-star restaurant and fucked you up against a dirty stall?"

"Yes," I breathe, clenching my thighs together at the prospect.

"Yes, what?" he corrects.

"Yes, Sir," I rush to tell him.

A devilish smirk paints his face. "Good girl. Let's go."

Chapter 44

Kabir

THEN

I've taken it easy on her for months. Resisted the primal urge to dominate her in the bedroom, to degrade her in the dirtiest, filthiest ways.

Happily holding back. I'd continue on like this for the rest of my life without a single complaint if it meant she was healthy and happy.

Tonight, though, she's asking for it. Practically begging me to give her the kind of depravity I crave. We're a perfect match, this woman and me. I've never been more eager to oblige.

I stalk down a narrow hallway, my grip tight around her wrist as I pull her behind me.

She laughs, giddy at my enthusiasm, I'm sure. When we pass a waiter coming out of the kitchen with an overflowing tray of food, I throw a hand over her mouth.

I take my chances and make a sharp right. Hand on the knob of a random door, I push it open with more force than necessary and shove her inside.

It's not a bathroom, though a supply closet will work just as well.

Once the door snicks shut, I press her up against it and make a meal of every inch of skin I can find. I'm rabid—a beast finally released from its cage, a man starving at the head of an overflowing buffet. I kiss and bite her neck, then trail my mouth between the perfect tits she's been flaunting all night.

"I'm going to fuck you hard," I tell her. "Fast." I cup her cunt and squeeze. "I haven't decided yet whether you get to come."

"What?" she gasps, already shimmying her arms out of the straps of the dress.

"Did I tell you that you could speak, you needy little brat?"

"No," she huffs as the dress puddles at her feet.

"No, what?"

She's naked before me. No underwear or bra. I take the opportunity to swat at her clit.

"No, what?" I demand again.

She sucks in a harsh breath. "No, Sir."

"That's my girl," I praise.

Dropping to my knees, I swirl my tongue around her sensitive bundle of nerves a few times, then quickly abandon it to stand back to full height.

She whimpers from the loss but doesn't protest. Though it's been some time, she knows better. She knows her place when we're together like this.

Fuck, she's a good girl. So responsive, so pliant to my whims.

Brushing her hair to one side, I bring my lips down to her ear. "You're going to need your safe word for what I have in mind. Is it still greedy?"

She pauses, holding her breath.

My heart stutters at the reaction. "It can be anything, love." I brush a thumb over her cheekbone. "Just something you wouldn't typically say during sex."

"It's still greedy," she tells me softly.

It isn't just a word. I know that now. Greedy is her stepbrother. The man who impregnated her. Hunter swears he had no idea of her predicament—that she was pregnant, nor that she miscarried. And yet he's the source of so much of her pain. I haven't even met the bloke, and I fucking hate him.

"Very well, then. Mine is still umbrella. If you need to pause, say loot."

Once she's nodded, confirming that she understands, I capture her mouth and feed my tongue between her lips a few times so she can taste the essence of herself.

I pull back, breaths sawing in and out of my lungs. I'm desperate to be inside her, but I have to be sure.

"Are you well, love?"

She gives me an exasperated sigh, even as she toys with her nipples. She sticks out her bottom lip and pouts. "Yes. Now fuck me before I give up and take care of it myself."

I grab both her wrists and pin them over her head, and her pout instantly transforms into a smirk.

Angling low, I bite down on one of her nipples and tug. "You bratty little cum skip." I lavish the raised bud before biting across her chest and giving the same treatment to the other nipple. "You're so desperate to be filled up," I taunt. "Don't move your hands. Don't move a fucking inch."

She keeps her arms above her head, motionless, as I shuck off my jacket, unbutton my fly, and line up at her entrance.

I zero in on her and wait for her to focus on my face as well, then I tell her a truth I've been waiting weeks to admit.

"I had a vasectomy." I nudge the head of my cock against her center.

Her pupils blow out, her breath hitching.

"What?" She half laughs in disbelief. "When?"

"A few months ago," I tell her, keeping my tone even. "I've already completed all the follow-up appointments. There's no evidence of sperm whatsoever."

She's silent, her chest heaving, causing her nipples to brush against my body with each desperate breath.

"I didn't want you to ever have to doubt or worry when we're together," I confess, pressing my lips into her forehead.

When I pull back and meet her gaze, her eyes shine with understanding.

"You had a vasectomy for me?"

It's then that I slam into her. Filling her cunt. Stretching her to the max and reminding us both of just how fucking incredible it feels when we come together like this. We groan in unison, and I nearly blow my load at the way she tightens and pulses around my cock.

Holding her face with both hands, I stare into her eyes, desperate to convey the intensity of my devotion. Desperate to know whether she feels the same sense of longing.

There isn't anything I wouldn't do for her. There isn't anything I wouldn't give her.

I hold myself inside her, pinning her to the door and crushing my pelvis into the apex of her thighs, unable to get as close as my mind and body want to be. With the base of my cock, I grind into her clit over and over again and capture her by the throat, claiming her.

I squeeze until she gasps for breath. When her lips part, I spit into her mouth.

"Yes, love. I had a vasectomy for you," I whisper, making sure she knows the truth before I resume the role we both crave.

Pulling back, I smirk. "I didn't have a vasectomy for you. I had it for me, you filthy slut. This way I can unload in all your holes whenever I want."

Despite my words, her eyes swim with understanding. She knows exactly why I did it.

We hold eye contact, barely moving, though our bodies connect and seize around each other in utter carnal desperation.

"Thank you." The soft words are punctuated by a gasp, signaling that she's on the precipice.

"Come, slut," I command, reaching between our bodies to rub her to completion. "Come so hard your cunt milks me dry and I can paint your insides with my seed."

She does, and it's exquisite. She comes, and she takes me with her.

Chapter 45

Hunter

THEN

I lie in bed, studying Spence where he lies beside me. I know myself well enough now to understand that these sleepless nights happen around the time I ovulate.

I set down my Kindle and watch the way his chest rises and falls rhythmically as he breathes.

He had a *vasectomy* for me.

My god.

And that isn't even the half of it. I'm alive because of this man, thriving because of his care. He saved me.

There within lies the tragedy of our timing. Just as we were on the brink—the precipice—of falling in love, he was forced to assume the role of caregiver. Of health care advocate. Of emergency contact and so many other roles not often bestowed upon a romantic partner so early in a relationship.

My therapist has warned about the possibility of developing a savior complex. Warm emotions flood me when I think about just how lovely he is and how happy I am because of him.

There's a little voice in my head, though, nagging me, telling me this can't be it. It could be the old me, the girl I used to be, throwing a hissy fit about the direction my life's taken. Or perhaps it's the voice of future me, whispering in my ear on sleepless nights that there's more for me than life in London.

It should be so easy to stay.

Should.

Spence and I are starting to build a life together. The man had a vasectomy with my mental health in mind. But despite feeling better than I have in months, I've yet to even consider what comes next. I could go to school, though that idea isn't particularly appealing at this moment. That alone is strange, because I loved high school and was genuinely excited about college.

I could go back to Splice or find a new job here in London.

I don't know what I want, nor do I like what my life feels like without a deeper sense of purpose.

It's like trying on a dress I used to love. One that no longer fits quite right. Or maybe it's my perception that doesn't fit anymore.

Here with Spence, every emotion is deep, amplified. It's incredible in so many ways. Still, could I build an entire life around him? And even if I could, would it be fair to the person I'm destined to become?

I snuggle closer and kiss his shoulder blade. He always sleeps on his stomach with his head turned off to one side.

He stirs on contact, turning to look at me through the dark.

"Sorry," I whisper. "I didn't mean to wake you."

"Are you well, love?"

He asks me at least a dozen times a day. He never asks if I'm okay, because sometimes I'm not. He doesn't ask how I'm feeling, because sometimes that question is hard to answer.

But am I well?

"I am," I promise him.

I really, really am.

He opens his mouth to say something else, but before he can, I rush to say, "Thank you for tonight. For... everything. I can't believe this is really my life."

He kisses my forehead, and then the tip of my nose. "You're welcome, love. Everything has a reason, and for everything, there's a season."

It's a phrase he's used before. Now, though, when he repeats it, it feels like an omen.

He turns his head and settles in again, and within moments, he's asleep once more.

I lie beside him and let myself daydream about what life could look like a year, five years, ten years from now.

Married, perhaps. Traveling the world.

It would work. It would be fun and fulfilling. Sexy and so satisfying.

Yet that vision for my life doesn't sit right.

I roll onto my back and exhale, counting on one of my breathing tools to help me relax.

My mind tends to spiral when I know that sleep won't come, so the best thing I can do is take care of myself.

Right now, I am okay.

Right now, I think I'm in love.

Chapter 46

Kabir

THEN

She's going to leave.

The dread churning in my gut when I woke was so acute, I expected to find the bed empty beside me.

It wasn't. She was right there. But something's changed.

What used to be listlessness has transformed into a restlessness. Where before, she feared herself, I sense she's eager to reacquaint with herself and learn all she can.

She's going to leave.

She's going to run.

I'm fighting every impulse screaming at me to make her stay.

It's Monday morning, so Gerald arrives bright and early, ready to review the schedule for the week while I dress.

Hunter hurries past the door, but quickly backtracks and stands at the threshold.

She's dressed in stretchy workout attire that shows off an expanse of creamy skin along her midriff. Her hair is piled on top of her head, and she's wearing a bright smile.

"Hey!" She practically skips into the room and pecks my lips. "I'm heading out to a yoga class. I didn't realize you were still home."

I smile at her enthusiasm, at the vivaciousness bubbling from her these days. "Have you done yoga before, love?" I ask, amused.

She shakes her head, her smile turning a little sheepish. "No, but I thought I could give it a try. Plus." She brightens again. "It's next door to this new patisserie I wanted to check out. I'll bring you home something yummy," she promises.

"Go on, then. Have fun."

She kisses me once more, then turns to the door. As she's exiting, she calls over her shoulder. "I'll bring you something, too, Gerald!"

"Ah, you're too good to me, lass," he tells her, his cheeks going pink.

"Hunter," I call after her. "Send me a picture of your ass in downward dog."

"Spence!" she groans, already down the hall based on the sound of her voice. She knows I'm teasing. Honestly, she's probably only acting offended on Gerald's behalf.

The elevator dings, then the flat falls silent once more.

I'm straightening my tie when I look up and meet Gerald's eye in the mirror.

"She's different, sir. More lively than when she first came to us," he remarks.

His fondness for her, I fear, rivals his fondness for me. Not that I blame him. I can be a true ass.

And Hunter? She's life itself.

She's brightness and sunshine—laughter and hope personified.

She's so very good. And she's finally on the right track.

"She is."

"She's happier," he observes. "And if I may be so bold, I think you are, too. She suits you, sir."

An ache grows in my chest as I consider his words.

She suits me.

She most certainly does.

Never before have I encountered another human I'm more compatible with and at ease around. From conversation to sex drive, we're a perfect fit. I could see myself settling down, committing to a single person, if that person was Hunter.

"Will you ask her to stay?"

His question irks me. Not because he asked it, but because it's vexing. I've been grappling with the same thought for days.

There's a desire for more there, beneath the surface. I first sensed it as she was coming back to life. Now it's there every day.

It's subtle. An untethering of sorts. But she's pulling away.

As she heals and grows more confident, she's clearing out the wilted versions of herself to make way for new growth.

Being anchored to me may have saved her, but it could ultimately hold her back, too.

Will I ask her to stay?

I won't.

I want her here with me, always. But I don't want to have to ask.

It could be tonight, it could be next week, it could be months from now. But she will leave. Because although she could be happy here—*we* could be happy—she could be happy elsewhere, too.

I want her to find her happiness. Whether it's with me or with another, she deserves all the joy life has to offer.

Gerald clears his throat, pulling me from my thoughts.

"No," I finally tell him with a firm shake of my head. "I won't ask her to stay. I don't expect she'll be around much longer either."

Without another word, I exit the bedroom.

Chapter 47

Hunter

NOW

Like a starfish, I splay my arms and legs out wide, stretching after a surprisingly satisfying night's sleep.

Yawning, I roll to my side and continue stretching and spreading out in the massive bed of the primary bedroom.

It hits me then. How much space I have, and dread instantly churns in my gut. I push up on one elbow and scan the room, my heart rate taking off.

I'm alone.

I didn't fall asleep alone. And yet...

The bedroom door creaks open, the sound startling me. I shoot up, gripping the sheets and duvet to my chest, even though I'm wearing pajamas.

Greedy steps inside, offering me a tentative smile.

"Hey." He gingerly holds a mug in one hand and shuts the bedroom door with the other.

"I brought you tea."

All the truths I've shared and the uncertainty woven into what lies ahead combine to form a ball of anxiety. So instead of responding with "thank you," or even "that was kind," I blurt out, "I thought you left."

Greedy's steps falter, and his face drains of all color. "What? No." He holds up the steaming mug as evidence. "I snuck down to make sure our parents are really gone and to make you this."

I blow out a long breath. Relief and a sensation akin to hopefulness settle inside me.

"Thank you," I finally squeak out, holding a hand out in acceptance of his thoughtfulness. The heat from the mug soaks into me as I cup it with both hands and bring it to my lips. As the warmth settles over me, I savor the notes of cardamom and mint.

"Did you want me to go?" he hedges, his throat working in a harsh swallow.

Heart dropping, I blink up at him. "Of course not," I rush to reply. Shifting over, I nod to the open space on the mattress beside me. "Come back to bed."

We weren't intimate last night. We weren't *sexually* intimate, I should say. Greedy held me. We talked half the night. We cuddled and spooned, and for the first time in a very long time, I felt at home in his presence.

A grin blooms on his face. The contrast between it and the look of uncertainty he wore before reminds me that he's probably just as unsure as I am about where things stand between us.

He climbs back into bed and perches against the headboard, holding out one arm to invite me in. I take another sip of tea and set it on the nightstand, then gladly shift over to snuggle into his side.

"It's going to take some time to get used to this," I admit.

He caresses my shoulder and down my arm, then repeats the motion.

"I know," he admits. "It's even more complicated thanks to His Royal Highness down in the kitchen right now."

I stiffen, but before I can come to Spence's defense, Greedy continues.

"He's acting like he's not going anywhere anytime soon. So I guess it's the four of us now."

Heat crawls up my neck at the thought.

The four of us.

Greedy and I are just beginning to find our footing. Things have evolved quickly with Levi, and it's like Spence and I were never apart. Is it really possible that the four of us could be together?

"Did you ever think we'd be here again?" I ask, purposely leaving the question open-ended. Here could be the cabin. This specific room. This entire place has been painted in heartache and grief, trauma and misunderstandings.

Shame washes over me when I think about the time we lost because I ran, foolishly thinking I could protect him and myself from the pain.

"Yeah, Tem," he tells me as he presses his lips to the top of my head. "I didn't know how or when, and some days it was damn near impossible not to lose hope, but I always knew we'd be back here."

I close my eyes and let his words reverberate in my mind. Illuminate my heart. Take root deep inside my soul.

He always knew we'd be back here.

Though I don't have a clue what comes next, his confidence in us is enough for now.

Chapter 48

Levi

NOW

The scenery here is exceptional. The crisp, barren tree line and a cloudless sky create a view that can be seen for miles.

I've made a point to spend as much time out here as possible over the last few days.

First, because Magnolia and Dr. Ferguson were here, and I felt it best to stay out of their way. Now, because I want to give Greedy and Hunter a little space.

Hunter is my girl, there's no changing that, and I'm certain we can make this work. That she can be *our* girl if that's the route they choose.

Regardless of my relationship with her, they deserve a moment to themselves. So much has happened over the last few days. I want them to figure their shit out. To untangle their past and to start on the path of healing.

I came out here for solitude, but that didn't last long.

"The reception really is shit," Spence grumbles, scowling at his phone. "I wonder how much longer we're staying here."

I'm half-tempted to joke about his private servers and whatever it was he was going on about with Kylian the other day.

Before I can, a memory of what transpired between us yesterday flashes in my mind.

I swallow hard, fighting back the urge to bring up the topic of the sexual tension rising between us. Not because I'm not eager to explore it, but because there are so many unknowns surrounding what'll happen next.

Between what's going on with Hunter's mom and now this reconciliation with Greedy, I can't afford for her to be upset, or for Kabir to rock the boat in some unexpected way.

"When will you go back to England?" I ask, feeling bolder than I anticipated.

He eyes me without lifting his head, cocking one brow at the directness of my question.

"Undecided," he remarks before focusing on his phone again.

"Well, you should get around to deciding. It's not fair to Hunter for you to just pop in temporarily."

Smirking, he glances at me, but immediately focuses on his device again. "I can assure you, champ. There's nothing temporary about my place in that woman's life."

Nodding, I push on. Now we're getting somewhere.

"So I take it you plan to stick around?"

Kabir sets his phone on the small table beside him and widens his stance. His spine is unnaturally straight, as if he's at full attention. We're sitting in Adirondack lounge chairs, for crying out loud, but he looks like he's presiding over a crowded boardroom table.

"If Hunter doesn't wish to return to London with me, then yes, I intend to stay."

"She's *not* going to London." I'm up on my feet without conscious thought.

One corner of Kabir's mouth tilts up in a smirk. "Ah, there it is."

Fire coursing through my veins, I glare. "You're not willing to let her go."

"Damn right, I'm not," he asserts. "Some people may call this predicament a stalemate, but knowing my girl—"

"*Our* girl," I correct.

Kabir breaks into a full-on grin as he regards me.

"Very well, then. Our girl. I'm sure we'll figure something out."

I sit back down, heating with embarrassment over my reaction. Embarrassed or not, anxiety still nags at me when I think about Hunter going anywhere at all.

"Why did you say that?" I eventually ask when my worries get the best of me. "Did she say something about going back to England with you?"

Kabir shakes his head. "No. Nor have I brought it up to her. Not yet, at least. Returning to London would resolve the Magnolia issue, though."

Shit.

My stomach sinks. He's right.

Hunter's so excited to get back to school, to kick ass for another semester, but given the line of conversation last night and what will inevitably be a lot of pressure from both her mom and Dr. F, maybe it would be better for her to get out of town.

"That's not the worst idea ever," I reluctantly admit. Rising to my feet, I cross my arms over my chest and assess Kabir. Then, bolstering my courage, I stride over to stand directly in front of him. "I'm not giving her up for anything. Where she goes, I go. End of story."

His expression is calculating as he inspects me. He's still wearing that smirk that would look smarmy on anyone else. But on him, it's really fucking sexy.

"All right, then," he concedes. He dips his head, picks his phone back up, and starts to scroll again.

Did he just let me win that fight? Were we ever even arguing to begin with? Either way, I'm counting it as a W.

I settle back down into the Adirondack beside him, close my eyes, and rest my head against the wooden slats.

Kabir clears his throat. "I guess now we just need to figure out where Garrett Reed stands."

That we do.

Chapter 49

Levi

NOW

Greedy's been putzing around the kitchen for the last twenty minutes. When I popped in to ask if he needed help, he insisted he had it under control. Whatever he's making smells heavenly, so I left him to it.

Spence excused himself to take a business call over an hour ago and hasn't emerged from his room since.

I see my shot. I'm taking it.

I climb the stairs two at a time, relishing the burn in my left quad with each stride. The cool, crisp mountain air combined with the daily stretches and strength training regimen I've adopted means I'm feeling better than I have in months.

I'm anxious to get back to South Chapel and return to physical therapy. It's time to up the weights, push my intensity, and add distance to my training. I've been reading everything I can about rehab and recovery. Over the last few weeks, I've even felt an inkling of hope.

When I came back to North Carolina, I accepted that any chance of a football career had been shot to hell. But I still love the game.

I've even started entertaining the idea of playing again. Even if I can't make it to the pros, there's a chance I could play at another school, or maybe a farm team, or for a different league.

If I keep up with my rehab and my healing continues the way it has been, maybe my days on the field aren't over.

It feels good to move. It's a reminder that I'm alive.

I'm alive, and my life has taken the most twisted turns over the last few months. Yet I wouldn't want it any other way. Not when I consider Hunter and Greedy and Spence.

Grinning, I reach the top of the stairs and knock softly.

There's no answer, so I peek my head inside. Finding the bedroom empty, I slip in and quietly walk to the opposite end of the room.

When I tap my knuckles softly on the doorframe, Hunter startles. A heartbeat later, her lips tip up in a smile and she beams at me, her eyes bright and her posture straightening.

Fuck if that doesn't make me feel like a goddamn superstar.

"How'd I know this is where you'd be?"

"I love it in here," she says, scanning the space wistfully. "I always have." Her smile softens. "Come sit with me?"

She sets a pink notebook and a pen next to her e-reader and shifts over on the chaise lounge to make room for me by her side.

Tipping at the waist, I greet her with a kiss, then I slip in beside her and scoop up her legs so they're in my lap.

As I settle, I survey the floor-to-ceiling bookshelves. They're jam-packed with books, old and new, but all are hers. Some are positioned with the spines displayed like the books on a library shelf. Others are flipped to display the brightly painted pages. A few are on full display in the middle of shelves, almost like trophies.

"He told me what he did," I remark, rubbing her bare legs mindlessly. "Updating it, adding your books."

"It's amazing," she admits, her tone breathy. "Although that's not how I felt when I first found out." She frowns. "I don't even know why I was angry."

"That was before," I remind her gently.

Before she confronted him. Before they came up with the bright idea of hate-fucking one another out of their systems. Before their animosity boiled over and they finally imploded.

Before her mother and Dr. F dropped the bomb.

I'm still reeling from the declaration. Greedy insisted he wanted to be the one to take care of Daisy last night. I allowed it and even convinced Kabir not to sleep outside her bedroom door.

I wanted them to have that time together.

Now it's my turn.

"Before," she eventually repeats, tracing the tendons of my forearm where I have it wrapped around her bare legs. She shakes her head and gives me a sad smile. "I hope like hell too much time hasn't passed."

"It hasn't." I pull her into my arms until she's snug against my chest. "We're together now, right?"

She nods, so I bite my tongue, leaving it at that. At some point, I'd like to define that word—together—and discover what she hopes for the four of us. What she envisions for the future.

My phone vibrates in my pocket then, causing Hunter to jump.

We both laugh, and I adjust my hips so she's not sitting directly on the device. Before I've even settled again, it vibrates a second time.

"Hold on," I mutter, shifting to one side and digging it out.

Before I even glance at the screen, I move Hunter where I want her. With a sigh, she leans into my side and curls her legs up on the opposite end of the lounger.

"It's just a text," I confirm, pulling up the first message from my mother.

I read it, then read it again.

I'm reading the second message when a third appears.

The tension in my muscles coils tighter as I process each word.

Fuck it all to fucking shit.

"What's wrong?" Hunter asks. She's perceptive as hell.

"What's today's date?" I ask.

"December twenty-sixth," she replies instantly. "Hope you wished Spence a happy Boxing Day." She pokes my side, but I don't feel it. I don't feel anything, honestly, as I stare down at the words on the screen.

I swallow past the lump that's lodged itself in my throat. "My mom says she can't keep me on her health insurance in the new year."

Hunter's eyes narrow. "Can't or won't?"

"Can't." I grimace. "Unless I commit to meeting with her friend from church."

This time, Hunter's the one who stiffens. "What kind of friend?"

I fight back a smile. Damn, I love that she gets feisty and jealous at the idea of my mom trying to set me up.

"The man who owns a branch of Chapel Hill Insurance. She wanted him to mentor me, remember? And she wanted me to eventually take out a small business loan and open my own branch."

Hunter wrinkles her nose. "She's manipulating you."

I shrug. Regardless, what other options do I have? I'm living on the goodwill of Dr. Ferguson and Greedy. Aside from daily rehab and hanging out with my friends, I don't have any plans for the new year. Greedy has another year of college to look forward to, and Hunter is already so excited for the new semester.

I don't want to be left behind or be the weakest link in the group.

"Maybe I should just hear him out?"

"Levi. No."

I stiffen at her use of my given name.

Sighing, I pluck my baseball cap from my head and run my hand through my hair. "You know what you're doing with your life. So does Greedy. Kabir certainly has his shit figured out. I don't want to be the bum not pulling his weight in this..." I trail off when I catch the direction my train of thought was headed.

Hunter pokes me in the ribs and grins. "In this *what*, Duke?"

"In whatever this is." I slump back, defeated. Reality is such a bitch.

A few minutes ago, I was pumped about getting back into the gym. About how maybe I would have the chance to play football again.

Fucking pipe dream is what that was. It's time to man up and figure out what I'm actually going to do with my life now that I'm back in South Chapel.

Hunter interrupts my thoughts with another caress of my arm. This time, she trails her fingertips all the way down my hand and interlaces our fingers. "You don't have to do what she wants, Duke. We can figure something else out."

No one else should have to figure out my shit for me, though.

"I don't want to be anyone's charity case," I lament. I don't know what the hell I want, but I'm almost certain I don't want to be an insurance dude wearing a polo and khakis, getting up early to go to chamber of commerce meetings and talking my family and friends into letting me provide free quotes for them.

Despite that, there's dignity in work. In pulling my own weight and contributing meaningfully to a relationship. So even if it's not the dream, it might not be such a bad thing, owning an insurance company. I could at least do my research. Remaining on my mom's health insurance would be a bonus.

"I don't have to actually make a commitment. I could just... see what the guy has to say."

I hold my breath, sure that Hunter's on the brink of arguing. I can sense it in her: the battle waging behind her eyes, her intense desire to protect me.

Yet when she finally replies, her tone is light. "If you decide to go, I'm going with you."

My heart catches in my throat. Her willingness to support me, even if she doesn't agree, means more than she could possibly know.

"She wants it to be this weekend," I hedge. *She* being my mother. *It* being the luncheon after church. "We'll have to attend service and then go out to lunch."

"Okay," Hunter confirms, emotionless. "I'll put it on my calendar. I'll make sure Greedy and Kabir know we need to be back in South Chapel by this weekend."

"Thank you," I say softly, tipping her chin back to kiss her.

"You're welcome," she whispers against my lips. She wraps her arms around my neck and interlocks her fingers. Instinctively, I grip her hips and guide her onto my lap so she's properly straddling me as I kiss her.

She swivels her hips, so I thrust up and match her movements, rubbing my hardening length between the apex of her thighs.

"Is this how you show your gratitude, Dukey?"

She's such a brat.

"This is how I show you something," I tease, gripping the back of her head so I can move her right where I want her.

Our tongues dance, and she lets me lead, softly murmuring with each swipe and opening farther for me so I can deepen the kiss.

She allows me to explore, and I take my fucking time sucking on her plush bottom lip. Nudging the tip of my tongue against hers.

As our kisses turn sloppier, needier, her body melts for me, yielding until she's soft and pliant in my arms.

Every time she brushes against my hard, aching length, she encourages me with her little pants and moans. God, I could listen to her make those noises all day long.

"Daisy," I say sweetly, running my nose along her jaw then kissing down her neck. "Can I go down on you, pretty girl?"

She squeezes her thighs in response and kisses me deeper. "Of course you can."

Pulling back, I search her face. "I've never done it before," I admit.

Sure, I've had a few girlfriends over the years, and I've done more with the opposite sex than just kiss. I may have had my mouth on her in the hot tub the other night, but that was a completely different scenario.

"You might have to... guide me. Tell me what feels good. Show me what you like." I gulp past the awkwardness that comes with asking for help. I want to be good for her. I want to be more than good.

"You're asking me to teach you how to eat pussy?" she teases.

I swat at her ass, then thrust my hips up. "No, pretty girl. I'm asking you to teach me how to eat *your* pussy. How to make her spasm, pulsate, and purr until you soak me with your pleasure."

"Fuck me," Hunter groans, planting her forehead on mine and looking right into my eyes. "I honestly might come from your dirty talk alone," she tells me, eyes dancing with mirth.

"Nah, I want to use my mouth on you in an entirely new way."

Keeping an arm banded around her, I stand. Once I'm sure my legs are stable enough to support her, I hoist her over my shoulder.

She laughs and playfully hits at my back. "Where are we going?"

I carry her out of the room. "I'm not about to go down on you for the first time in Greedy's mom's library, Daisy."

She snorts, bouncing on the mattress when I drop her down. "Greedy says it's my library now."

I stand to my full height, take off my hat, and pull my shirt off with one hand. As I slip my hat back on, I don't miss how Hunter's eyes rake up and down my body appreciatively. "There's sharing, then there's disrespect. I'm not crossing that line with him."

Hunter's teasing gaze softens just a bit.

"Plus," I add, lowering myself over top of her. "I want to lay you out and properly take you in before I feast."

She grins, and together, we make quick work of pulling off all her clothes.

Once she's bare for me, she lets her knees fall open, revealing the pink, glistening lips of her sex. She runs a hand down her torso, letting the other linger on her chest as she plays with her own nipple.

I'm mesmerized, my attention fixed on her fingertips as she uses them to spread herself open for me.

"You're so fucking pretty," I tell her, arousal coursing through my veins and making my cock throb angrily.

Licking my lips, I home in on the spot where she centers her touch. I'm fascinated by the way she strokes herself, capturing her clit between her fingers and pulling gently.

When I tear my focus away, I find her watching me, her pouty lip caught between her teeth and her eyes sparkling with desire.

"Lick me everywhere, but give me more pressure here." She uses both hands to pull apart her pussy lips, exposing herself to me and pressing softly into her folds.

"Then, if you can get my clit in your mouth and suck—"

Unable to resist any longer, I sink to my knees and pull her hips to the edge of the bed, dipping my head between her thighs.

Using my tongue and my teeth, I nip along the inside of her thighs.

When I finally reach my target, I falter, but just for a second.

Her breath hitches, and her leg muscles tense where they're propped over my shoulders.

Reverently, I whisper, "I'm going to lick you now, pretty girl. And I'm not going to stop until you soak my tongue with your juices."

As I approach her center, her body trembles subtly. With a slow swirl of my tongue around her folds, I savor the taste, committing her unique flavor to memory.

Daisy's breath hitches. Then, as I connect my tongue to her cunt, she lets out a soft cry.

I lick and suckle, savoring the tanginess of her flavor and devouring her every moan. Arousal rises through my limbs in waves as she knocks the hat from my head and grasps my hair to guide me. Fuck, her responsiveness sends me soaring. Knowing I'm the one making her buck her hips and moan in pleasure is a high I've never experienced.

"So good, so fucking good." Her praise transforms into a whine, and her thighs clasp around my head like she can't control herself.

Soft gasps crescendo into ragged pants. She bucks her hips wildly, driving her pelvis higher and higher until she's practically fucking my face.

"That's it, pretty girl," I rasp, my voice thick with desire. "Let me have that cum."

Locking my arms around her thighs, I pull her as tightly to my face as I can. Then I close my mouth around her clit and mound.

Sucking hard, I pull up, driving her body into my mouth as I flick my tongue over her pleasure point.

"Levi!" My name is a ragged scream.

Without letting up, I eye her, searching for cues. She's pinching both her nipples, her head thrown back in ecstasy. I take that as a sign to continue what I'm doing.

"I'm coming," she announces on the next breath.

Her hips rock in time with the orgasm as moisture coats my tongue and lips and even drips down my fucking neck.

"Thatta girl," I praise, lapping at her cunt as I keep gently sucking.

When her body finally stops convulsing, I pull back, grinning.

I run the back of my hand along my chin, then spread her wide and really take her in.

Eyes closed and wearing a blissful smile, she absentmindedly strokes her fingertips over her breasts and down her midsection. Her pussy's all red and engorged with arousal, thoroughly eaten and fully sated.

I feel like a goddamn champion.

I also have the urge to go back in for another taste.

"I fucking love eating you out." I press a quick kiss to her clit.

With a squeal, she pulls away from me. "Too sensitive!"

Grinning ruefully, I grab her legs and force her to stretch back out for me. "Let me see you, pretty girl. I'll be good." I plant soft kisses along her legs, then on her lower belly, before traveling higher. My lips savor every inch of skin. I need to make sure she fucking knows how I feel about her.

This isn't infatuation. This isn't just sexual attraction.

This woman is the epitome of everything I want and need. I want to spend every day for the rest of my life making sure she knows it.

When I reach her mouth, I peck her softly on the lips. "How did I do?"

"Don't tell the others," she deadpans, "but I think you're a pussy-eating prodigy."

"Yes!" I give my fist a pump, then dive back down to kiss her neck until she's laughing in my arms. "The others are gonna have to get over it. I'm telling them, and I'm putting it on a T-shirt."

"Don't you dare!" she squeals as I tickle her sides.

Pussy-eating prodigy. Maybe I could turn that into a full-time job. Hell, I'd work for free if it meant satisfying this woman every day and hearing her scream my name when she comes. Suddenly, my future doesn't look so bleak after all.

Chapter 50

Greedy

NOW

It's our last night at the cabin. Levi needs to be home by this weekend, so tomorrow morning, we're heading back to South Chapel.

All of us. Together.

Last night, we discussed our trip back, agreeing that it's best if we stick together and stay at the house. For logistics, more than anything. If Kabir left the group and found his own accommodations, it would mean Tem having to go back and forth. It'll be so much easier if we're all together, full stop.

Before bed, Hunter pulled me aside to ask if I was really planning to stay.

The sheen of tears she blinked away as she searched my eyes and the way she gnawed on her bottom lip? Fuck. I couldn't reassure her fast enough that I wasn't leaving. I never wanted to leave, even the day I told her I would. If I had my way, we'd never be apart again.

That's a big part of why I'm about to bring up the wild suggestion I've been toying with all afternoon.

We're all together. It's now or never.

Hunter is stretched out on the couch reading while Kabir sits at one end with her feet in his lap. Levi's spread out on the floor stretching, watching Hunter like she hung the moon and all the stars.

I feel the same way.

Entering the space, I clear my throat.

"Teach me."

Three sets of eyes land on me: Sea-glass green, familiar and calm, from Hunter. Dark denim blue, questioning and curious, from Levi. Then a piercing, icy gray that commands respect and honor.

I swallow past the hesitation I've grappled with all evening, lock eyes with Kabir, and repeat: "Teach me. I want to learn what she likes. About her limits. I don't know anything about... degradation... but I can learn. I *will* learn," I correct, my focus shifting to Hunter.

More than anything, I want to be everything she needs. I just hope like hell she sees the earnestness in my request.

Rising to her feet, Hunter worries her bottom lip. As she approaches, she ducks her head and gives it a shake.

My cheeks heat and my stomach sinks as I steel myself for her dismissal.

Dammit.

"Greedy..." She pushes up on tiptoes and loops her arms around my neck. "I don't want you to degrade me."

Stiffening, I balk. "But you said you like it."

With a glance over her shoulder, she exhales, then fixes her attention on me, her expression thoughtful. "I like when Spence degrades me. In the bedroom only. Within the boundaries of our dynamic."

Right. *Their* dynamic. I avert my gaze, rejection stinging behind my eyes.

"Hey." She catches my face in her hands, guiding me back to look her in the eye. "You own so many of my firsts. I like"—she clears her throat then, pressing her lips together as she considers me—"no, I *love* what you and I share in the bedroom. How you worship me. I love when you encourage me and the way we connect on such a deep level during sex."

My shame is quickly washed away, replaced with pride. We do have a sizzling, all-consuming connection.

"I don't want you to treat me the way he does. Or talk the way he does." She loops her arms around my neck again and pulls me down until her lips are at my ear. "I love who you are and what we have when we're together. You're enough, Greedy. You're more than enough."

I ease back a fraction, meeting her gaze, then lick my lips hesitantly and kiss her. It's a soft kiss, full of tenderness and sorrow, forgiveness and the promise of all that's still to come.

A throat clears across the room before we get too carried away.

"Perhaps there's a middle ground," Spence suggests, first regarding Hunter, then turning to Levi, and finally me. "A way for us to explore certain proclivities within the confines of the bedroom. Together. As a group."

I hold my breath, waiting for Levi or Hunter to speak up first.

But when I glance around, hopeful for an assist, I realize once again that all three sets of eyes are focused on me.

After what feels like a lifetime, Levi finally pipes up.

"I'm in. I want to try…" He trails off, looking earnest as fuck. "I'll try anything. Everything. I want to try it all." His tone has gone gravelly, his cheeks pink. "And I'd really like to be with… all of you."

"Tem?" I ask.

Hunter's gnawing on her bottom lip. I lift one hand and trace the raw skin she's abusing with her teeth.

She sighs, then gives me a sheepish smile. Leaning in close so her words are just for me, she asks, "Are you okay with this? Truly?"

"I want you any way I can have you, baby," I whisper back, nodding. "And I'm open to… more."

"It's settled, then," Kabir announces, rising to his feet and offering a hand to Levi. "Shall we take this to the bedroom?"

As he pulls Levi up from the floor, I drape an arm around Hunter's back, hanging on as we make our way to the stairs.

"Let's go figure out exactly how Garrett Reed personally defines the word *more*."

Chapter 51

Greedy

NOW

"Undress," Kabir tells Hunter, a one-word command that pisses me off while also setting my blood on fire.

Dutifully, she removes her clothing, layer by layer, until she's unhooking her bra and peeling her panties down her legs.

Through each step, my mouth waters. In my periphery, Levi's mouth is agape, and he's practically drooling.

"In this room, tonight, I am in charge."

That gets my attention. Levi, too.

Kabir stalks around the space as he unfastens his cufflinks, regarding Hunter with a seemingly uninterested sweep of his eyes.

Fuck. I don't like this. Based on that move alone, I'm already fighting to keep my mouth shut.

"On your knees," he commands.

She drops instantly.

Beautifully.

But still...

"Hunter and I have a rhythm. An understanding. Irrevocable trust thrums through us. That's why I can command her like this, and it's why she so eagerly and willingly obeys. You two..." He regards Levi and me, blinking dismissively. "I can teach," he says, removing his button-down and draping it over a chair. "But you must agree to listen and learn."

Levi half nods while turning to look at me.

Trepidation rushes through me, but I join him, bobbing my head and committing to—fuck. I don't even know.

This was my fucking idea, dammit. Why the hell do I feel so off-kilter now?

"You're hesitating."

Wincing—because how the hell can he read me so easily?—I clear my throat. "I am."

"Why?"

God, he's bossy. Does he really just expect me to—

"Garrett." I force myself to zero in on him. Then I look to Hunter, who's kneeling, naked, silent, and perfectly still. My gaze drifts to Levi, who appears more eager than hesitant. I'm honestly jealous he's not struggling more.

"If this is to work—if you'd like to explore *more*—we have to communicate. A scene is only successful when it is accompanied by deep-seated trust between all parties involved."

My cheeks heat at the call-out. I feel like I'm being scolded.

"Do you have any limits we should be aware of?"

I rack my brain and come up empty. I've only ever been with Hunter—and Levi, sort of, that one time—I don't have enough experience to know where my limits lie.

"I don't know," I answer honestly.

"I don't have any," Levi declares. Fuck, how is he so confident about all this? "I don't have much experience with group stuff, but I'm willing to try just about anything."

Kabir smiles at that.

"Do we—" My voice cracks, so I clear my throat and start again. "Do we need safe words?"

"Always."

Kabir's assuredness calms me. He looms over Hunter and regards her. I'm entranced by their interactions, by how easily she's silenced, kneeling before him, waiting for further instruction. A lick of jealousy courses through me. Fuck. What they share is clearly so deep, so ingrained, in the both of them. I'm desperate to be on that level.

Clenching my jaw, I check myself. I'm here. With them. We're exploring more *together*. I owe it to Hunter, Levi, and hell, even Kabir, to commit to this idea that I so boldly suggested.

"Firecracker." Still cradling Hunter's chin, Kabir tilts her head back so she's staring directly at him. "For simplicity's sake, could we establish safe words for when we're all together?"

Something akin to relief flashes through her eyes. "Yes, Sir," she says. "Thank you, Sir."

Her chest heaves, then her shoulders lower. Angling forward, she rubs her cheek on his pant leg. Quickly, she pulls her hair into a messy bun, then she lowers herself farther and presses her lips to his shoe.

"The fuck?" Levi groans beside me. I suck in a breath, ready to wholeheartedly agree, but all the air escapes me when he adds "why is that so hot?" and adjusts his erection.

"Enough," Kabir declares, calling my attention back to Hunter. She's still low, literally worshipping his feet. From this angle, I can see the two little dimples right above her ass, the curves of her breasts as they swing freely, grazing the floor.

The surge of arousal traveling through my body at the sight is impossible to ignore.

"Red will be the safe word. If anyone says it, all activity stops, no questions. You could say red for a number of reasons," Kabir explains. "You're physically uncomfortable. You're unsure of the scene. Your head isn't in it. It just doesn't feel well with your soul."

He looks at me pointedly. "There's no shame in safe-wording. Ever."

Hunter tips her chin back. She doesn't speak, but Kabir obviously recognizes her silent request. So, brows lifted, he nods.

"Pink for pause," she murmurs.

"Very well," he confirms.

Attention on Levi and me again, he says, "If you need a break—a physical breather, a moment to check in with yourself, or with someone else—say pink. Pink pauses the scene. Sometimes, it permanently ends a scene, too. There's also no shame in pausing."

I'm nodding. Beside me, Levi's doing the same. How I went from eager to completely unsure to nodding along in the span of a few minutes is beyond me.

"One more thing."

We all look to Kabir.

"Tonight, I'm in charge. You'll do as I say. You'll follow my lead. You'll commit to this experiment. You'll submit if I require it"—his heated stare lands on Levi, then drifts up to me—"and I guarantee you will not be disappointed."

Chapter 52

Kabir

NOW

"Hold it. Just like that."

Garrett Reed's abs ripple as he holds just an inch of his cock inside Hunter's cunt.

Her pussy reacts, fluttering from the loss of sensation as she fights the urge to shift and pierce herself on his length once more.

"You're drenched, Firecracker." My voice is laced with false disdain. "Dripping and making a mess." I trace one finger through her sex, circling Garrett's straining cock in the process. "Such a needy little slut, desperate for her brother's cock."

Garrett drops his head back and groans. I allow it.

Hunter freezes, her body tensing. She yearns to sass back, to declare that he's not her brother. The urge emanates from her in violent waves. Thankfully, her mouth is much too full of Levi's heavy sack to allow such backtalk to escape her.

She's spread out on the bed, with Garrett fucking her hard and fast, then pulling back as soon as she nears the edge. Levi is positioned at her head, on his knees, jerking himself in almost violent strokes as she sucks his balls.

I've remained at a distance from most of the intimacy in this scene, giving the guys, especially Garrett, time to acclimate.

Though try as I might, I can't fucking resist the temptation any longer. Not when Levi's fat cock is practically weeping for me to have a taste.

"Hands off," I instruct, focused on his throbbing erection.

I lick my lips in anticipation, and Levi immediately obeys.

"Good boy," I praise, causing Hunter to softly moan.

Lowering, I take the mushroom head of his cock into my mouth. I swirl my tongue around the circumference, getting it nice and wet.

Then I pull back, spit, and look to Hunter.

"Don't waste a single fucking drop."

She nods enthusiastically, my beautiful, perfect girl. Then she sticks out her tongue below Levi's body.

I suck him hard and fast, pausing occasionally to spit again. Soon, the fluid coating his cock begins to drip down his length.

Hunter obediently laps at each drop, cleaning Levi and swallowing down his pre-ejaculate mixed with my saliva.

When his abdomen starts to tense, I stand up.

"Everyone off the bed."

The room is silent and still for the space of two heartbeats. Then each of them is obeying. Sheets rustling and soft footsteps are the only sounds.

"Get on your knees where you belong," I tell Hunter dismissively, then I turn to the boys. "Stand on either side of her, above her head."

Levi quickly complies. Garrett, though, remains in place, looking at Hunter.

She gives him the slightest nod. She's a rockstar. For the last hour, she's offered him soft, subtle assurances, and she's guided him through the scene in ways I never could have navigated. She's always in control when we're together, and she knows it. It's beautiful to witness her command him as well.

Satisfied, Garrett takes his place on her other side.

"Such a needy little cum bucket," I pronounce as I step directly in front of her. I stroke her face affectionately, encouraging her to tip her head back and look me in the eye. "Filthy American whore."

Greedy's jaw ticks, but Hunter's eyes are ablaze with carnal lust.

I grip her chin and turn her to face him, allowing him to properly take her in. To see how she responds, how she flourishes.

"Look at how she aches for you, Garrett. Your stepsister. On her knees. Practically begging for your cock."

Turning her face back to me, I rub my thumb along her lower lip, and as she opens in response, I spit into her mouth.

"Do you want their cum, Firecracker?"

"Yes, Sir," she replies without hesitation.

"And who should be the one to give it to you?" I ask.

"You. I want you to give it to me, Sir."

I grin. She's perfect. My filthy, cum-obsessed princess. Desperate for cock. Desperate to please me.

"You heard her." I look from one man to the other. "Get closer."

Without even a second of indecision, they inch forward, each nearly straddling one of Hunter's shoulders.

Slowly, I grip their cocks, one in each hand.

The warmth. The heft. *Fucking hell*. These American boys may have me ruining my trousers at this rate.

I give them each a stroke, keeping my motions simultaneous, then another.

Levi leans into it immediately, rocking his hips forward, seeking more friction.

Garrett tenses, his face screwed up, though the look appears to be one of concentration rather than discomfort. I keep going, focusing on his face, searching for any indication that he may need a break or to stop entirely.

Yes, we have a safe word, but he's new to this dynamic. He may be too far gone to remember to use it. It's my responsibility to guide him through the scene safely and consensually.

His expression doesn't relax. If anything, it morphs into an almost pained grimace. I'm moments away from pausing when he says, "This is so fucking hot. Why is this so fucking hot?"

Smiling, I look down at Hunter, who's beaming.

"You want them to mark you, Firecracker? Do you want me to smear their seed all over your face?"

"Yes, Sir," she pants.

"Touch yourself," I instruct. "If you can come before they do, I'll allow it."

"Thank you, Sir," she practically sobs, snaking one hand down between her legs while she uses the other to tug hard on her own nipple.

Desire courses through me as I lock eyes with Levi. I spit on his cock, and in response, he groans, his head thrown back in ecstasy.

I turn to Garrett, and with a smirk, I repeat the action.

"My cum slut wants your seed. Desperately. Are you going to give her what she wants, boys? Do you think you can hold off until she detonates?"

I jerk them faster, fascinated by the similarities and subtle differences between their cut cocks. One thing is for certain: they look exquisite with my fingers wrapped around them, the dim light glinting off my rings.

"Hurry up, whore," I bait. It's unnecessary. She's right there. It's written all over her face, and it hangs in the air around us, the tension she's radiating.

The moment she lets go, I grip the boys so tightly my knuckles ache.

Surprisingly, they respond positively to the edge of pain: Garrett first, pulsing and spewing seed with force, then Levi, his length weeping with cum in rolling waves.

Aiming for my target, I jerk them through their orgasms, then guide their leaking cocks along Hunter's cheeks, over her lips and her chest. She's painted in cum when they're finally done. Glazed and glossy and coated in the claiming she so beautifully accepted by my hand.

My own cock begins to soften—as predicted, I came in my fucking pants.

I drop to my knees before my girl and cup her face. "You're perfect," I tell her, kissing the tip of her nose, then savoring her lips. I lap up the salty, musty spunk she's coated in and kiss her thoroughly. Pulling back, I groan at the sight of her, then get to work kissing and cleaning her neck.

Surprisingly, Garrett lowers to his knees, mirroring my position. Levi follows suit.

"Didn't she take it so beautifully, boys?"

"Hottest fucking thing I've ever seen, Daisy." Levi angles in, kissing her without hesitation.

"That was incredible." Garrett is intent on Hunter, his expression filled with awe.

She watches him, too, as if the two of them are having a silent conversation.

"*You're* incredible," he lauds, leaning in and resting his forehead on hers.

He doesn't kiss her, but he sees her. Recognizes her. Whispers additional words of praise as Levi and I make quick work of cleaning her skin.

Once she's licked clean, I resist the urge to pull her into my arms. Instead, I look to Garrett and allow him the honor. "Hold her."

"Gladly." Rising to his feet, he scoops her up. Then, tucking her in close, he carries her to the bed.

Pride and hope surge through my system as I observe their interaction. I rise, then offer a hand to Levi. When he's on his feet, we stand side by side, watching Hunter settle on her side while Garrett strokes her hip and kisses the back of her neck.

"*More* worked out pretty well for us," Levi remarks.

That it did. That it fucking did.

Chapter 53

Hunter

NOW

I wake up in the middle of a tangle of bodies. We've formed a human knot in our sleep. Though someone's lying on my arm, and my legs are twisted up in the sheets with someone else, I love it.

I close my eyes, intent on drifting back to sleep.

For a moment, I breathe deeply, reveling in what we shared. Thrilled that they're still here, that they stayed, and that this feels like the start of something familiar but new.

Despite my best efforts, I'm not comfortable enough to drift off again. My body aches, but not just in the delicious, well-fucked way.

There's a tightness in my lower back that stretches around my hip and down my quads.

The longer I'm awake, the more noticeable the pain. It only takes a few moments to recognize the cramps radiating through the front of my pelvis.

Quietly, slowly, I untangle myself from the boys.

Once I'm out of bed, I take a moment to drink in the scene. Greedy and Levi are in bed, both still out. Though they flanked me when I woke, they've already readjusted in my absence.

Levi's flat on his stomach, head turned on the pillow, and Greedy's got one arm wrapped around his waist.

My heart pangs. They're adorable.

After another moment where I soak in the details, I force myself to trudge into the bathroom.

I avoid looking in the mirror. After last night, I can only imagine that disheveled wouldn't even begin to describe my current status.

Tapping the switch for the dim light over the shower, I shuffle my way to the toilet. I relieve myself, and when I wipe, the slickness tells me exactly what I'll find before I even glance down.

I take a deep, cleansing breath, and then another, and wipe away all the reddish-brown discharge that signals the start of my period.

I dig through my toiletry bag and grab a menstrual disc, insert it, then wash my hands thoroughly.

On my way back into the bedroom, I grab the first T-shirt I can find on the floor.

It's unlikely that I'll sleep anymore tonight, but I could use a glass of water. Maybe a snack, too, if I'm going to take ibuprofen for the cramps.

I venture downstairs and am not at all surprised to find Kabir set up in the main living area.

He doesn't see me as I quietly watch him from the shadows. He's wearing lounge pants and nothing else. God, he's gorgeous.

He's focused on his work, with a computer, a tablet, and a few notepads spread out on the coffee table. I don't know whether he's up because he's also not tired or if this is necessary, since I'm keeping him away from his work.

"Hey," I whisper as I approach, not wanting to startle him.

Regardless of my intent, his gaze snaps up.

Assessing me from head to toe, he sets his notepad aside. Then he closes his computer.

"Everything all right?"

With a nod and a yawn, I make my way over to him. "Can I sit with you?"

He holds out an arm and rests it on the back of the couch. Gratefully, I plop down into his lap.

One hand caresses my nape, and his lips find my temple, giving me the most tender, loving kiss.

"Are you well, love?" he asks.

Another yawn catches me by surprise. Once it passes, I answer.

"My period just started." I curl up into a smaller, tighter ball.

"Really?" He moves a hand to my low back, massaging and applying pressure where it always aches during the first few days of my cycle. "This is you on your period?"

"I guess," I admit, tucking my chin.

I can't fault him for being surprised. Based on his tone, he's impressed, too. The way I handle the symptoms of PMDD these days is a far cry from what he remembers, I'm sure. These days, I'm so much better at dealing with the physical pain and the mental anguish of this awful disease.

"This is me on hormonal birth control and a daily SSRI, plus using an additional anxiety med for sleepless nights. This is me meditating daily, drinking minimal caffeine, and staying locked away from the world for three or four days a month to cope. But yeah. This is me on my period."

Spence's hold on me tightens. "It's night and day, love. I'm so proud of you."

I peer up, basking in his praise.

"I always assumed things continued to get better, that you were well and that you were thriving. But when I didn't hear from you…" He trails off, and I know he won't push.

But now that he's here and that it's clear he isn't going anywhere anytime soon, I want to fill in the blanks. He deserves to know what happened between London and now.

"I met someone after I left London."

He remains stoic, but in true Kabir fashion, he asks a clarifying question.

"You met someone who isn't me, Levi, or Garrett Reed?"

Pursing my lips, I nod. "His name is Sione."

"You met him in Italy, I take it?"

I murmur a noncommittal sound. Did I tell Kabir where I went or where I stayed after I left him in the UK? I don't recall getting into those specifics—

"You fell in love in Italy," he surmises, his voice even and knowing.

I guess I didn't have to fill in the blanks for him after all.

"I didn't mean to—"

With two fingers, Spence tips my chin back, forcing me to meet his gaze.

"You didn't have to. I know you, Hunter St. Clair. I know your heart. When you didn't come back to me, I knew you'd found someone worth staying for."

I gulp past the shame that washes over me as he speaks the very real truth. Kabir and I were never supposed to be anything but sex. Instead, he became my savior, my anchor, a person I could see myself spending the rest of my life with.

And yet I ran.

I ran just like I always do.

A version of myself who could have been content exists inside me. I honestly believe I could have been deliriously happy living in London with Spence. But I wasn't whole enough at the time to commit to him or to the idea of what I wanted my future to look like.

I was different after my time in London. I wasn't broken anymore, but I wasn't the same.

"I missed you," I assure him. "I thought about you every day."

"Tell me about Sione," Spence encourages, turning the conversation back to my time in Italy.

"His grandparents own a handful of villas near Lake Como. He's my age, also a student, but he spends his summers helping them with tourist season. He plans to go into holistic healthcare or alternative medicine. He taught me yoga and how to meditate. He taught me so much about myself," I confess, my heart aching at the thought of the boy who helped restore my spirit in so many beautiful ways.

"So I was dumped for an Italian bohemian?" Spence jibes.

Snorting, I duck my head. He's kidding, but the sting of shame is ever-present when I consider the way I left. The way I always leave.

"Sione's not Italian," I explain, forcing myself to look him in the eye. "He's Tongan-Romanian. His grandparents are Romanian. They just live in Italy during the summers."

My chest warms at the memory of Mammamia and Moulshi. I miss them.

"And where is he now?"

I turn my head away, ashamed to admit what he probably already knows.

"Did you part on bad terms?" Spence presses.

I'm silent again, even as I know he won't let me get away with it.

Gently gripping my chin, he turns me back to face him. "Answer me, Firecracker. Where is your Italian lover boy, and did you part on bad terms?"

"We didn't part at all," I admit.

His eyes flash when it clicks. "You ran."

Holding his gaze, I nod. Then, sheepishly, I add, "It's possible he thinks we're still together..."

Kabir raises both brows, offering me an amused expression. "Are you?"

I hit him with a glare, but when heat flares behind his eyes at the challenge, I force a neutral expression.

"You just choreographed a three-way between me, my boyfriend, and my stepbrother, Spence. Then you made them both finish on my face. I think it's pretty clear that I'm with you now."

He swats playfully at my ass, shaking his head and chuckling. "You're lucky you're on the rag and your hormones are all out of whack, love. Besides, it was an excellent three-way, if I do say so myself."

Heat swirls in my belly, even as I snort in response to his cocky comment. "It really was." Settling into his chest, I trace along the hard muscle on either side of his breastbone. "I miss him," I admit.

"Sione?"

"Mm-hmm," I hum, finally feeling the pulls of slumber. "He still texts me sometimes. Sweet messages, usually around my period, like he's still tracking it, even though I haven't seen him in half a year."

Kabir brushes my hair out of my face, tucking it behind my ear. "Do you want to see him? We could go to Italy on holiday before your classes start back up."

I shake my head. "I can't leave Levi." Then there's the whole debacle with my mom.

"Don't say no yet." Kabir drops his arm around me and pulls me closer. "Think about it. We could all go."

"We?"

"You, me, and the boys," he explains, his tone the definition of casual. "We should start to consider ourselves a unit if we plan to carry on in this manner."

Hope sparks inside me. Not for the first time in the past twenty-four hours, it feels like we have a real shot.

"I'm sorry I left London the way I did," I tell him.

With a shake of his head, he grunts. "I'm not. You're doing so well, love. This version of you wouldn't be possible without your time in Italy. Without any of the events that happened between then and now."

He kisses the top of my head again.

"Besides, I knew it wasn't really goodbye for you and me."

"How?" I ask through a yawn.

"I've told you before, love. We're endgame."

Chapter 54

Greedy

NOW

I sneak out of the room just as my phone stops vibrating. Instantly, it starts up again. I take a few steps away from the primary and head down the first flight of stairs so I won't wake anyone.

"Hello?" I finally answer as I reach the second floor.

"Son."

The way he says that one word makes my heart lurch and my feet falter.

"Hey, Dad. Is everything okay?" With a hand on the banister, I force myself to continue down the next flight of stairs on shaky legs.

"No. Everything's not okay."

"What's going on?" I step into the living room and immediately freeze.

Kabir is sitting on the sofa, cradling a sleeping Hunter in his arms. He's looking down at her like she's the most precious, cherished thing in the world.

I'm starting to believe that to him, she is.

Rather than being prodded with spikes of jealousy at the sight of them, a warmth grows in my chest.

The way he looks at her? The unyielding trust she has in him? It's all starting to make sense.

"Are you there, son?" my dad asks, pulling me back to the present moment.

"Yeah, sorry. I'm here now."

Kabir looks up quickly, meeting my gaze and lifting one finger to his mouth.

Obviously, I realize Hunter is sleeping, but at the tension in my father's voice, I'm locked in place, no longer keen on scurrying over to the kitchen. I zero in on Kabir, who's watching me just as intently, and silently urge him to understand. I'm on high alert. The way his eyes go a steely gray confirms he sees it and is instantly there, too.

"I missed some of what you said. Can you explain it again?" I keep my voice soft and shuffle to a chair on the far side of the room, far enough away that I shouldn't disturb Hunter, and rest my arms on the back of it.

My dad exhales, the sound weary. "It's Magnolia," he says. "Something's wrong. She's hysterical."

"Did something happen?"

"Not that I'm aware of. She was okay when we left the cabin yesterday morning, but as the day went on, she got more and more agitated. She keeps saying she can't get through to Hunter."

"All right..." That sounds like the Magnolia we all know. Fuck, I hate that he's going to discover the truth about the woman he loves the hard way. Though it's about time he sees her true colors.

Honestly, there's a good chance Hunter was ignoring her mom. I wouldn't blame her, and there's no way in hell I'll even try to convince her to respond.

"Reception is terrible up here," I remind my dad. It's the truth, after all. "Maybe Hunter hasn't seen the texts or calls?"

"That could be," he admits. "I tried to ask Magnolia, but it was like she didn't even hear me. She's not herself. She's hysterical. I think Hunter needs to come back and be with her."

"It's the middle of the night," I protest.

Kabir arches a brow in question. I shake my head, because there's no way in hell anyone's going anywhere right now.

"You're right," my dad replies. "But can you pass along the message in the morning? Tell Hunter her mom needs her. Have her come straight home. Actually, have her call me. In case we end up at the hospital."

"I'm sorry you're dealing with this, Dad. I'll make sure Hunter checks her phone first thing in the morning."

"Thank you, son. I love you. I'll keep you posted."

After he disconnects, I pocket my phone, then lift my head and meet the curious gaze of His Royal Highness.

"It was your father?"

"Yeah." I blow out a long breath and scratch at the back of my head. "Magnolia's freaking out. She wants to talk to Hunter and needs to get through to her immediately."

"Come sit."

I do as he says, taking a seat on the couch beside him, closest to where Hunter's head is cradled against his chest.

"You know that her mother is toxic," I say, looking from the beautiful girl in his arms up to the man who—fuck. The man who made me come tonight.

I should feel embarrassed. Off-kilter. I should be questioning so much, trying to make sense of what's next. Instead, there's no awkwardness whatsoever. Not during sex; not afterward, when we were cleaning up; and not now, as we sit side by side.

"I know enough, yes."

Raking my hand through my hair, I examine Hunter. For a girl who struggles with insomnia, she's having no problem sleeping through this conversation.

"I have half a mind to not even tell her," I murmur as I admire her soft, pretty face. She looks so peaceful. So at ease.

Kabir clearly doesn't agree, if his grimace is any indication.

"I can understand your thought process, but it has to be her choice," he tells me.

Her choice. Right. Must be nice to be given a choice.

I grit my teeth as a lick of anger dances up my spine.

"Garrett," Kabir says softly.

I force myself to focus on him, noting that for the first time, he's dropped my middle name.

"She didn't think she had a choice, mate. Back then? With you? She'd be the first to admit now that her decision was foolish, but at the time..." He shakes his head sadly. "She never wanted to hurt you."

Just like that, my anger dissipates. He's right.

Even so, I'm still licking the wounds. They're deep and have been festering for three years, and they were ripped wide open when Kabir showed up and dropped that bomb last week.

Fuck. Has it really only been a week and change? How did we get here so quickly?

Was it quick? Or was this all meant to be? Maybe every move, every decision, was leading to this.

No wrong moves.

It's what I used to say all the time. I stopped believing the sentiment after Hunter left. Our lives fell apart three years ago, but what if that had to happen for us to get here, to the place we are now?

"It needs to be her choice," I concede, playing with a loose strand of hair. "But there's no sense in waking her tonight."

"On that, we agree."

I look around the room, noting Kabir's setup. There's a tablet and a headset off to one side. He's got his laptop cracked, and there are notebooks and a few files open on the coffee table.

"Do you still have more to do?" I ask.

He nods, but he doesn't seem like he's in a hurry to get back into his work. "She doesn't always sleep well," he says softly, gazing down at Hunter.

I snicker, because for the first time, His Royal Highness is not catching me unawares.

"Believe me, man. I know. Want me to take her upstairs?"

With a nod, he shifts so I can stand without disrupting her. I scoop her up into my arms, and, thankfully, she barely stirs.

I've got her braced against my body tightly, ready to take her upstairs so she can get a good night's sleep, but before I turn, a warm hand brushes my forearm.

"Garrett," Kabir says, his blue-gray eyes solely focused on me. "Earlier was... enjoyable. Fulfilling. Scorching hot. For a moment, it felt like so much more. I think we could make this work. All of us. If you're willing to give it a go."

A zap of surprise courses through me at his directness. Though I can't deny I appreciate it. I had no idea what would come of us going down this road. But if we're all in agreement and willing to travel it together...

"I feel you, sir." With a grin, I shoot him a wink, which I think catches him off guard. "I'm in."

Chapter 55

Hunter

NOW

I stir, but I can't force my eyes open. The pull of exhaustion is too great. It feels like I took a sleeping pill but didn't sleep long enough for it to work its way out of my system.

A yawn fights to escape me, but it's like my body doesn't remember how. I can't recall the motions my mouth is supposed to make. How to open wide. How to exhale.

I had the weirdest dream, too.

Spence and Greedy talking—speaking kindly to each other, even. That's how I knew I was dreaming. Then I was being laid in the softest bed, kissed on the head, and tucked in just how I like. It was lovely.

Moments later, though, the dream turned nightmarish.

I woke with a start and was immediately shushed and soothed. Then I was guided downstairs. I was thirsty—so thirsty—but couldn't voice the thought.

It was like I was sleepwalking, yet I remember the journey.

I'm floating in and out of consciousness now, on the precipice of being pulled under more firmly.

My cramps are ever-present, but I don't have the strength to get up and find more ibuprofen. Sooner or later, one of the guys will make their way upstairs.

The pull of sleep is heavy, and my eyes are so tired.

So much so that I don't even peek them open to see whether one of the guys is still lying beside me.

I attempt to reach out, but the effort is too great.

A shiver racks through me. Half my body is cold, but the other half is far too warm.

Not only that, but my cheek is stuck.

In fact, I'm sweating, and my cheek's sticking to the surface beneath me. Maybe I'm draped over one of the guys' bare chests? Though it feels like it could be leather.

I spend nearly a minute trying to convince myself to sit up. Roll over. Readjust.

A strange sensation nags at me. A thought in the back of my mind, trying to spur me into action. I can't quite pinpoint it. It's the same feeling I get when I can't remember whether I took my meds or where I was when I fell asleep. I just need to sit up. Readjust.

But the best I can do is crack my eyes open.

Instead of seeing Levi or Greedy, or even Kabir, all I see is a wall of beige.

Cream and beige leather, if the scent is any indication. It's mixed with the chemical smell associated with used cars.

That's it.

I'm in a car.

I force my eyes open a fraction of an inch wider, but no matter how hard I try, I can't will myself to sit up.

Am I restrained? No. I don't think so. Shit, I don't even think my seat belt is buckled.

But I'm lying against a leather bench, and the longer I survey my surroundings, the clearer it becomes.

I'm in a car.

I'm in the back seat of a car.

My heart plummets. Why the hell am I in a car?

Chapter 56

Levi

NOW

I wake up achy, sore, and so fucking satisfied.

Last night plays back in my mind like a movie. One I never saw coming but that just might be my new favorite.

With a groan, I push down the morning wood that won't go away anytime soon if I lie here and fantasize about the highlights reel of last night.

It's not a great line of thinking to go down if I want to be productive today.

Grunting, I sit up and massage my leg. It's stiff, as it always is when I wake, so I work the muscle, warming it up so it'll relax enough for me to stand comfortably. While I knead away at my healing leg, my thoughts go to the messages from my mom, to the heaviness of her request.

Request is a mild term for it, really. A trap is more accurate. One I'm about to knowingly walk into.

Hunter's words tug at me, easing the trepidation. She'll go with me. She'll be by my side.

I swing my legs over the side of the bed and peer over my shoulder, only to realize then that Hunter's not in bed like I thought. In fact, I'm the only one still up here.

I get up, hobble to the bathroom to take a piss, and make my way downstairs.

In the kitchen, I find Greedy and Kabir sitting across from each other at the table.

My heart rate picks up, and I go on high alert the second I take them in, readying myself to be a buffer and step between them when necessary.

But Greedy's scrolling on his phone, nursing a cup of coffee, and Kabir is reading an actual newspaper.

They're both relaxed in their seats, posture casual.

When Kabir rises, he turns to Greedy and asks, "Need me to top you off?" nodding toward his coffee.

"Nah, man, I got it," Greedy tells him, pushing his chair back.

What the fuck? I've yet to see even cordiality between them, let alone a friendliness like what I just witnessed.

"Uh, hey, guys," I say as I make my way over to the coffeepot.

Greedy beats me to it. He pulls out a mug and pours a fresh cup, then passes it over to me.

"Morning, champ," Kabir greets.

"Champ, huh?" Greedy smirks, his eyes dancing with mischievousness.

Kabir regards him across the kitchen, his expression deadpan. "Don't be jealous, Garrett. It's unbecoming."

"I'm not jealous," Greedy answers a little too quickly.

"Dude." I elbow him in the ribs. "He's teasing you."

Greedy eyes me, his teeth sinking into his lower lip. "I liked it better when he was teasing us both last night."

My dick twitches in interest. *Fuck.* I was prepared to deal with a decent amount of awkwardness this morning, yet it's like any other day. Okay, maybe not, because I can't say I've ever visualized standing beside my best friend while another man strokes us both to completion.

"Good morning," I tell him huskily.

"Morning," he replies, scanning me—my bare chest, athletic shorts, and nothing else—in a way that makes me feel like a fucking king.

Kabir better watch himself. Greedy's gonna have to call me His Royal Highness if he keeps it up.

I bite back a smirk at the thought. Pretty sure none of us are at that level yet. Though with the way things are headed...

Yawning, I dump a few spoonfuls of sugar into my coffee and give it a stir. Then I turn back to Greedy.

"Where's Hunter?"

With a shrug, he tops off his own mug. Then he saunters over and sits back down at the table. "She's still sleeping."

"She wasn't in bed," I tell him, my heart thumping against my sternum.

Or at least...

"She wasn't in the primary bed when I woke up," I clarify.

With a hum, Greedy nods. "She woke up in the middle of the night. I put her up in the room you had been sleeping in after she fell asleep again."

That makes sense. I didn't think to check the other bedrooms on my way down. Even so, I want to find her. Talk to her. Check in after last night, both for her sake and just to see where things stand.

Decidedly, I fill a mug with water from the tap, then stick it in the microwave. When the microwave dings, I snag a tea bag from the drawer.

"Please tell me you're not doing what I think you're doing," Kabir groans.

Shrugging, I give him a smirk. "What do you think I'm doing, *sir*?"

Kabir cocks one eyebrow, and that's all it takes. My dick's already half-hard.

I'm gonna pay for that. I can't fucking wait.

Before I let myself get distracted, I head out of the kitchen. Carefully, I climb the stairs, mindful of my leg and the piping-hot mug of tea.

Once I make it to the second floor, I knock twice on the door of the bedroom I've been using.

There's no answer, so I push in.

"Daisy." The bedding is rumpled, and the sheet is draped over one side so it's puddling on the floor. A quick survey of the room confirms she was here but isn't now. If she's not here, I know exactly where to find her. Smiling, I turn and head up the second flight of stairs back to the primary.

I should have known to check there first.

I make my way all the way up to the top floor without so much as sloshing a drop of tea. "Hey," I announce when I push through the bedroom door and head toward the opposite side of the room.

Only when I step into the library, it's empty, too.

Dread churns in my gut.

It's the same sensation that hits me when the football slips out of my grip, and the fumble is inevitable.

Or when the pastor starts preaching about the sanctity of marriage, but deep down, he really means the alleged sin of homosexuality.

Something's not right.

I peek out on the balcony, but no one's there. I check the en suite just to be sure. Finding it empty, I abandon the mug and take the stairs as quickly as my still stiff leg will take me.

On the second floor, I check all the bedrooms, flipping lights on and grabbing a shirt off the floor. By the time I'm dressed, I'm panicked and sweating.

My breaths come in shallow pants, and my nerves fire off like I've had too much caffeine, even though I've only had one sip of coffee so far. I bound down the stairs, ignoring the pain that shoots through my leg when I land a little too hard.

"Hunter's not upstairs," I inform Kabir and Greedy as I enter the kitchen.

They're both back at the table, exactly how I found them earlier.

They look up at me, their expressions curious but calm. Why isn't anyone else worried right now?

"Did you check the library?" Greedy asks.

"Yeah, of course."

"The bathroom?" Spence suggests. "She just got her period."

"Yes. I checked *everywhere*."

"You couldn't have checked *everywhere*," Spencer argues mockingly.

Greedy rises, and Kabir follows. Good. At least now they can help me find her.

"Tem!" Greedy calls out as we head up the stairs as a unit.

Kabir makes a sound of disgust. "Must you holler, Garrett?"

I let Greedy take the lead—it's his house, after all. I'm both satisfied and slightly terrified as we venture from room to room and come up empty-handed.

Where the hell is she?

"Tem!" Greedy yells again, louder this time, after we've checked all the rooms and both levels of outdoor spaces. We're back upstairs in the primary, all three of us standing in the center of the room, perplexed.

"Honestly, Garrett..." Kabir chides.

"How do you suggest we find her, Your Royal Highness?"

He smirks. "Easy."

He pulls out his phone and taps at the screen. The moment he hits send on the text, Hunter's phone pings on the bedside table.

Greedy's the first to make his way over.

"Her phone is still plugged in."

The pit in my stomach grows with each step as I make my way across the bedroom. Something is wrong here.

Greedy meets my gaze. "She wouldn't go anywhere without her phone, right?"

"Bloody hell, this can't be right." We turn back to Kabir, who's still in the middle of the room, scowling at his phone as if he's personally offended by whatever he sees on the screen.

In unison, we stride to him.

He thrusts the device out to Greedy. "Do you know where this is?"

Sidling up beside my best friend, I survey the map on the screen. It's the East Coast. South Carolina, North Carolina, the Atlantic Ocean.

"What are we looking at here?" Greedy asks.

"Answer the question, Garrett. Is that place familiar to you? That dot? Right there on the screen? Do you know where that is?"

Greedy uses his thumb and forefinger to zoom in on the pink dot Kabir is referring to. "That's Virginia," Greedy says, "and the dot looks like it's on Route 95. It goes all the way up the coast."

Kabir snatches his phone back and stares at the screen again, cursing under his breath.

"What's wrong?" I demand, my stomach twisted into painful knots. "What's happening?"

Kabir meets my gaze, his expression a mix of horror and pain.

The look is like a punch to the jaw. He hasn't even uttered a word, and yet I know his next words will knock the wind right out of all of us.

"That *dot* is Hunter."

"The fuck? What do you mean that dot is Hunter?" Greedy demands, his body rigid beside me.

"I can track her. She's in Virginia, and based on my calculations, she's currently traveling 120 kilometers an hour on Route 95, heading north."

To Be Continued

Coming Fall 2024
Available for Preorder now

Afterword

I make no excuses for what I just put you through. Two books down... two more to go.

Tell your friends, enemies, and every stranger you meet to read this series. Then get ready to meet Sione, aka the One and Only, when So Rare releases later this year!

Acknowledgments

Thank you to every single reader who (legally) reads my stories. I hope you find an escape and also feel seen whenever you visit the fictional worlds of Lake Chapel, South Chapel, Hampton, and beyond.

Special shoutouts to the individuals who helped me drag myself over the finish line of this project, including:

Beth—for putting up with my BS, correcting my Abby-isms, and not being afraid to ask "Where's Greedy?!?" even if it did make me a salty bitch for a few hours. I FLOVE you and I couldn't do this career (or life!) without you.

Megan—for letting me send long voice memos and for being #TenseForSpence despite your love of Greedy. I'm so grateful for all the ways you lift me up and support this amazing business we're building!

Linds, Mica, Robin, and Amy—thank you for the sensitivity and context reading you provided to make Hunter's story the best it could be.

Adah, Brittany, Alina, Jen, and Tricia—thank you for beta reading and providing invaluable feedback that shaped the heart of this story.

The readers who aren't scared of cliffhangers—you are my people. I love you, and I appreciate your commitment to the angst, even when you know it's going to hurt.

My therapist—thanks for those emergency seshies when I clearly trauma-ed too close to the sun. This book wouldn't exist without you. You're the real MVP!

Finally, to anyone suffering with PMDD who battles cyclical demons month after month after month—You are not alone. Now is not forever. Take care of your body, mind, and spirit, and don't be afraid to seek help when you need it. You are so much more than a diagnosis. Never forget that even on your lowest days, you are whole, wanted, and wonderful.

By Abby Millsaps

presented in order of publication

When You're Home
While You're There
When You're Home for the Holidays
When You're Gone
Rowdy Boy
Mr. Brightside
Fourth Wheel
Full Out Fiend
Hampton Holiday Collective

Too Safe: Boys of Lake Chapel Book One
Too Fast: Boys of Lake Chapel Book Two
Too Far: Boys of Lake Chapel Book Three
So Wrong: Boys of South Chapel Book One
So Real: Boys of South Chapel Book Two
So Rare: Boys of South Chapel Book Three
So _____: Boys of South Chapel Book Four

About The Author

Abby Millsaps is an author and storyteller who's been obsessed with writing romance since middle school. In eighth grade, she failed to qualify for the Power of the Pen State Championships because "all her submissions contained the same theme: young people falling in love." #LookAtHerNow

She's best known for writing unapologetically angsty romance that causes emotional damage for her readers. Creative spicy scenes and consent as foreplay are two hallmarks of her books. Abby prides herself in writing authentic characters while weaving mental health, chronic illness, and neurodiverse representation into the fabric of her stories.

Connect with Abby
Website: www.authorabbymillsaps.com
Patreon: https://www.patreon.com/AbbyMillsaps
Instagram: @abbymillsaps
TikTok: @authorabbymillsaps
Email: authorabbymillsaps@gmail.com
Newsletter: https://geni.us/AuthorAbbyNewsletter
Facebook Reader Group: Abby's Full Out Fiends

www.ingramcontent.com/pod-product-compliance
Lightning Source LLC
LaVergne TN
LVHW030317070526
838199LV00069B/6487